THE PERILOUS GARD

ELIZABETH MARIE POPE ᙭

᙭ THE PERILOUS GARD

Illustrated by Richard Cuffari

Houghton Mifflin Company Boston

First published in the United States of America by
Houghton Mifflin Company, 1974

Library of Congress Cataloging-in-Publication Data
Pope, Elizabeth Marie, 1917–
The perilous gard / by Elizabeth Marie Pope
p. cm.
Summary: In 1558 while imprisoned in a remote castle, a young
girl becomes involved in a series of events that lead to an under-
ground labyrinth peopled by the last practitioners of druidic magic.
HC ISBN 0-618-17736-1 PA ISBN 0-618-15073-0
[1. Druids and druidism — Fiction] I. Title
PZ7.P792PE 1992 Fic — dc20 73-21648

Printed in the United States of America
QUM 10 9 8 7 6 5 4 3 2 1

CONTENTS

For the family at Fenwick

I 🦢

The True Sister

"She won't be angry with me," said Alicia. "Why should she, Kate? Every word I wrote her was true. This *is* the most horrible place in the world. You know it is."

Kate did not answer. She was standing by the window, with her back to the room, staring out at the overgrown gardens and the dripping trees of the great park. Hatfield in the rain might not be the most horrible place in the world, but it was certainly the dreariest royal palace in all England — perhaps that was one reason why Queen Mary had chosen it for her sister Elizabeth's house — and it had been raining steadily for almost two weeks. The summer of 1558 had been a late one, miserably cold and wet; unless the weather cleared soon, they were sure to have floods or another bad harvest. It was nearly August, yet even with the windows shut, the room would have been much the better for a fire on the hearth.

Needless to say, there was no fire. The Queen's jealous hatred of her sister was continually breaking out in curious little acts of petty spitefulness, and one of them was to keep the household short of fuel. The sea coal at Hatfield always seemed to be smoky, the kindling wood green; sometimes there was barely enough to supply the Princess's own apartments, let alone the dormitory allotted to her maids of honor. There were never enough blankets to go around comfortably either, and they were

thin too. Katherine and Alicia Sutton, who were the youngest
of the maids and had been at Hatfield for the shortest time, had
the thinnest of all. Alicia, perched on the foot of their bed,
poked at the coverlet with an accusing finger.

"It's wrong!" she said. "Wicked!"

Kate swung about to face her.

"You never wrote the Queen that?" she demanded.

"Don't plunge at me, Kate!" begged Alicia. "I can't think if
you plunge at me. And do *try* not to lurch with your shoulders!
You know what Mother said."

Kate drew back a little, stiffening. She was a tall girl, all
arms and legs, and her awkward shoulders were the despair of
Lady Sutton at home in London. Her father and his father before
him had both married beautiful women, but Alicia was the only
child who had taken after her mother. Kate, most unfortunately,
looked like her father and still more like her grandfather, Sir
Giles, who had founded the fortunes of the family back in the
days of old King Henry the Eighth. Sir Giles had started life
as a common merchant seaman (the malicious rumor that he
had been a pirate was almost universally discredited), and though
in the end he had grown rich and died knighted, it was not for
his grace or good looks. Even King Henry once remarked, in an
exasperated moment, that he could never have told Giles Sutton's
face from a stone wall if the stone wall had not been so much
the handsomer of the two.

"And she's the image of him!" poor Lady Sutton was accustomed to complain bitterly. "His very image! That walk, if a
walk you could call it! And the way those eyes of his went
through you, exactly like a knife!"

"And his brains too," said Kate's father dryly.

"Brains!" snapped Lady Sutton. "Tilly vally, Sir Thomas!
She's not a boy! What does a woman want with brains? I'm

sure I never had a brain in my head, and no more does Alicia!"

"Alicia doesn't need a brain," said Sir Thomas, more dryly still. "Not with *her* eyes."

Alicia's eyes were enormous, as golden as honey, and innocently trustful as a baby's. When she looked up at Kate, standing by the window, they suddenly melted, and a faint sparkle of tears appeared on the lashes, like jewels on a fringe.

"You could say you wrote the letter yourself," she suggested hopefully. "That's what you'd do if you were a true sister."

Kate broke in on this romance without ceremony.

"Did you sign my name to it?" she asked.

Alicia's eyes widened. "Sign your name?" she said, in a rather puzzled voice. "How could I sign your name to the letter when you didn't even know I was sending it?"

"Did you copy my writing?"

"I've told you before, Kate," said Alicia, "and I tell you again, that I will not learn that foolish newfangled Roman handwriting Father taught you, and let that be an end of it."

"Then it wouldn't do much good to say I sent the letter, would it?"

"Oh." Alicia blinked. "Wouldn't it?"

"No."

"But if you *said* you —"

"No. We'll have to find some other way that I can be a true sister to you."

Alicia flushed and began to wriggle one foot in its soft embroidered shoe. "Very well: sneer at me," she said. "Don't be a true sister. I was only trying to help the Lady Elizabeth. The Queen can't know how bad it is here. All I did was write and tell her."

"*What* did you tell her?"

"It was only setting her straight. All I wrote was that the

Princess was an excellent lady, and loyal, and noble, and everyone loved her, much better than the Queen, and it's wrong to
keep her shut up in this horrible place where she can't even
put her nose outside the park gates, and there isn't any company
except old Master Roger to read her Latin, and no fresh fish in
Lent except carp from the pond, and no warming pans for the
beds not even in January when it snowed for three days, and —"

"Never mind the rest," Kate sat down limply on the window
seat. "You ought to be in a book, Alicia. That's where you ought
to be, in a romance. Riding on a white horse, with a good
brave knight to take care of you. Whatever do you suppose the
Queen will think? She'll never forgive you."

"I'm not afraid of the Queen."

Kate thought of the Queen sitting in her high-backed chair
on the day she and Alicia had been taken to court to be presented
to her before they went down to Hatfield. The Queen's hands,
never still for a moment. The tight lips. The hot, sick, unhappy eyes darting from one to the other and back again.
"Well, I'm afraid of her," she said.

"Yes, but she liked me," Alicia insisted. "Don't you remember,
Kate? She said I had a sweet face and reminded her of my
mother."

"She wasn't angry with you then."

"Oh, she isn't going to be angry with me now, not for only
one little short letter."

"Alicia —" Kate stopped, helplessly at a loss. She did not know
how to explain. Nobody had ever really been angry with
Alicia, whatever she did: the whole world had been her apple
tart since the day she was born.

"Think of what happened to Catt Ashley," she persisted.

"Who cares about her? The Queen isn't going to be angry
with me," Alicia repeated comfortingly. "It was only a *little*

letter. Why, the whole of it was hardly three pages long." She slipped to her feet, stretching like a kitten, and began to tidy her hair.

"The Queen may not read it," said Kate. "She must get hundreds of letters. And she's ill again. Or it may have gone astray on the road."

"Oh, no, it couldn't have," said Alicia proudly. "I put it in the royal courier's packet with the one from the Princess."

Kate, giving up, merely nodded and turned again to look out of the window. Two sparrows were trying to shelter from the rainy wind in the ivy that grew on the palace wall, and she felt a little sick as she watched the storm tear one of them out of its hold and blow it fluttering away from the leaves. The Queen was capable of anything when she was in one of her furies, particularly a fury with her sister or anyone belonging to her sister's household. Catt Ashley was the Lady Elizabeth's favorite attendant, her old governess, but she had been sent to prison in the Tower of London all the same only for being found with some ballads and pamphlets attacking the Queen's policies; and Blanche Parry had said that she was very lucky not to be there still.

Blanche Parry herself opened the door at that moment and came frowning into the room. She too had been with the household ever since the Lady Elizabeth was a child, and was now the Keeper of the Princess's Jewels, not that there were many jewels for her to keep, and the "Mother" in charge of the maids of honor, not that there were many maids either.

"I've been looking for you," she said. "Why weren't you down in the hall, where you belong? Stop preening yourself, Alicia! Don't sit there like a stone image, Kate! Her Highness wants you."

Kate heard what seemed to be her own voice asking a question.

"No, I don't know what it's about. She was working with Master Roger when the rider came from London. It's put her in a wicked temper, that's all I can tell you," said Blanche Parry, shepherding them before her down the stairs. "More trouble with That Woman, I suppose. If some people were locked up as lunatics instead of sitting on thrones . . . Come along now, don't keep her waiting, remember your curtsies both of you, try not to trip over your skirts again, Kate, I never saw such a clumsy girl. This way. They're in the little parlor."

The little parlor was a small gloomy room — all the rooms at Hatfield were gloomy — with narrow latticed windows and a couple of damp logs smoldering in the fireplace. The table had been covered with a rug from Turkestan, according to the fashion; but it was old, and the colors looked dingy and worn. Master Roger Ascham, the Princess's Latin Reader, was standing by the table, the book he had been working with still impatiently open in his hand. Master Roger was apt to regard politics and riders from the court as mere interruptions to the more important business of scholarship.

The Lady Elizabeth sat in a big carved chair by the window, reading a letter. She was a slender young woman, very plainly dressed in a gown and kirtle of ash-colored wool with knots of black velvet — the Queen did not like to hear of her sister wearing finery or bright colors — and at first glance there was nothing remarkable about her except the brilliant hazel eyes and the blazing red-gold hair she had inherited from her father King Henry. That afternoon the hair was braided down, half-hidden under a small black velvet hood, and the eyes bent over the letter were quite calm, only a little disdainful. But as Kate and Alicia came through the doorway, the Princess deliberately

closed her hand and crushed what she was holding into a mass
of twisted paper and broken sealing wax.

Kate and Alicia took the regulation two steps across the
threshold and sank curtsying to the floor. Kate immediately
tripped over her skirts in spite of everything Blanche Parry had
told her; and before she could recover her balance, Alicia had
crossed the room in one lovely curving rush like a wave to the
shore and was kneeling at the Princess's feet.

The Lady Elizabeth looked down at her.

"So you think it is wrong to keep me shut up in this horrible
place?" was all she said.

Alicia had begun to cry. Her big tear-fringed golden eyes
lifted adoringly to the brilliant hazel ones above her.

"Oh, Your Highness!" she whispered. "I was only trying to
help you! Truly I was!"

The Lady Elizabeth leaned forward with one of her swift
decisive movements and touched Alicia's shining hair. "Little
fool, how would it help me for you to have your head cut off?"
she demanded, but in a much more gentle voice. "You should
hear what the Queen my sister has to say of your conduct. All
in her own hand, too. 'I have never known your household,
Elizabeth, to show me anything except treachery and ungrate-
fulness —' " She swept open the crumpled papers on the arm
of the chair, her eyes hardening again as they ran down the
thick, heavily blotted lines. " 'It was much against my judgment
to place any of my subjects in your charge, but their mother
wished for it, and I trusted they were too young to engage in
plots or to suck up malice and corruption —' Fine phrase, suck
up corruption! What next? 'God knows I am accustomed to
insolence and rebellion, yet I am the Queen of England still,
and if Alicia Sutton thinks I can endure to be so baited, so

attacked, so defied and tormented it will go very hard with her —' "

Kate's heart gave one sickening lurch, and then seemed to stop beating altogether.

" 'But —' " the Princess went on, "(and did you ever hear the like of this for a piece of good logic, Master Roger?) — *'But* I am not yet so dull that I cannot perceive she is too sweet and fair a child to have thought of such mischief for herself; and I have no doubt at all that if one of them contrived that letter, the blame should be laid chiefly on that sister of hers, who I did very well note to be of a cold, hard, and secret countenance, like her father; and he is a man whose face I could never bring myself to trust.' "

"There, Kate!" said Alicia, triumphantly, quite forgetting where she was. "I *told* you she wasn't going to be angry with me!"

"Her Majesty's powers of reason are extraordinary," observed Master Roger, looking up from his book.

The Lady Elizabeth's eyes were still on the letter in her hand.

" 'It remains now,' " she read on, " 'only to make an end of this wickedness and folly. I have therefore determined to take Alicia Sutton and place her here among my own ladies at the court, where with good company and maidenly pastimes she can shake off the infection of your household. As for Katherine Sutton —' "

The clear voice hesitated for a fraction of a second.

" 'As for Katherine Sutton,' " it continued, " 'she is young; and I am not a cruel or a hardhearted woman. My command for her is only that she shall be put into the care of Sir Geoffrey Heron, a man I *can* trust in wholly, and kept by him under strict guard at his house called Elvenwood Hall in Derbyshire;

and so let me hear no more of the girl, I have done with her.' "

There were two or three other sentences — something about "he is to fetch her away within the week," and "deliver her promptly into his hands," but Kate did not really hear them. She could see the Lady Elizabeth's lips moving, and the paper in her hand, but the words made no sense to her. She had never heard of Geoffrey Heron or of Elvenwood Hall. She knew nothing of Derbyshire except that it was in the north somewhere, forest and mining country, very wild, full of streams and caves. There was a castle in Derbyshire that had a great cave underneath it, Peak Castle, and other places — the Blue John Cavern at Treak Cliff where the purple spar came from, High Tor, Great Matlock: but the names only darted and tumbled about her mind like a scatter of loose beads in a box-lid. They had no meaning. The one thing that seemed clear and fixed was that Alicia had been right after all. Whatever happened, the Queen was not going to be angry with *her*.

Alicia had begun to realize that something was wrong. "But, Your Highness!" she protested. "It wasn't Kate's fault. What is she sending her away for?"

"Because she is not a cruel or a hardhearted woman."

"Then how can she? She mustn't! Our father won't let her!"

"Your father can do nothing to stop her," said the Lady Elizabeth gravely. "Nor can I. We would only make the matter worse if we tried."

"But it wasn't Kate's fault! It wasn't!" repeated Alicia, springing up and burying her face on Kate's shoulder in a storm of tears.

"Alicia!" Kate came back to her senses with a jerk. "Alicia, for the love of heaven! Be quiet!"

"I won't be quiet!" wept Alicia. "And if the Q-queen thinks I

I want any m-m-maidenly pastimes when my poor sister is chained up eating dry bread in a black dungeon full of snakes and toads —"

"Who said a word about chaining me up in a dungeon? She only means I'll have to keep within a mile of the house, or something — you know, like Her Highness here at Hatfield. I'm not being sent to the Tower, you little goose! Sir Geoffrey won't hurt me."

"He-he won't?"

"Didn't you hear the Queen say he was a man she could trust?" Kate demanded, hoping that nobody would raise the question of exactly what the Queen thought she could trust Sir Geoffrey to do. The Lady Elizabeth was looking down at the letter again, her face troubled. It was, unexpectedly, Master Roger who spoke.

"Your sister's right, Alicia." He gave Kate a reassuring nod. "No, I'm not trying to comfort you. It's true."

The Lady Elizabeth turned to him. "Do you know the man, then?" she asked eagerly.

"Not to say know him, Your Highness. My old pupil, Thomas Corget — a good lad, though no great hand as a scholar — told me once that he was of some estate in the fen country about Norfolk, and had a great reputation there for his honesty and fair dealing. He was one of the gentlemen who came to the Queen's help at the time of a Somerset rebellion; and it seems she took a liking to him, for she gave him a high post in Ireland and he was there for some years, never returning to England until last winter, after his wife died. Elvenwood Hall must have come to him from her. She was Lord Warden's daughter, and her father's only heir."

"Warden?" the Princess interrupted him. "I have heard of Wardens in Derbyshire, but Elvenwood Hall was not the name of their house. It had another name, and there used to be some curious tale about it."

"Tom Corget said there were so many curious tales about the Perilous Gard running about in Derbyshire that after a time he did not trouble himself to listen to half of them."

"The Perilous Gard?"

"That was the other name, my lady. The last Lord Warden tore down much of the house and rebuilt it when he came into the title, and would have changed the name too, if he might have; but country folk all call it by the old one still. Tom Corget and I were disputing about the name: it was so that we came to speak of Sir Geoffrey."

"Sir Launcelot had a castle called the Joyous Gard," remarked Alicia, in a rather muffled voice from Kate's shoulder.

Master Roger's bushy eyebrows twitched together ominously. As a classical scholar and a defender of the New Learning, he held the tales of King Arthur and his knights in the deepest contempt, and was always doing his best to root them out of the Princess's household.

"Since the word 'gard' signified a 'castle' in the old days, I have no doubt it was a castle once," he observed severely. "Tom Corget and I were disputing about the 'perilous.' Tom (no scholar) held that it was nothing but a by-name meaning that the place was a strong one — hard to attack, or dangerous to meddle with. It was *my* contention," went on Master Roger, now well away and settling briskly into the stride of his argument, "that the word 'perilous' was often given in the former age to such places as foolish and superstitious persons chose to believe were of a magical nature. Like the Perilous Chapel in the monkish legend of the Holy Grail; or the Perilous Seat in King Arthur's court where no one except the best knight in the world was able to sit. When I was a boy there was a hill near

my cousin's house in Northumbria that was always called the
Perilous Hill because it was said that the Fairy Folk used to
live underneath it. The story went that they had all been driven
away long since; but the country people still go in terror of the
place, and the bravest of them would not set foot on it after
dark for a hundred pounds. As I told Tom Corget, it was my
belief —"

The Lady Elizabeth stirred restlessly in her chair.

"Master Roger," she said.

"Yes, my lady?"

"I was asking you about this house of the Wardens. What
were the curious tales Thomas Corget spoke of?"

"Yes, my lady. I am coming to them. As I told Tom Corget,
it was my belief that places like the hill near my cousin's house
must once have been the centers of some heathen worship in
ancient times now forgotten; and the stories of the Fairy Folk
living there were only memories of the old heathen gods, overlaid with fantasies and superstitions. When I was young, the
country women all believed that the Fairy Folk would steal
children away with them if they could; and this — so I told Tom
Corget — goes back to the days when the old pagans did take
human beings to offer in sacrifice to their gods, like the Druids
of Britain and France according to the report of Julius Caesar.
Then also the Fairy Folk are said to deck themselves out with
gold, and live in great ceremony, dancing and singing, as the
heathen gods were accustomed to do. I have never learned the
truth of the matter; but certainly, the people near my cousin's
house still dreaded the very name of the hill, and thought it was
unlucky to go near the place, even by day. Now it came into
my mind when I was disputing with Tom Corget that the
Perilous Gard might likewise stand near some old center of
heathen magic, such as I considered the hill to be. That would

account for the name, and also for the curious tales that are told of it. It is a very remote and solitary place, and the Wardens were a strange family, or so Tom said to me. I saw myself when I was a boy what country people can believe in with no more than old rumors and idle tongues to set them going."

"And what were the curious tales they believed in?"

It seemed to Kate that Master Roger glanced at the Princess before replying and very slightly shook his head.

"Oh, much the same foolishness," he answered quickly; "no need to weary you with the ins and outs of the matter. The Wardens are all dead and gone now — Lady Heron was the last of them — and Sir Geoffrey is an honorable man. You may take Thomas Corget's word for that, Your Highness. Mistress Katherine here should find nothing to trouble her at Elvenwood Hall."

"Very well, then." The Lady Elizabeth let the Queen's letter drop from her hands to the floor, and glanced across the room at Kate. "Come here, girl."

Kate detached herself from Alicia and knelt down cautiously by the arm of the great carved chair. Her knees were still shaking, and she was afraid that she might trip over her skirts again.

"This is a hard business," said the Lady Elizabeth. "I will not make it harder with more talking."

"No, Your Highness," Kate replied thankfully. She knew she ought to say something about suffering gladly for the Princess, or acting like a true sister to Alicia, but she could not think of anything to say. She was not suffering for the Princess, and she did not want to be a true sister to Alicia. She was conscious only of a furious irritation at the maddening senselessness of the whole affair.

"You heard what Thomas Corget said of Sir Geoffrey?"

"Yes, Your Highness."

"I shall see that your father hears of it, too. And if I ever have the power I give you my word —" her eyes met Kate's in a long, grave, deliberate look, "I give you my word that I shall send him at once to bring you away."

"But I don't see why Kate should have to go at all," Alicia's voice broke in on them. "Listen, Your Highness! Listen, Master Roger! All I have to do is write to the Queen again and *tell* her —"

"*No,*" said Kate and Master Roger and the Lady Elizabeth simultaneously.

II 𝔤

The Elvenwood

Katherine Sutton reflected gloomily that here she was, like a lady in a romance, riding through the forest on her white horse with a good brave knight to take care of her. At least the horse was white — or as much of the horse as she could see for the mud splashes that covered its hide — a big, lumbering beast of a mare with an infuriating habit of chewing the bit like a cow on a cud. She pulled it up for the fortieth time as it stumbled over a root, and then, straightening her back, lifted her face to look for a break in the sky.

It was raining again, a thin, cold, misty rain that penetrated to the bone. Even under the huge trees there was very little shelter. The rain threaded and beaded every branch and leaf and twig, dripping mournfully at the jarring thud of the horses' hoofs. It clung to the shoulders of Kate's heavy cloak and glistened in the long gray folds of her riding skirt. The instant she raised her head it began to gather on her lashes like tears.

The narrow, leaf-strewn track of a road was thick and sodden with water. The twelve mounted men and the four heavily loaded pack-carts behind her must be beating it into a mire. She was almost the first in line. Ahead of her, there was only the square back of Diccon carrying his master's pennon on a short lance. He and most of the others had soldiered in Ireland with Sir Geoffrey, and even now they looked far more like an armed guard than a troop of ordinary household serving men.

Kate glanced over her shoulder for a moment at the long file of riders, with their heads bent against the rain, and then turned back to watch the clouds again. But it was no use. She could not get even a glimpse of the sky. The great arching boughs of the trees had met overhead and shut it out completely.

Kate had never seen such trees. In her part of the country, the last of the forests had been cleared long before she was born, and there was nothing left of them but open woodlands and hunting parks. This was different. It might have been the wild forest of another age, centuries ago. Except for the sound of the horses' hoofs lifting out of the mud and the faint shivering drip of the rain, it was utterly silent. In the silence, immense, dark, overwhelming, shouldering over the road, towering like castles, the great trees rose and pressed about the horses and their riders, melting away on every side into depth on depth of green shadow that opened a little to let them through and then closed in behind them again.

"They look taller because the road is so low," Kate told herself. "It must be very old." The road could never have carried much traffic — it turned and dodged among the trees like a footpath — but over the years the passing of men and horses had little by little worn it away until now it was far beneath the level of the ground. The bank on her right was nearly as high as the wall of a house, laced and knotted with enormous twisted roots all overgrown with moss and little dripping tongues of fern.

There was a sudden crash and a warning shout behind her, and she reined up. Something was wrong with one of the pack-carts at the end of the line. Heads were turning and shadowy figures running through the mist; she heard the shrill neighing of a frightened horse, and then, riding over the confusion, the clear stern voice of Sir Geoffrey: "Let be! Give them room:

it's only the rope broken. Dirk and Ned, lash those boxes again. Quickly now! We can't spend the night roosting here in the forest. Dismount and rest, you others. There's no harm done."

Everybody halted obediently in a jingling of spurs and a creaking of leather as the men swung down from their saddles. Sir Geoffrey came looming out of the mist, on foot, with the rain blowing about his head, and paused beside Kate's stirrup. He put his hand on the pommel of her saddle and looked up at her. He had a big, craggy face with a jaw like iron, and level, rather forbidding gray eyes.

"How do you, Mistress Katherine?" he inquired stiffly.

Kate lifted her chin and looked back at him.

"I thank you, Sir Geoffrey," she replied. "Well enough."

"Is there anything you want?"

"I thank you, Sir Geoffrey," Kate repeated. "No."

Sir Geoffrey took a step as if to move away, and then swung around on her again, frowning. But he did not appear to be angry. He stood watching her for a long moment, and finally said: "There's no need to cry."

"I haven't been crying," Kate answered indignantly. Her father had said once that thank God, she wasn't always melting into tears like her mother and Alicia; and it had been a matter of pride with her never to let herself cry afterwards. "I haven't been crying," she repeated. "That's only the rain on my face."

The shadow of something that might have been a smile glinted an instant in Sir Geoffrey's forbidding eyes and was gone before she could be sure of it. "Wipe the rain off your face, then," he told her. "And stop trying to look down your nose at me! I've been on the road with you six days now, and all I've had out of you is yes-Sir-Geoffrey and no-Sir-Geoffrey and I-thank-you-Sir-Geoffrey like a stone speaking. Come now, you don't seem to be a fool: deal with me plainly — *is* there anything you want?"

The corner of Kate's mouth flickered suddenly in an answering smile before she could stop herself.

"Indeed yes, if you please, Sir Geoffrey," she replied. "I want a roof over my head and a blazing fire and some dry clothes and a hot roast chicken and a goose-feather bed with three coverlets on it. Will you be so kind as to fetch them at once?"

The glint of amusement deepened in Sir Geoffrey's eyes. "Stay where you are," he ordered, and striding away, returned after a moment with a slab of yellow cheese and a hunch of bread wrapped in a napkin.

"You can have your roast chicken tomorrow when we're safe at the Hall," he said. "Try a bit of this now, and eat as much as you can: you'll need it. We've a long road still ahead of us."

"How long?" asked Kate promptly. Though she had never until now brought herself to put questions to Sir Geoffrey, one of her chief trials during the last six days had been the riding blind into completely strange country. It had not been so bad at first, on the way up from the south, while she could at least recognize the names on the signposts and the towns where they had stopped for the night. The inns had been large and bustling, and there were other travelers on the road. But early that morning they had turned off the road and ridden away over a desolate moor seamed with ridges and outcroppings of rock, as if the bones of the land were forcing their way through it, with nothing alive on the wide gray folds of the hills except for an occasional flock of sheep so far away that it could hardly be told from one of the low drifting clouds. And after they had crossed the moor, it was only to pass through a narrow gap between two stony tors and down deeper and deeper into the forest.

"How long?" Sir Geoffrey shrugged his big shoulders. "If this rain won't stop and the carts go on breaking down, God knows. Not long as the crow flies. We're on Warden land now, in the Elvenwood. It's winding about among these cursed trees that makes the going so slow."

Kate frowned up at the looming green shadows. "Don't they ever cut them down?" she demanded.

"I asked my wife's father that same question once," said Sir Geoffrey, "and he told me it would be a bold man who'd lay an ax to any tree in the Elvenwood."

"Why?"

"I don't know," said Sir Geoffrey. "For then his daughter came into the room, and the matter went out of my mind."

Kate looked from the trees to the road. For a few feet around them it was churned into black mud and hoofprints where the horses had trampled it; then the leaves covered it again. A few feet more, and it was out of sight.

"Isn't there any other way we could go?" she asked.

Sir Geoffrey shook his head. "We're in a valley between two cliffs," he explained briefly, "and we have to go the length of it to come to the Hall. What's the matter? Afraid of the dark?"

"No," said Kate, rather more loudly than she meant to. It was already dusk on the deep pathway under the overhanging branches, and her eyes were beginning to play tricks on her as the moving leaves wavered and shifted in the uncertain light. There was one old stump covered with ivy at the top of the bank that looked exactly like a hooded figure in a green cloak, leaning forward to listen.

Then, somewhere in the distance, through the trees, she suddenly heard a voice singing. It came blowing towards them on the misty rain — a high clear voice, curiously piercing and sweet. It was singing a verse from the old ballad about the minstrel who met the fairy lady under the elder tree.

> *Her skirt was made of the grass-green silk,*
> *Her mantle of the velvet fine,*
> *And from every strand of horse's mane*
> *Hung twenty silver bells and nine.*
> *'O harp and carp, True Thomas,' she said,*
> *'O harp and carp along with me —'*

"Good Lord, it's Randal," said Sir Geoffrey. "I'd know his voice if I heard it in the Indies. Listen! He's coming this way."

"Who?" asked Kate, bending forward to catch the notes through the rustling of the leaves.

"Randal," repeated Sir Geoffrey. "Old Randal the harper. I wonder where he's been all the winter? I haven't seen him since I came back from Ireland."

"Is he one of your men?"

"He's been known to call himself that when it would keep some town from putting him in the stocks for a vagabond," replied Sir Geoffrey dryly. "And I suppose you could say that he lives with me when he lives anywhere. He's a minstrel — one of the old wandering breed, always on the road. I took him in one harvest time years ago when he came ill with the fever to my door in Norfolk, and he's been drifting back now and again ever since. Don't be frightened when you see him, will you? The fever nearly killed him, and he never got his wits back properly afterwards."

"Do you mean," Kate ventured, "that he's mad?"

"No — only touched in the head, as my old nurse used to say. He can't remember much before the fever, and sometimes he talks a little wildly. You needn't mind that. He's as gentle as a baby, and you can hear for yourself that it did no harm to his voice."

The voice was singing again, higher and nearer. This time

it seemed to be a "riddle song," but not one that Kate knew, set to a gay, curiously dancing air:

> *O where is the Queen, and where is her throne?*
> *Down in the stone O, but not in the stone.*
> *O where is the Queen, and where is her hall?*
> *Over the wall O, with never a wall.*
> *O where are her dancers, and where are they now?*
> *Go out by the oak leaf, with never a bough.*

"Randal!" called Sir Geoffrey. "Randal, lad! Come here!"

The air snapped off suddenly in the middle of a note, and a slight figure dressed in rusty brown came scurrying like a dead leaf around the bend of the road. Under one arm, cradled against his shoulder, he was carrying something that looked like a small harp, covered with fine canvas to shield it from the rain. A broken crimson quill-feather dangled from one corner of his battered cap.

"Welcome, Sir Geoffrey," he said, pulling off the cap and somehow contriving to bow gracefully in spite of the harp and the rain. He had a pointed brown face and spoke with a sweet, lilting, musical accent very unlike the harsh Norfolk voices of Sir Geoffrey's other retainers. "It is many and many a day since I saw you riding down the road with all your armed men at your back. Where have you been so long away?"

"Where have you been yourself?" demanded Sir Geoffrey, glancing at the little stream of water that was running off the tip of the crimson feather and splashing down past Randal's knee into the mud of the road. "Put that cap back on your head, man: it's no weather for courtesy. You ought to be sheltering at the Hall. What are you doing here?"

Randal's mouth drooped like a scolded child's.

"I was looking for the way in again," he explained, twisting the cap between his hands. "I knew the way in as well as the door to your house before they took my wits away from me, if I could only call it back to my mind. There is one way in through the stone of the tower, and another way in over the wall by the well, and another way in by the oak leaf, with never a bough."

"No more of that talk!" said Sir Geoffrey. "Do you want to work yourself into the fever again? What you need is a corner by the fire and something to eat. How long have you been starving this time?"

"Not a bit of bread have I had since morning," Randal admitted, "nor," he added winningly, with his eyes on Kate's hand, 'cheese."

Sir Geoffrey smiled and shook his head. "No, that's the last of it," he said. "There'll be more at the Hall. Find Diccon and tell him you're to ride with us in one of the carts when we go."

But Kate had already tumbled the bread and cheese back into the napkin and was leaning down from her saddle. "May I give him the rest of mine?" she asked. "I've had all I want."

Sir Geoffrey nodded. "If you choose," he said. "This is Mistress Katherine Sutton, Randal, and you must play your harp for her one of these days. She is coming to stay at the Hall for a time."

Randal looked up at her, and then suddenly made another of his fantastically graceful bows, the crimson feather fluttering in the rain.

"A blessing on your gentle heart, my lady," he said.

Kate stiffened again at once. She had never liked to be thanked; and what was the sense of making such a to-do over a morsel of bread and cheese?

Randal went on standing by her stirrup, the bread and cheese in his hand.

"Sir Geoffrey says you will be staying at the castle," he told her. It did not seem to occur to him that she must have heard what Sir Geoffrey had said.

"Yes, Randal."

Randal took a step forward and touched her bridle with the tip of his finger.

"You won't be lost, will you?" he asked anxiously. "Like the other one?"

"What other one?"

Randal's gaze faltered and then went uncertainly from Kate to Sir Geoffrey and back to Kate again. He seemed puzzled and unhappy about something.

"The — the other girl," he stammered at last. "The little girl who was lost. I was told there was a little girl. Some say that she went of her own free will, and some that she was taken, but she found the way in, and then she never found the way out again."

There was an odd, breathless sort of pause. Kate, turning her head, saw that Sir Geoffrey was standing stock still in the road, his big hands clenched at his sides. All the friendliness was gone from his face, and his jaw looked more than ever as if it were made of iron.

"Do you know what it is that he means?" he demanded curtly.

"No, Sir Geoffrey."

"You will, soon enough," said Sir Geoffrey, in his grimmest voice. "Take that food now, Randal, and come along with me: it's time we were away."

He tramped off without another word, Randal trotting obediently at his side. Through the blowing mist, Kate saw the driver of the wrecked cart go running up to speak to him. There was a jingling stir and a confused trampling of hoofs as the men began to mount again. She turned to haul the white mare's nose up out of the ferns on the bank.

Then, low but very distinct under the rough noises from the road, she heard the last sound in the world that she had expected to hear.

Someone was laughing.

Startled, she looked up, and saw a woman at the top of the bank, among the branches.

She was standing so still, her long dark hair and shadowy green cloak melting in and out of the shifting leaves, that for an instant Kate thought she was not real, only a trick of light and color like her first illusion about the ivy-covered stump. But she was real. Kate could see the hard delicate bones of her face, and the glint of a gold bracelet on the wrist under the edge of the cloak. She was gazing down at the scene on the road beneath her with an amused, faintly disdainful laugh still lingering about her mouth, as if she were watching a pack of half-grown puppies all yelping together in a kennel-run.

The next moment there was a great noise of shouts and cracking whips as the carts began to move forward. The white mare snorted and plunged, and by the time Kate got control of it again, the woman was gone.

III ૐ

The Young Man at the Window

By the time they had ridden another two miles, Kate had made up her mind that the woman among the branches must have been a gypsy tinker or a charcoal burner's wife pausing to watch them out of curiosity: it was not a very good explanation, but it was the best she could think of. All the same, she could not rid herself of a foolish notion that the woman was still with them, flitting from tree to tree, though in the deepening shadows it was getting impossible to distinguish the trees or much of anything else except the solid, square-shouldered shape of Diccon's back on the road just ahead. She was tired now, too tired to reason; presently, her thoughts began to run together and everything faded into a blur of weariness like a dream, the endless bone-racking trot of the mare, the wet discomfort of her cloak, the clang of a gate, torches and running feet and hands lifting her down from the saddle, and then more feet and firelight and warmth and darkness, all slipping away at last into another confused dream. The woman in the green cloak was watching her again, but after a while she went away, and Master Roger had his hand on her shoulder and was telling her to listen to what it was that Randal was singing, only Randal was singing a long way off, and try as she might she could not seem to catch the words because she had lost the way in and there was a light that kept shining on her face and bothering her. She put up one hand to thrust it away, and turning over drowsily, opened her eyes.

She was lying in a great carved bed, its four towering posts hung about with embroidered curtains. The curtains had been drawn to darken the room, but somewhere beyond them the sun was out, and a long ray of light was slanting in through a narrow parting where they did not quite meet on the left-hand side of the bed.

"It must be afternoon," Kate thought hazily, fumbling for the pull-ring of the curtains and jerking them back.

Her first impression was that she must still be asleep and dreaming. She remembered that the last Lord Warden was supposed to have done some rebuilding, but nothing had prepared her for what she actually saw. There was no sign that the Perilous Gard was "old" or even "a castle," as Master Roger had supposed. The walls were paneled in polished oak, finer even than the Princess Elizabeth's own bedchamber at Hatfield, and one wall was hung with a great tapestry showing ladies dressed in green, with garlands of oak leaves on their heads, dancing hand in hand through the trees of a flowery wood. The plaster ceiling was exquisitely moulded in an intricate strap-work design. The lattice windows flashed and sparkled with coats of arms painted on the glass. There were blue velvet cushions on both window seats; the long mirror that hung on the wall beside the bed was framed in gold and must have cost a fortune. She found her gray riding dress, brushed and sponged, laid out for her in a beautifully fitted garderobe opening off the main room.

The gray riding dress had been considerably battered by six days on the road; and Kate, surveying her reflection in the glass, could not help feeling a little out of place as she combed out her tousled hair before the golden mirror. The whole room would have made a much better setting for Alicia. Alicia would have looked lovely sitting on one of the blue velvet cushions with her shining head bent over an embroidery frame while she waited for the time when a knight on a white horse would (inevitably) come riding through the dark forest to rescue her.

Kate rose to her feet, and pushing back the lattice of the nearest window, leaned out to see if she could get any idea of the shape of the house.

Then she saw that Master Roger had been right after all. She was looking down into a paved courtyard surrounded on three sides by high gray battlemented walls and towers. At her side of the courtyard the whole of the castle had been rebuilt — she could make out fine oriel windows giving on a terrace below, and clusters of new chimneys rising from the roof above. The work was apparently not yet finished: there was a tangle of scaffolding around one of the chimneys, and the balustrade along the edge of the terrace was only half constructed, ending in a litter of raw stone and an ugly gap. Everywhere else the ancient walls and battlements and towers remained untouched. Most of them seemed to be abandoned, overgrown with ivy and gradually falling into decay. Only in one of the towers — a great square hulk of blackened limestone like a Norman keep on the far side of the courtyard — was there any stirring of life. There was a dark archway open at the foot, with a handcart standing before it. A man was unloading sacks and a pile of flat wooden boxes from the cart and carrying them inside.

The sacks held grain or something of the kind — she could tell that by the shape — but the boxes puzzled her until one of them suddenly toppled over and fell with a crash to the pavement. The catch of the lid broke open, and a shower of yellow tube-shaped objects fell bursting out over the stones of the courtyard. The man swore and scooped them back into the box again, jamming down the lid hurriedly, but not before Kate had seen what they were.

Wax candles — the yellow tube-shaped objects were wax candles, and they ought to go somewhere else before half of them were eaten by rats and the grain as well: her father had always said that old keeps were fit for nothing but charcoal or other rough stores. Kate stood watching the man at his work for another moment or so; then she shrugged and went back across the room to the door. It was, after all, no business of hers to decide what Sir Geoffrey did with his household supplies. She ought to be getting downstairs to find out what he intended to do with her.

The door opened on a short passage, and this in its turn opened on a carved oaken gallery overlooking an immense echoing hall of stone hung with arms and trophies. It was one of the "great halls" where in earlier times feasts and assemblies had been held, and was evidently much older than the part of the house from which she had come. From the gallery a flight of stairs ran down to the raised dais set aside for the lord of the castle and his family, three steps above the level of the floor.

Sir Geoffrey was sitting at the long table on the dais, a wine cup in his hand and two serving men bustling about him with silver-gilt dishes and platters and flagons. Randal was there, too: Kate, hesitating at the top of the stairs, could see him curled up on the steps of the dais, his harp resting against his shoulder as if he had just finished a song. A little old woman with a bunch of keys at her girdle was pattering to and fro supervising the serving men; and a very small fat man — from the chain of office about his neck, Kate thought that he must be the castle steward — was leaning over the table by Sir Geoffrey's side, apparently making some kind of report. Beyond them, with his back to one of the great oriel windows, stood another and much younger man, dressed in plain dark green like a forester or a huntsman, a little apart from the rest.

Sir Geoffrey glanced up and caught sight of Kate on the gallery.

"Awake, are you?" he called to her. "Dorothy here told me you were sleeping like the dead an hour ago. Come down and have your hot roast chicken. Humphrey, fetch a seat for Mistress Katherine."

Everybody in the hall immediately slewed around to stare at her except the young man at the window, who had turned his head and was looking out at the courtyard. One of the serving men ran to set a chair at the table beside Sir Geoffrey's, and the little old woman came fluttering up behind him with a dish of hot manchet-bread and a choice of honey or thick cream to eat with it.

"Honey, please," murmured Kate, stiffening under the gaze of so many curious eyes and slipping into the chair as quickly as she could.

"This is Dorothy," said Sir Geoffrey, nodding at the little woman. "My wife's old nurse, who sees to the house for me. She put you to bed last night, though I don't suppose you remember it. Randal you know. And this is Master John, the steward. I've been telling him about you. He'll be the one to care for you until I come back again."

"Oh, are you going away?" asked Kate, in a rather dismayed voice. She was beginning to feel at least accustomed to Sir Geoffrey by this time, and she had taken an instant dislike to Master John. Master John was bowing to her respectfully, with a welcoming smile, but the small black eyes in the fat smiling face were watchful and extraordinarily cold.

"I'm needed at home in Norfolk," said Sir Geoffrey curtly. "And I can't take you there: the Queen's orders were that you keep strictly to the Hall. Now, John, about the brick for the new chimneys —"

He turned away from her and took up his interrupted talk with the steward again. It was the sort of talk that Kate had often heard before, sitting in a corner while her father did the business of the merchant fleet that had grown up out of the one small trading brig in which her grandfather had first put out to sea — sales and repairs, records and accounts, the rise in prices, the purchase of supplies, though that talk had all been of shipping and voyages, and this was about sheepshearing and lead mining, manorial customs, the autumn sowing, a shipment of wine from Bristol that had mysteriously gone astray, the weight of the woolpack, the failure of the hay crop. Some of the discussion she could not follow, but most of it was plain enough. That was chiefly thanks to Master John. Master John was talking very well, all the facts and figures at the tips of his fingers: bills, prices, profits, and bargains (he seemed to have a remarkably good eye for a bargain), quite unruffled, never at a loss. He was, Kate gathered, already Lord Warden's steward when Sir Geoffrey inherited the estate — Lord Warden had died only that April — and it was clear that for some time the management of the whole place had been very largely in his hands. Sir Geoffrey evidently planned to leave it there. He was speaking rapidly and impatiently, with few questions and short answers, as if he had no heart for the discussion and his mind was really on something else.

"He's leaving everything for Master John to settle," thought Kate to herself. "What's the matter with him? . . . I don't believe he's listening to half of it. All he wants to do is get away."

She ate her hot roast chicken gloomily. It was plain to see that Sir Geoffrey was not going to linger at the Perilous Gard an hour longer than he had to; and once he was out of reach, who would be left to her? Old Dorothy seemed kind enough, but she was tottery with age and had a foolish trick of pursing up her lips in a condescending, now-now-your-old-nurse-knows-what-is-best-for-you manner. Kate glanced at the young man by the window. He was still standing there, his eyes on the court-yard, so quietly that in the talk and confusion she had not yet really looked at him. Sir Geoffrey did not seem to be aware that he was even in the room.

He was a very young man — only two or three years older than she was — and a handsome one, as tall as Sir Geoffrey, and with much the same kind of thick tawny-yellow hair. From his plain green dress, and the knife at his belt, she had taken him to be one of the foresters on the estate, a keeper or a huntsman per-haps, waiting to make his report when Master John had finished; but now, as she looked at him more narrowly, over the rim of her cup, she was not so sure. The hand resting on the hilt of the knife was long and finely made, with a heavy ring on one of the fingers; the hilt itself was studded with amber and inlaid with gold. He was standing bolt upright and curiously rigid, his jaw set, the mouth shut in a hard straight line. His face was very white, and he carried his head stiffly, as if he went on holding it erect only by the sheer force of his will.

Kate put down the cup, startled. She had seen that look before, during her grandfather's last illness, when he was suffer-ing almost unendurable pain.

"Oh, see to it yourself, John, see to it yourself, can't you?" Sir Geoffrey demanded, suddenly and violently. He rose to his feet. "Do anything you like. I've no more time to waste on you now: I want to be out of here at sunup. Have you done, Mistress Katherine? I told Dorothy to show you the house and settle your room for you. Randal, come with me." He set his untasted cup on the table, with a savage thud, and strode away. The young man at the window drew back a step to let him pass.

Sir Geoffrey went by him without a word or a glance, and on down the hall to the outer door. Master John, all bows and smiles, scurried after him; and when Kate turned her head again, the young man had disappeared.

Nobody else seemed to think that what had happened was in the least out of the ordinary. Humphrey and the other serving man were already clearing away the dishes on the table, and old Dorothy came pattering up to her again to ask her if she would care to look at the house before she went back to her chamber.

Kate nodded politely. She longed instead to sit old Dorothy down on the nearest stool and start asking her questions, but it seemed a little soon to try anything of that sort. From behind the great standing screen across the lower end of the hall, she could hear what sounded like a vast range of pantries, butteries, and kitchens still clattering with plates and voices; but Dorothy, pursing up her lips, led her firmly past these interesting noises to a side door opening back into the newly constructed part of the building, where they went solemnly through one beautiful, empty room after another.

"I did not know it was such a rich house," said Kate at last, looking about her wonderingly. They were standing in a long gallery of the kind that was becoming fashionable as the old solar chambers fell more and more out of style. The gallery was the most sumptuous she had ever seen, magnificently paneled, with one entire wall cut into a sweeping line of windows through which the sun fell dappling on polished floors and portraits and cabinets of rarities. From the windows she could see the ground below falling away sharply to the roofs and fields of a little village huddled at the foot of the hill on which the castle had

been built. Beyond the village was a stretch of open land dotted with groves of trees; and beyond that, as far as the eye could reach, the greens and far misty blues of the Elvenwood, with the cliffs closing in on either side of it.

"A rich house," she repeated, turning from the window to gaze around the gallery again. "A marvelous rich house."

Old Dorothy seemed pleased.

"The Wardens were ever great builders in their day and their time," she said, complacently. "My young lady's father finished this room the year after Queen Mary came to the throne." She had a high voice, and spoke with much the same curious, lilting accent as Randal. It seemed to be a peculiarity of the district. Master John, Kate remembered, had a touch of it too.

"They were an old family?" Kate decided she had better not mention Thomas Corget's report that the Wardens were a strange folk.

"*Old?*" Dorothy threw the word away from her with a contemptuous toss of her head. "Old, did you say to me? Look you here." She opened a small door in one corner of the gallery, and beckoned Kate through it onto a narrow walk that ran along the top of an ancient curtain wall, behind a battlemented parapet.

"Do you see that yonder?" she asked her, pointing west across the courtyard.

Kate nodded. It was the great square tower with the dark archway at the foot. The man with the handcart had gone away, and only a flight of rooks was wheeling and calling about the blackened stone.

"Lord Richard out of Normandy set that there to be his strong place many and many a hundred years ago, when he came into this land with Duke William the Conqueror, and took the old lord's daughter for his wife," said Dorothy, through the clamor of the rooks. "And even so it was not the first strong place that ever was built on that ground — no, nor the second, for the old lord's line had been in the land for many and many a hundred years before Lord Richard drove him out. He was a fierce proud man, Lord Richard was; they say he brought a master builder all the way from France to lay that tower, and killed him when the work was over so that no one would ever make another the like of it. But the old lord's daughter was a match for him, and she taught him the way of the land, and he reared his sons according to the custom of the Gard; and for many and many a hundred years they held the Elvenwood in their turn, and kept it free and safe from all the world. Oh, they were a great family, the Wardens, as mighty as kings in their day and their time, yet my poor lady's father was the last of them, and who's to have the care of us now?" She looked almost imploringly at Lord Richard's tower, her wrinkled hands shaking.

"Sir Geoffrey —" Kate began tentatively.

"And whoever heard of Sir Geoffrey before he came thrusting himself in where nobody wanted him?" old Dorothy snapped, with another contemptuous toss of her head. "My lady — she was young, and full of fancies, and she could twist her father around her thumb whenever it pleased her. Nothing would do but she must marry the man, and he no more than a beggarly knight who came to the door when he was lost in the Elvenwood. 'Let her alone, let her alone,' was all my lord would say. 'She can teach him the way of the land too, when I'm dead and gone; and better this one than another, for he loves her.' I told them what would come of it, over and over again I told them. You could never teach *him* the way of the land. They're all soft, the Herons."

"*Soft?*" Kate's chief impression of Sir Geoffrey had been that he was made entirely out of granite and steel.

"Big and soft and stupid," said old Dorothy, viciously. "Haven't you eyes? You saw him with his brother."

"What brother?"

"Christopher Heron." Dorothy spoke the name almost as though she were spitting it out of her mouth. "You saw him. He was over by the window while you were eating your bit of a dinner."

"That was Sir Geoffrey's *brother?*" Kate knew now what the height and the thick tawny hair had reminded her of. "B-but why does he treat him so, then?"

"Because he's softhearted, I said! It was his own child — his own child, the only child my poor lady had; and Christopher Heron was crazed with jealousy of her, wanting the whole inheritance for himself. He's always been mad to have land of his own. Any of Sir Geoffrey's men will tell you that."

"Are you saying," Kate demanded incredulously, "that he *killed* her?"

"I'm not saying it; he says it himself. What more do you want? There's some that will make another tale of it, but don't you believe them. I know what I heard with my own ears. 'I killed her,' he said to his brother, standing there before all of us as white as his shirt; and not a thing did Sir Geoffrey do but turn his back on him and walk away. They say he has a great name for justice in his own country. Justice! What he ought to have done was tie his hands behind his back and hang him to a —"

"Dorothy."

Sir Geoffrey had opened the door from the gallery, and was standing at the end of the walk, Master John at his shoulder. Dorothy stopped short, and in spite of her belief in his softheartedness, made a noise like a frightened hen.

"You can go now, Dorothy," said Sir Geoffrey. "You're

wanted in the hall. John here will take you down." He did
not raise his voice, and it was impossible to tell from his face
just how much he had overheard, but Dorothy went scuttling
past him as if in a high wind, Master John kindly taking hold
of her arm to steady her through the doorway. Kate thought she
saw the fat white fingers close very hard in the flesh of the arm as
he did so, but they were both gone so quickly that she could not
be sure. She and her guardian were left facing each other along
the line of battlements.

"Come here," said Sir Geoffrey.

Kate went. She hoped that she did not actually scuttle, like
Dorothy, but it seemed a long way.

There was a pause, while Sir Geoffrey regarded her grimly
and she felt herself slowly shrinking to the size of a very small
pebble that lay on one of the stone corbels near to his hand.
It must look so dreadfully as if she had gone sneaking off to
whisper scandal in a corner the minute he let her out of his
sight.

"Sir Geoffrey —" she began, stiffly.

Sir Geoffrey apparently did not even hear her.

"Mistress Katherine." It was the same level voice he had
used with old Dorothy. "Before I go to Norfolk, there is something I have to make clear to you."

Kate waited helplessly for the storm to break.

"Did the Queen tell you the terms on which you are to live
here?"

"T-the — the —" Kate stammered. "No."

Sir Geoffrey picked up the little pebble and stood for a
moment turning it over in his fingers, and looking down at the
courtyard. Kate, following his glance, saw that Christopher
Heron had come out of the door to the hall below and was
crossing the pavement. His head was bent; the afternoon sun

glinted on the thick tawny golden hair. He went on past the dark archway to Lord Richard's tower, turned around a corner, and disappeared from view.

"Her Majesty was very plain with me," said Sir Geoffrey, still in that level voice. "You are to be lodged and served like a lady of your rank, but not to go out of the park — there's no park, so we'll call it the village and a mile from the house. Do you understand that?"

"Yes, Sir Geoffrey."

"You are not to send or receive letters for any reason whatsoever."

"Yes, Sir Geoffrey."

"Your friends and your family are not to visit you, and you may not have other company except in my presence and with my express leave. That," Sir Geoffrey added, "means, at this time, Master John's leave. It will be his business to see to you as long as I am away. If you're in any doubt as to what you can do, go to him and he'll tell you."

Kate swallowed hard. After her day in the forest, she felt no particular desire to go anywhere further than the village and a mile from the house — but the thought of being told what she could or could not do by Master John did rather stick in her throat.

"When are you coming back?" she inquired hopefully. It might not be so bad if it was only for a couple of weeks.

"Some time after All Saints' Day," said Sir Geoffrey, flicking the little pebble across the courtyard.

All Saints' Day was the beginning of Advent, the first day in November, just after the harvest festival, and half the summer away.

"Yes, Sir Geoffrey," she said, swallowing again.

The old reluctant hint of a smile came slowly back into her guardian's eyes.

"That will be enough of the yes-Sir-Geoffrey," he informed her. "And I don't want to hear any more of the no-Sir-Geoffrey or I-thank-you-Sir-Geoffrey either, my girl! I know I'm in a foul humor, but I'm always in a foul humor these days, and it's nothing to do with you. There! Now give me your hand and cry friends with me, can't you?"

Kate took an awkward step towards him. "I hadn't meant to gossip with Dorothy," she ventured to apologize. "It was only —"

"I know that too." The big hand closed over hers and held it. "All I'm asking of you is to be a good lass while I'm away and mind your book and don't go cumbering your head with other folks' troubles. You know the old proverb that there's no sense meddling in what you can't mend? — Didn't your father ever say that to you?"

Kate nodded a little doubtfully. "Well," she began, "he —"

"Then you take his advice if you won't take mine. He has the name of being a wise man, your father."

The corner of Kate's mouth quivered very slightly as she followed him meekly through the door of the long gallery. She had often heard her father quote that proverb; he said it was invented by fools to save them the trouble of thinking. " 'Don't meddle in what you can't mend!' " he would growl at her. "And how do you know it's past mending? There'll be time enough not to meddle after you've looked into the matter. At least you could try to satisfy your mind first."

IV 🦢
The Holy Well

Kate was sitting by the window in the long gallery, with her hands clasped about her knees, watching old Dorothy mend the frayed edge of a tapestry on the wall. Old Dorothy was a wonderful needlewoman, and in spite of her age did a great deal of work that she might better have left to the sewing maids, if, as she was complaining at the moment, they hadn't been a pair of young slatterns, barely able to hem sheets. Now back in her lady's time, before Sir Geoffrey —

She stopped short with a jerk of her thread.

"Yes, Dorothy?"

"No matter," said Dorothy, rather flurriedly. "Never you mind. I'll thank you for that ball of silk, Mistress Katherine. The green one in the basket, next to your hand."

Kate bent to pick up the ball with a little sigh. She had been at the Perilous Gard now for over a week, and she was no nearer to knowing the true state of affairs there than she had been on the day of her arrival. Whatever Master John had said to Dorothy on their way down from the battlement walk — and Kate had the clearest possible memory of the fat white fingers sinking into the old woman's arm — it had cut off any more talk about her lady and Sir Geoffrey and Christopher Heron as clean as a knife. Kate could do nothing with her. Dorothy would only turn flustered or stubborn, and go scuttering away from anything that looked even remotely as if it might be dangerous ground. But at least Kate was allowed to follow her about and pick up an occasional ball of silk or a crumb of conversation, though the conversation was now made up entirely of complaints about the younger servants or long rambling tales about dead-and-gone Wardens, all tiresome. The Wardens had certainly been great builders and lived richly as dukes, but they did not seem to have done much of anything else. They had not gone crusading; they had somehow contrived to stay out of the wars of the Roses; the unending aristocratic struggle for power, rank, office, court favor, and advantageous marriages appeared to have passed them by. They had evidently wanted nothing, fought for nothing, and occupied themselves with nothing except what was necessary for the maintenance of the Perilous Gard. They stood almost as aloof from the world as if they were members of some religious order — but there was no sign that they had ever been religious; they did not even keep a household chaplain of their own, like other noble families. So much and no more Kate had learned — and even the learning of that much, she reflected bitterly, was beginning to seem like a feat to be proud of.

It was not that Master John treated her badly. To Mistress Katherine Sutton, once a royal maid of honor, Master John was always smiling and affable, with a bow and a sympathetic glance whenever he was obliged to refer to Sir Geoffrey's orders from the Queen, or his own orders from Sir Geoffrey. She was not locked up, or insulted, or abused. She was only quietly and deftly shut out of the life of the castle. With its foresters, clerks, grooms, and serving men, its falconers and dog boys, its cooks, pantlers, and scullions, its chambermaids, sewing women, laundresses, pages, and all the other ragtag and bobtail of a "great household," Elvenwood Hall was a community in itself;

but Kate was almost as alone as though she had actually been chained up to the wall in the black dungeon of Alicia's imagination. From her windows she could sometimes see a couple of grooms saunter across the courtyard, or carters carrying another consignment of stores into Lord Richard's tower, or the porter lumbering up from the gate; but as soon as she appeared the grooms would be sure to move off, the carters vanish around a corner, and the porter go by her in a great hurry to see to some business of his own. When she came upon a maid dusting one of the rooms, the girl would hardly wait to drop a curtsy before whipping away like a mouse; and she never saw the serving men or pages except while she was eating her meals in the great hall under the cold eye of Master John, humbly erect in his proper place by the cupboard. Randal had gone back to Norfolk with Sir Geoffrey, and Christopher Heron she had not met at all. She thought she had caught a glimpse of him once, through the archway that led to the outer bailey court and the main gate; but when she ran out there was nobody in the court but Master John, who merely smiled and remarked that it was a fine evening for a walk, did she mean to go as far as the village?

Kate, strong in Sir Geoffrey's ruling about the "village and a mile from the house," had nodded and marched rather defiantly past him out at the gate. That was on the first day after her arrival, before she had seen the village or had any real taste of Master John's quality.

The village proved to be only a scattering of stone cottages about a green, with a tiny alehouse at one end and a very small, tumble-down church at the other. Beyond the church, there was a mill clacking away by a little river, and corn fields carefully shared out into long strips for planting, according to the old custom. The sun had just begun to set; a handful of men were gossiping with the priest by the church porch, and a mother or so had already come out on her doorstep to call the children in to their beds. A last game of tag was dashing and shouting around the green.

It all looked so pleasant and so blessedly ordinary after the Perilous Gard that Kate paused to watch for a moment at the turn of the path. Nobody saw her: she was in the shadow of a high stone wall, and the village was wholly taken up with its own affairs. The racing line of children wheeled nearer; one little boy, running wildly, swerved, collided against her, and went down on the grass almost at her feet. Kate stooped to pick him up. He was a very small boy with a shock of dirty hair, and a drip at the end of his nose.

"There, you're not hurt," she said quickly. "Don't be afraid; it's only —" and suddenly realized that something was wrong.

A redheaded woman drawing water at the well had straightened up and was staring at her. Everybody was staring. The men by the church porch had broken off their talk, the children had stopped playing and were huddled uneasily together, all staring at her with hostile, terrified eyes. The little boy tore loose from her hold and darted frantically across the path to the redheaded woman.

Kate stared back at them in bewilderment. The village was so far off the beaten road that she would not have been surprised to find the people shy of outsiders — silent, awkward, suspicious even — but she was entirely unprepared for the sort of fear and hatred that had swept over their faces when they saw her with the little boy. "He isn't hurt," she repeated, taking a step forward. "I didn't mean —" but the woman only caught the child up in her arms and began backing away. The other men and women scattered to let her through. The next instant there was nobody left on the path except Kate herself and the priest, still standing his ground by the church porch. He was an old man, with a careworn, gentle look; but he held himself very straight, and his faded blue eyes met hers sternly, full of repudiation and horror. Then he raised his hand and made the sign of the cross on the air between them.

It was too much. Kate, white with shock, stood for a moment as if he had struck her and then, lifting her chin, turned away without another word and walked back up the steep path that led to the castle. Master John was still at the gate, apparently enjoying the evening air, and moved aside with a respectful bow when she came in.

"Here again so soon, Mistress Katherine?" he inquired solicitously. "You shouldn't have troubled yourself with the villagers. They're a little distrustful of strangers, if I make myself clear."

"Yes, Master John," said Kate in her stoniest voice. One thing at least was perfectly clear. Master John had known what would happen and was laughing up his sleeve at her. She could still see the flicker of malicious amusement in his eyes as she sat by the window of the long gallery listening to old Dorothy chatter about the sewing maids and gazing down at the cluster of roofs in the valley below.

The sky was overcast again, but the corn fields had begun to change color at last, and it looked as though there might be some hope for the crop. Two men on horseback had just emerged from the shadows of the forest and were coming slowly down the road towards the castle. They paused for a moment under the last of the great oak trees; then they dismounted, and started to make their way up the winding path to the gate on foot.

Kate, surprised, leaned forward to get a better view. The path, though very steep, was well cared for and quite safe for riding; even a stranger ought to have been able to see that. And one of the men should not have been walking at all: he was lame, with white hair, and pitifully slow.

"Dorothy!" she said over her shoulder. "Come here, Dorothy! Look! Who are those men? Why are they leading their horses?"

Dorothy gave them one brief glance and returned to her tapestry.

"They always do," she answered indifferently. "Pluck an oak branch from a tree by the hill and walk up the rest of the way — that's the rule of the land. Don't fall out of the window, Mistress Katherine. It's only a couple of pilgrims coming to the Well. They'll have to spend the night here now, it's so late."

"Pilgrims?"

It was the last word Kate had expected to hear. The old custom of going on pilgrimage to the holy places had been dying out in England ever since King Henry had plundered the great shrines during his quarrel with the Pope; and even at the best of times, the Perilous Gard could never have been a holy place like Walsingham or Canterbury, if the miserable condition of the church in the village was anything to go by.

"Pilgrims?" she repeated incredulously.

"Didn't you hear me? Pilgrims, coming to the Well."

"What well?"

"The Holy Well," snapped old Dorothy, like a Londoner being asked for the third time what he meant by Saint Paul's Cathedral. "Over the wall westward, at the back of Lord Richard's tower."

"Oh," said Kate, beginning to understand. There were holy wells in other parts of England. They were usually springs or fountains which some saint was supposed to have blessed in the old days, and country folk in the neighborhood were likely to believe that a certain power of healing still lingered on the waters. "We had a maid at home once who came from a place in Kent where they had a holy well," she told Dorothy. "The girls used to go and bathe their faces in it every May Day for a charm to make them prettier."

"Did they, indeed!" said Dorothy, with a disdainful shrug. "And what's a pretty face? Could the water in Kent take away sorrow and pain and the grief of a wound, like the Holy Well here at the Gard?"

"I don't know," said Kate doubtfully, feeling that given the pretty face, the sorrow and the pain could be left to take care of themselves. "What is it that you do here? Bathe your faces, the way they did in Kent?"

"Bathe your face in water from the Holy Well?" Old Dorothy sounded scandalized at the very idea of it. "No, no, Mistress Katherine: it's only to drink for a cure. You must first go up to the cave where the Well is, and dip your oak branch in the spring outside. Then you must offer a gift to be taken by the Well, speaking your trouble aloud, so that Those who rule over the Well can hear you."

"You mean there's some special saint that you pray to?" asked Kate, finding this a little hard to follow.

"I mean Those who rule over the Well," said old Dorothy obstinately. "Why should we trouble ourselves with the saints? Those who rule over the Well were here in the land for many and many a hundred years before *they* were heard of. But —" she broke off again, fumbling nervously with the ball of green silk. "Now, don't you go fretting about the Well any more, Mistress Katherine. It's not for me to talk of such matters. Master John's the one to tell you. You ask him if you're so wishful to know."

And much good that would do me, thought Kate to herself, watching Dorothy patter hastily out of the room. After what had happened in the village, she would not have asked Master

John for so much as the time of day; and when she heard his voice from the back of the courtyard early the next morning, she slipped quietly into the dark entry of Lord Richard's tower to wait until he went by.

Master John came walking briskly past, followed by two other men. One was a young serving man in an unfamiliar livery, with a leather traveling-bottle slung over his arm; but the second was the elderly pilgrim she had seen coming up the road the day before; or so she judged from his white hair and the branch of oak leaves he was carrying with him. His face was almost as white as his hair, strangely rapt and exalted, and the branch he held had been dipped into water. Drops still hung gleaming on every leaf and twig and ran down over his fingers. Even after he had passed her and was gone up the steps to the terrace, the way he had come was marked by a faint line of dark wet splashes scattered along the pavement.

There was no time to work out a plan — Kate's first thought was to move quickly before the trail of splashes could dry out again. The faint dark line led her around the corner of Lord Richard's tower, through an old broken passage with ivy clustering between the stones, and finally out into a tiny circular courtyard, furred all over with thick fine moss as green as an emerald in a ring. To her left a flight of cracked and uneven stone steps went up to the battlemented walk that ran along the top of the outer wall. Below the walk, set in the mid-curve of the wall, was a narrow archway framed with blocks of carving that were pitted by age and hard weather. Through the archway she could see grass and rocks and a glimpse of open country.

Kate crossed the courtyard very slowly, frowning: her eyes on the archway. She was thinking of the fortifications at the other side of the castle, the massive walls rising out of the hill, the one steep road winding up to the gate, the gatehouse with its portcullis and arrow slits and towers. Even now, with its defenses neglected and the walls beginning to decay, the place had appeared overpoweringly strong; in the old lords' time it must have been impregnable. Yet here there were no defenses whatever, not so much as a door in the archway, not so much as a trace on the stone to show that a door had once been there before it had fallen away.

It was only when she passed through the archway and came on the grass beyond that she understood why. What she had thought was open country was actually a small deep valley, hardly more than a gorge, lying between high cliffs that were flung up sheer hundreds of feet into fantastic pinnacles and crumbling overhung masses of rock. The Perilous Gard was backed into the mouth of this gorge as though it were an old lion crouching in the entrance to his den, its great shoulders touching the cliffs on either side and filling the gap completely. The whole valley was sealed off. It could not be attacked or even approached except through the castle itself.

The archway from the castle opened on a wide flat stretch of grass, cut to a rough lawn; and at the far side of this lawn was an enormous standing stone, like the ones on Salisbury Plain, more than twice the height of a tall man. It was a gray cloudy day, smelling of wild places, with the promise of rain in the air. The only living thing in sight was a hawk circling and soaring on the wind above the cliffs.

Kate stood hesitating a moment in the archway. She did not care for wild places, and nothing but curiosity and a rankling determination to get the better of Master John made her go on. There was a thread of a path running along the turf to the right of the Standing Stone, and she began to pick her way along it.

Beyond the Standing Stone the ground fell away and dropped sharply to the floor of the valley, so sharply that Kate would not have been able to keep her feet if the path had not been thrown back and forth across the steep decline of the slope instead of going straight down. The floor of the valley was all rock, littered with great boulders and loose scree and shards washed from the cliffs; only the path was free of them. The valley grew steadily narrower and deeper, the cliffs closing in and the path winding down until it finally came to an end in a little bay of green grass with the crags towering all around it.

The little bay was cool and very quiet except for the sound of running water. It came from a spring that fell from a crevice in the cliff wall on her right, and ran murmuring for a few feet through moss and clustering ferns and tufts of wild flowers clinging precariously to the stones before it was lost again among the rocks. In the cliff wall opposite the spring was a dark jagged opening like the entrance to a cave.

It was not a large cave. Even by the dim light that filtered in through the narrow opening, Kate could see that it was only a sort of chamber, walled and roofed and floored with living rock. The Holy Well lay in the center, a black circle surrounded by a curb of carved stonework, so old that the figures in the carving had worn away to nothing but blobs and lumps.

The Well was unusually wide and the curb very high — long-legged though she was, Kate's breast was barely level with the rim. The rim itself was made of flat hewn stones, carefully fitted together but very unequal in size. Those towards the back of the cave were fairly narrow, while those towards the front, facing the entrance, widened abruptly and came thrusting out to form a broad shallow lip. Standing on this ledge was a deep bowl of greenish bronze, fastened by a long chain to a bronze ring sunk into one of the stones. The bowl was empty, but still wet, and the stone on which it rested was splashed with water. There was no other sign that a pilgrim had been there that morning.

There was also nothing to account for the rapt, ecstatic look she had seen on his face as he passed her. What any sane person could have found to reverence about the Holy Well was beyond Kate's comprehension. The round black cavity with its out-thrust lip reminded her unpleasantly of an open toothless mouth; and the air that came from it was cold, dank with the smell of wet moss and old decaying rock.

Even when she found a toe hold on the carving and scrambled clumsily part way up the curb, she could not see anything over the ledge except a ring of slimy stones going down a few feet and then vanishing into total darkness. Far below there rose the sound of running water again, unexpectedly loud, as if the Well were not fed from a spring or pool, but opened directly on some fast-moving underground stream. She found a heavy shard loose on the rim and pushed it off into the hole, scrambling a little higher and leaning still further forward to try to gauge the depth of the shaft.

The shard disappeared completely. Not the faintest tin-kling splash came up to her through the booming depths of the water.

Kate drew back. She was beginning to feel cramped and dizzy with stooping; and the cold air rising from the Well seemed stronger.

Then, from behind her in the shadows, a hand suddenly shot out and closed over her wrist. She was torn from her hold, pulled down off the curbstones, lifted bodily, and hauled, scuffling ignominiously, to the grassplot outside the cave. And the angriest voice she had ever heard in her life was shouting at her.

"What are you doing up there, you fool?" it cried. "Come down, do you hear me? Come down!"

Christopher Heron was standing between her and the entrance to the Well. He was dressed now in a tattered old blue shepherd's smock that he might have picked up on a rubbish heap, and the fine gold-hilted knife was gone from his belt; but Christopher Heron it certainly was. The hand was still clamped like iron about her wrist.

Kate looked back at him, almost as angry as he. She had never liked being swept off her own feet and dangled helplessly, even as a game in the nursery.

"I *am* down," she pointed out coldly.

Christopher Heron stared at her. His eyes went from her hair, which was tumbling crazily about her ears, to the skirt of her dress, which was dark with slime and streaks of moss where he had dragged her down the curbstones; and a slow, painful flush began to pour over his face But the hold on her wrist did not slacken. "I thought you were going over the edge," he said. "You might have been killed."

"I might have been if it was a moonless night and the curb wasn't nearly five feet high," Kate retorted "How could anyone go over the edge? A child would be perfectly safe in there."

The grip on her wrist tightened savagely for an instant; then it loosened, and he took a step back, away from her, his hands dropping to his sides. All the color and excitement had suddenly drained out of his face, and it looked very faintly, almost contemptuously, amused.

"You'll be telling me that Cecily's safe and alive next," he said.

"And so she may be for all I know," Kate snapped at him. "Who *is* Cecily?"

"The child you were speaking of."

"What child?"

"His child," said Christopher impatiently. "Surely Geoffrey told you what became of her."

"Well, he didn't. I never heard of anyone named Cecily in my life."

"Somebody must have told you. Master John, or old Dorothy."

Kate's mind went back all at once to that first afternoon when she had stood on the battlement walk outside the long gallery looking across the courtyard to Lord Richard's tower. "Dorothy did say —" she began.

"I thought as much. What did she say?"

"She said —" Kate suddenly realized just what was coming and tried to stop; but it was too late: the words were already out of her mouth. "She said you'd killed Sir Geoffrey's daughter to get the whole inheritance for yourself — I didn't believe her," she added hastily.

Christopher Heron only shrugged his shoulders.

"Why not?" he asked. "It makes a far better tale than what really happened."

Kate frowned at him. She had always detested being laughed at, and the mysteries and uncertainties of life at Elvenwood Hall were becoming more than she could bear.

"What *did* happen?" she demanded bluntly.

The look that came into Christopher's eyes made her regret the question the instant she asked it. They were no longer amused, or contemptuous, or even angry — only cold, level, and as implacably stern as his brother's. He stood there before her in silence for a long moment, while the question — which seemed to Kate to grow louder and ruder with every passing second — hung unanswered in the air between them. Then he said, very slowly and deliberately:

"I'll tell you."

And Kate realized with a start that the look in his eyes had not been meant for her at all. It was himself that he had considered and judged. The "I'll tell you" did not mean that he liked or trusted her, only that he had passed a sentence on himself.

"No!" she said sharply. "Don't! I'm sorry. I shouldn't have asked you."

Christopher Heron went straight on without heeding her.

"There is one thing you ought to hear first," he said, in that deliberate voice. "It is what Geoffrey did for me. I am twenty years younger than he is. My mother was too old to have another child: she died when I was born, and my father never forgave me for it. He could no more bring himself to look at me or speak to me than — than Geoffrey can, now."

"Do you mean to say," Kate asked incredulously, "that your own father never spoke to you *at all?*"

"Well, I remember him telling me once that I was born damned," said Christopher calmly, "but he didn't live long enough to see how right he was. Geoffrey was the only one who cared for me. He saw to it that I got some learning, and gave me a horse — not a pony, a proper horse — and taught me to ride himself. He was a stern man in many ways, but a very kind brother too. If it hadn't been for his wife —"

"What was wrong with his wife?"

"Nothing — as far as I can tell. I never saw much of her. He didn't have a wife until five years ago, and then he married Anne Warden, God knows why. She was a little sickly thing, always ailing, and afraid of her own shadow; but Geoffrey thought the sun rose and set in her. She made him leave home and take that post in Ireland: I know she did."

"It was Queen Mary who sent Sir Geoffrey to Ireland."

"There were plenty of other men she could have sent to

Ireland instead. Geoffrey didn't have to go: he went because Anne wanted it so much. For some reason she was bound and determined to get him out of the country and away from us all."

"You didn't like her, did you?"

Christopher paused, and then went on as if he had not even heard the question. Whatever sentence he had passed on himself, there were evidently some things that it did not bind him to tell her; and the nature of his private feelings was one of them.

"They stayed in Ireland until she died, and Geoffrey came home with the child. That was last winter. Cecily was four then."

This time Kate knew better than to ask him whether he had liked the child.

"Geoffrey was still grieving for Anne, and very concerned to keep Cecily happy. My sister Jennifer — she's married and lives in London — wanted to take her to bring up with her own children; but Geoffrey couldn't bear to part from her. We were afraid she'd miss her mother, and her old home, and — well, I suppose the truth is that we both fell into the way of making too much of her. Jenny said that if we didn't take care we'd ruin her between us; but Geoffrey had seen too much of taking grief out on a child, and so had I . . . Then this April, Lord Warden died too, and we had to come down and settle what was to be done with the estate. Cecily ought to have stayed at home with her nurse; but she kept crying and crying to go with us, and we didn't reckon on what she might do when she got here. It was bad enough the first night, when she wouldn't go to sleep without one of us on each side of her bed singing her lullabies; but it was worse in the morning. Geoffrey had to be off by himself, working on accounts, so he gave her over to me and told me to take care of her until it was time for dinner. I didn't mind that. But there was one game she wanted to play — a silly thing we called Cecily-is-lost. I'd look away and count to a hundred while she hid somewhere, and then run up and down calling O-Cecily-is-lost-where-is-Cecily? until she jumped out and laughed at me. I wouldn't have cared if we'd been alone to ourselves, but we were out on the terrace by the hall, and half the household was hanging out the windows to see what the new young master would do next. I told her to come indoors and be quiet, but she only stuck out her tongue and ran away — she was very quick on her feet and harder to catch than a butterfly — and a fine fool I felt, my first day at the place, chasing her around the courtyard with Master John and old Dorothy and all the rest of them looking on and snickering up their sleeves at me. As if that mattered!"

Kate bent to pick a flake of wet moss from the folds of her skirt. She supposed that the whole thing had served Christopher right — he and his brother must have spoiled Cecily outrageously, but . . .

"Tell me," she said irrelevantly, "did she have golden eyes? Big golden eyes, almost the color of honey?"

"Cecily?" Christopher looked puzzled. "No: her eyes were gray, like Geoffrey's and mine. Why? What has that to do with it?"

"Nothing," said Kate. "I'm sorry: go on. What happened then?"

"By that time I didn't care *what* happened. All I wanted to do was to be rid of her. I shouted to Master John to see to the child — she'd ended up hiding behind him in one of the doorways — and went away by myself to walk it off by going to look at the Holy Well. Randal was always talking of the Holy Well, and old Dorothy had been crooning to Cecily about it too, the night before, while we were trying to put her to sleep.

"When I was past the Standing Stone I saw that she'd gotten

away from Master John somehow and was following me. She was keeping behind the rocks, ready to run if I started after her, but I didn't. I went on to the Well without looking around, and threw my penny in the water, and had my drink; and when it came to speaking my troubles aloud, I called out that Cecily Heron was a pestiferous brat and I wished that somebody else had the charge of her. I could see her out of the corner of my eye, over by the spring, peeping between those two big stone slabs, and I knew she was listening; but I was still so angry that I didn't try to go after her. I only sat down by the edge of the path with my back turned, and waited for her to come to me. I was sure she'd come to me sooner or later if I didn't pay any heed to her, and it was better to have her up here than playing off any more of her tricks down at the Hall. *I* thought it was perfectly safe, too. There were the cliffs on both sides of us, and I was sitting by the path, and the curb of the well was — how did you put it? — nearly five feet off the ground. Even when I looked for her and didn't see her, I couldn't believe it. I only thought she'd found an especially good place, and was hiding again."

"You — you mean she slipped past you?"

"No. I was watching for that. She was behind me all the time. If she went anywhere, it was —" He turned his head and looked at the narrow dark opening among the rocks.

Kate caught her breath.

"But she couldn't," she said desperately. "She couldn't — it's not possible. She couldn't have climbed up and fallen. She *could not* have climbed up there. The carving isn't deep enough to give her a hold. I had to catch at the rim before I could get any grip myself."

Christopher Heron put his hand into the breast of his smock and held something out to her. It was a very small slipper, made of fine leather, bright crimson, the toe scuffed, and a loose lace trailing from a broken eyelet at the ankle.

"I found that on the lip by the edge of the shaft," he told her. "The lace had caught between two of those flat stones. She must have climbed up somehow and torn it off when she fell. We never got her body back. Master John says that no one knows how deep the Well is. It goes down into a chasm below the rocks, some sort of underground river. The water runs very strong there; didn't you hear it? Everything you throw in gets carried away. They call it 'being taken by the Well.' That was what old Dorothy kept screaming — 'The Well's taken her! You let the Well take her!' over and over again."

Old Dorothy screaming, feet running, the empty gaping circle of stones with its wet lip like a mouth, the useless torches and ropes, the shouts, the questions, the crowd of faces, Sir Geoffrey's face, Christopher Heron's —

Kate's eyes went from the narrow dark opening among the rocks to Christopher Heron, standing by the spring with his back to the cliff wall. He was still looking at the entrance to the cave, steadily, and without moving.

"Well?" he said.

Kate lifted her head, groping among her scattered wits for one fragment of the story that had puzzled her.

"How did Master John know that there *was* a chasm under the rocks?" she inquired shakily.

"Lord, girl!" Christopher Heron was startled out of his immobility. "Is that all you can say?"

"I-I'm sorry," Kate stammered. "I was only wondering —"

"I didn't murder anyone to inherit Elvenwood Hall. The whole of the Elvenwood can sink in the sea before I'd lay a finger on it. But what old Dorothy said to you was true. I killed Cecily. She was the dearest thing in the world to Geoffrey, and he trusted her to me, and I brought her to this place, and I killed her. Is that clear?"

"Yes, but —"

"And you want to know why Master John thought there was a chasm under the rocks?"

Kate flushed. What had he expected her to do? Start screaming at him, like old Dorothy?

"Yes," she repeated stubbornly.

Christopher Heron shrugged his shoulders again.

"I can't tell you why Master John thought so. From what I've seen of Master John, I should say he was down in the chasm trying to fish out some of the pilgrims' gold. Master John doesn't strike me as the sort of man to let a little thing like superstition stand in the way of his picking up an honest penny."

"Could he do it?" asked Kate promptly.

"No. The current down there would carry anything away. I only said he might try. It must go to his heart to see all that good money lost in the water."

"Does it really cure sorrow or pain and the grief of a wound?" said Kate, frowning a little.

"The water, or the money?"

Kate decided to ignore this frivolity. "Dorothy sounded so certain that it did," she persisted.

"I don't know. I never tried."

"You told me you drank some of the water. What did it taste like?"

"It tasted like water to me," said Christopher Heron. "Cold plain water. But old Dorothy would certainly tell you that that was because I only gave a penny to the Well."

"Why?"

"The story goes that the more you cast in, the stronger the

water you draw out will be. A penny only brings you luck. A silver piece, and the cup will cheer you. To cure sorrow or pain and the grief of a wound, it has to be gold or precious stones. Pure gold and rubies are the best, but any small diamond or pearl you may happen to have about you —"

"You're laughing at me," Kate interrupted him. "That can't be true."

"I didn't say it was true. I said it was the way the story went."

Kate sighed. She had thought there was a chance that the water might actually be medicinal, like the mineral springs at Buxton — she had passed through Buxton on her way north with Sir Geoffrey — and instead it was only a pother of outlandish magical nonsense like something in a romance.

"What's the matter now?" asked Christopher Heron. "Are you suffering from sorrow or pain and the grief of a wound? Throw a diamond or a ruby into the Holy Well, and that will ease you."

"I'm not a heathen savage," said Kate. "Diamonds and rubies! I never heard such foolishness."

"What a good clear mind you have."

"It doesn't take a very clear mind to keep from throwing diamonds and rubies down a hole in the ground. As if anyone would!"

"Anyone? What about old Dorothy?"

"Anyone who had a diamond or a ruby to spend wouldn't be a poor ignorant creature like old Dorothy."

"Oh, would they not!" Christopher's mouth twisted wryly for an instant. "In the last four months I must have seen almost fifty pilgrims go up to the Well. About half looked to be charcoal burners or gypsies or servants from the Hall with a penny to spend for luck. The other twenty-five or so were rich folk, no mistaking it — what our old bailiff in Norfolk would call 'gentry born': velvet and fur and Master John to escort them, big purses at their belts and big rings on their fingers and big clinking gold chains around their necks. When they come down from the Well, the chains are gone and their hands are bare and the purses are flat — and it isn't only for the one time, either. Some of them come back over and over again. Did you see the old gentleman who was here this morning?"

"Yes," said Kate reluctantly.

"That was the third time he's gone up to the Well since I've been here. Then there's a woman in mourning black — she comes very often, almost every two weeks — and a dark girl with some sort of scar or blotch on her face, and a one-armed man, and five or six others, all holding wet branches and bottles of water to their bosoms, happy as drunkards, the poor ignorant creatures."

"Are you sure?" Kate could still hardly believe it.

"Certain. One of the Wardens about a hundred years ago had a son called Henry who was a leper. They built a hut for him to live in down yonder among the rocks. You can watch the whole valley from there. Nobody could go by on the path without my seeing them."

"Why?"

"I told you why," said Christopher impatiently. "The man was a leper. He had to stay where he could see people coming if he was going to keep out of their way."

"No, no, it isn't that. You said, without *your* seeing, nobody could go past without your seeing them. As if you were there all the time. As if —" An appalling thought suddenly flashed into Kate's mind. "Sir Geoffrey doesn't make you *live* in that place, does he?"

"Geoffrey has nothing to do with it," said Christopher Heron. "He hasn't concerned himself with me or my affairs for a long time now, any more than my father did. I live as I please."

"In that place?"

"I go back to the Hall whenever Geoffrey comes."

"But when he's away you live in that place?"

"I have to live somewhere."

Kate looked up the narrow valley with its litter of fallen stones and the bare rock shutting it in on either side. The gray clouds that had filled the sky all morning had begun to close down and were pouring over the cliffs like smoke. "But surely you haven't any need —" she began.

"No: Henry Warden saw to all that," Christopher cut in before she could finish the sentence. "It's not far to the spring, and there's a flat rock by the door of the hut where a boy from the castle could come and leave food without troubling him."

"I don't care what Henry Warden did," said Kate fiercely. "You aren't a leper like Henry Warden."

"No, I'm not. He shut himself away before he could kill anybody."

"You didn't kill Cecily."

"Why is she dead, then?"

"You didn't mean to kill her. Any more than you meant to kill your mother."

"I could have kept her safe at the Hall, I could have tried to catch her on the path, I could have gone to look for her sooner, I said I wanted to be rid of her, perhaps in my heart I always wanted to be rid of her without knowing it. How can *you* tell what I meant to do? How can I? How can anyone? I think the damned souls in hell must spend half their time wondering what it was that they really meant to do."

"If you think the damned in hell spend their time doing that, then you can't know very much about the damned in hell," Kate retorted furiously. "I am utterly at squares with this childish dealing. Why in the name of heaven don't you go down to the village and make a proper confession to the priest and let him tell you what penance you ought to be laying on yourself? You aren't one of the damned in hell. We're all of us under the Mercy."

"I'll lay my own penance on myself," said Christopher Heron. "And I wasn't born under the Mercy . . . Good lord, it's starting to rain again! Look at that sky."

Kate disregarded the sky. "You could at least go away somewhere else where you wouldn't have to think about her all the time," she suggested, as a last resort.

"I could go digging for pearls in the ground too, and much good that would do me," said Christopher Heron. "Must you leave now?"

"I wasn't leaving."

"Oh yes, you are," said Christopher Heron. "Leaving to my great regret because I don't want you to get caught in the rain and die of a cold or ague. How otherwise could I courteously put an end to this stupid and profitless conversation? I told you what I did because I laid it on myself to do it, but I've told you now and it's over and done. Why should we go on quacking over the way I feel — or the life I lead — or anything else I may choose to do? Be off with you."

He said it very quietly, without stirring a step, but something in his voice swung Kate around like a hand on her shoulder and sent her almost running up the path back to the castle. She was halfway to the Standing Stone before she paused and glanced back.

Christopher Heron was still standing where she had left him. He had turned his head again and was looking through the rain at the dark opening in the cliff wall.

V ﴾

The Redheaded Woman

The rain lasted three days. By the time Kate went to bed, it was falling steadily, and by midnight it was coming from the northeast in great gusts that lashed against the windows and made it impossible to rest. She lay awake a long while staring into the dark and wondering how far a leper's hut that had been deserted for a hundred years would serve to keep out the weather or shelter anyone, even supposing that anyone had sense enough left to get under shelter. He had more likely laid it on himself to tramp about in the rain.

She sat up, punching her down pillow vindictively into shape. It was all very well for a hero in a romance, like Sir Launcelot, to break his heart and — how did it go? — "run mad in the wilderness"; but in her opinion Sir Launcelot had behaved very foolishly. Somebody ought to have stopped him.

But who was to stop Christopher Heron from doing as he chose?

For one instant, she had a brief dazzling vision of Katherine Sutton back in the valley again, facing Christopher Heron with cool certainty, winning all the arguments, reducing him to a state of stammering admiration and apology; but this dream did not survive a moment's inspection: it would have to be somebody else. Not Master John — if it suited Sir Geoffrey's heir to spend his days repenting in a leper's hut while Master John went on ruling over the whole estate, Master John would doubtless be only too pleased to oblige him. Sir Geoffrey? Sir Geoffrey was far away out of reach in Norfolk, but when he returned in November — ? When he returned in November, Christopher would come back and stand in the great hall again, with his fine green suit and his hand on the gold-inlaid hilt of his hunting knife, to keep his brother from knowing where he had really been spending his time. It might be a foolish proud way to act, but it was his last dignity, the only one that was left him, and how was it possible to tell Sir Geoffrey without stripping him even of that? She could not do it. She could not, as a matter of fact, do anything at all.

The worst of it was that she kept having a strange, restless feeling that there was something she ought to be doing. She could not think what it was, but there was something, flickering at the back of her mind where she could not get at it, like a mote on the edge of her eye. Even when she finally drifted off into a half-consciousness filled with the sound of falling rain, it was only to hear Master Roger's voice again, as she had on her first night at the Hall, very faint and far off, telling her to listen, there was something she had forgotten, something urgent, listen, there was something she ought to be doing, but though she listened frantically all that came to her was a confused echo of more voices, Randal's voice singing,

> *O where is the Queen, and where is her throne?*
> *Down in the stone O, but not in the stone,*

and mingled with it another voice, a child's voice crying pitifully, "O Cecily is lost! Where is Cecily?" over and over, until she woke shivering with the room still dark and the rain tearing at the windows.

The morning was no better. The storm had risen higher during the night, turning to gales that ripped along the roofs and sent tiles and chimney pots crashing down in fragments over the stones of the courtyard. By noon they were having trouble with all the fires, and dinner was a matter of bread and cheese and lukewarm broth and yesterday's roast duck cold. Pages and menservants with errands to do stood huddled in the doorways, eyeing the sky like uneasy animals before they pulled their cloaks over their heads and darted out into the rain.

Kate spent most of the day wandering restlessly about the house. She hated storms, and the queer sense that there was something she ought to be doing still nagged at her. Old Dorothy had taken to her bed with the rheumatism, and that meant she had no one to talk to. There was a great carved case full of books in the long gallery, but most of them seemed to be ancient manuscripts of works on alchemy and medicine, illustrated with obscure designs and written in languages that she could not read. She finally stumbled on a small, badly printed *Lives of the Saints* in English, thrust away behind the others. It had apparently belonged to Anne Warden; her name, looking oddly familiar, was written on the title page in a thin, delicate hand. Kate riffled over the leaves idly, catching at a passage here and there:

. . . and then came a night of great rains and wind, and in the midst of it the ferryman was awakened by a child's voice crying pitifully, "It is very late, and I am lost far away from my home, O come and carry me over the river." So he arose, and took his staff in his hand, and set the child on his shoulder, and went his way into the water; but ever as he went that water rose higher, and he felt the burden of the child grow heavier and yet heavier, as though he were carrying the whole weight of the world on his own back, until he cried out, "It is more than I can bear!" and then —

and then she broke off without finishing the story. She knew how it ended, it was one of the most familiar of all the legends, the sudden radiance of light surrounding the Child at the end of the crossing, the divine voice saying, "And your name henceforth shall be Christopher, the Christ-bearer, because you were moved by pity to carry your Lord tonight." But that had been in the morning of the world, when miracles rose out of the wayside grass as easily as larks; it was not to be expected that such a thing would happen again. She closed the book and went over to the window to see if the storm showed any signs of slackening off.

The wind had quieted a little, but the rain was falling harder than ever. The line of stone discharge-spouts jutting from the roof gutters was choked and strangling with water. More water was running from every slate and tile and pane, sheeting down walls and buttresses, gathering in streams among the rocks of the hill, making its way to the flat lands around the village in the valley. The tranquil little river that wound through the corn fields to feed the mill weir had become a raging brown torrent.

By the second day, the damp was steadily eating its way into the house, and a finger touching the velvet of a cushion left a spot. The rain continued to fall. Down in the valley, the river had swept away the mill weir and was pouring in floods over the fields through the broken bank. From the long gallery, Kate could see figures, dwarfed by the distance, toiling like ants with rocks and hurdles and logs and sacks of earth to close the gap and save what was left of the standing crops. There was no telling what might have happened in the little valley where the Holy Well lay, on the other side of the castle. The battlement walk that opened off the long gallery ran all the way around the old curtain wall until it joined the walk above the archway that overlooked the valley; but when she made her way there, staggering under the wind, it was only to find that the whole gorge was so full of mist and rain that she could not see beyond the Standing Stone.

The third day the wind shifted towards the end of the afternoon, and the rain began to fall more and more softly, but by that time the change was too late to be of any use to the village. The waters were still coming down from the hills in floods, tearing out hurdle and log and earthwork, and spreading in a great widening sheet further and further over the wreck of the grain.

The morning of the fourth day was different. All that was left of the storm was a fleet of huge white clouds racing like splendid ships over the flawless blue of the sky, with their shadows racing below them on the drowned fields that sparkled in the sun. Elvenwood Hall threw open its windows and began to sort itself out in a fine bustle of kindling fires, flourishing brooms, running feet, and chattering laughter. Kate was forgotten in the confusion; nobody had any time to think of her. She took a breakfast apple from a fruit dish on the high table, and slipped through the door out onto the terrace.

She glanced at the walk leading past Lord Richard's tower as she crossed the courtyard, and then turned aside — she was not wanted up at the Holy Well; and even if she had been, she could not have gone there: one of the castle pages was loitering about the overgrown passage, whistling and swinging a bundle wrapped in a white napkin. She went instead to the outer gate and dropped down the path towards the village.

There were figures in the distance picking their way through the wreckage on the banks of the river, or standing in forlorn twos and threes looking out over the waste of the fields, but she turned aside again when the path forked and took the road by which the pilgrims had come from the forest. She would not be wanted at the village either.

She passed on into the grove of oaks where the pilgrims cut their branches, and had not gone far when she found that the river had taken a bend and was coming to meet her. It was still very high, roaring with yellow foam and tearing great snatches of grass and clay out of the banks as it passed; but dappled with green leaf-shadow and cut off from the tragic fields by the trees of the grove, the coursing waters were a fine sight. Even Kate, who disliked waste or extravagance in any form, lingered along the path to watch them plunging and racing away into the deeper shadows of the Elvenwood.

The sun had grown pleasantly warm, and she was looking for a place to sit down and eat her apple when there was a piercing cry and something came blundering and hurtling through the trees further down the bank. It flung itself on her, snarling, sobbing, scrabbling at her cloak, its hands outstretched and clawing wildly. "I see you! I see you!" it wailed. "You give him back to me! I see you!"

Kate caught at the flailing wrists and thrust the creature away. It was the redheaded woman who had snatched up the little boy in the village, her face blubbered and her eyes wide with panic and hysteria. Kate shook her.

"Why shouldn't you see me?" she demanded furiously. She had had enough of being seized and pulled about by total strangers. "Certainly you see me! I'm not invisible! What do you want?"

"Give him back, give him back, give him back!" the woman shrieked, writhing against Kate's grip. "I warn you! I've a holy cross made of the cold iron in my bosom, and I'm warning you! You give me back my child!"

"I haven't got your child," Kate informed her coldly. "And if he's the dirty little boy with the snotty nose, I don't want any part of your child! What in heaven's name is the matter with you? Has anything happened to him?"

"You took him," the woman sobbed. "Just as my eye fell on you, he was behind me on the bank, throwing sticks in the water, and when I looked around for him, he was gone." She collapsed all at once on her knees, burying her face in Kate's old green cloak and fawning horribly. "Oh, give him back to me!" she cried.

Kate snatched with relief at the one piece of solid information that had flown past on this preposterous storm of demands and accusations. "Well, if he's lost, why couldn't you say so?" she asked. "Is everybody mad in this place? Be quiet, will you! He can't be far away. Be quiet, and listen! How do you expect to hear him if you keep screeching like a lunatic?"

The woman clutched at her convulsively, gasping for breath, but she did not scream again; and as the echo of her wailing cries died away, they both heard what sounded like a muffled chirp somewhere down among the noises of the flooded river. It came from a fallen oak tree that overhung the water a short way upstream in the direction of the village.

The little boy, trotting after his mother, had evidently run around the tree to watch the progress of his stick, and the waterlogged clay of the bank had collapsed under his weight, carrying him down with it. Fortunately, the tree was enormous; and the great gnarled roots that had interlaced the bank had kept him from being altogether swept away. He was half in and half out of the water, his feet swirling helplessly in the racing foam, his small hands clinging to the tangle of roots, crying and calling for his mother.

The redheaded woman darted forward, and had to be hauled back, struggling and flapping like a mother hen, while Kate

tried desperately to think of some way to get the child without bringing down the whole bank and drowning all three of them. She had never rescued anybody from a flooded river, and did not have the least idea of what she ought to do next.

"You'll have to lie flat and throw him my cloak to catch at," she said, turning cold at the calm assurance of her own voice. "Do what I tell you, do you hear me? Take your time. I've got you by the feet . . . Edge forward slowly to ease the strain on the bank. Slowly — slowly — steady, that's right . . . No, don't just scream 'Darling! darling!' at him. Call to him to grip hold of the cloak and keep quiet . . . Tell me when you're ready to pull . . . There! Don't cry, it's all over, he's not hurt. Let's get him out of those wet clothes."

Between them, they somehow got him out of the clothes and dried him off and wrapped him in the green cloak, Kate's hands shaking and the redheaded woman overflowing with gratitude and apologies.

"I never meant to speak so rough," she explained imploringly. "But there was my Harry gone in a flash, and when I saw the color of the cloak I thought sure you must be the Lady in the Green."

"Oh?" said Kate. She was busy feeding Harry with bites of her apple. "Mind the core, poppet. — Who's the Lady in the Green?"

The woman drew back a little. "You'd be the one should know that," said she in rather a stiff voice, "seeing as you live up at the castle."

"I'm a prisoner up at the castle," Kate corrected her. "And as for what goes on there —" she hunched her shoulder, "anybody in the village would know more of that than I do."

"Na na, I know nothing at all," said the woman quickly. She leaned forward, lowering her voice to a whisper. "It's not good to speak of such matters. She walks among the trees in her green cloak, and if we talk of her too loud she may hear us and be angered."

"But —" Kate began, and then paused, her eyes narrowed as if she were trying to see something a long way off. The forest road; the broken cart; the thickets blowing in the mist; and among the trees in a green cloak . . . "Tell me," she said abruptly, "does she have dark hair, very long dark hair? And a gold bracelet on her left wrist, just under the edge of the cloak?"

The woman caught her breath. "She's showed herself to you, then?" she asked, almost as though she were frightened. "There's not many who can say so."

"Yes, she showed herself to me." That, thought Kate, remembering the delicate aloof mouth and the disdainful eyes, was exactly the right term for what had happened. "She stood on the bank over my head and looked down at us, the — the way you'd look at a clot of worms crawling about in the road."

The redheaded woman nodded. "Yes," she said without resentment. "That would be the way of her and her people."

"What people?"

The woman leaned still closer, one hand fumbling at something hidden in the bosom of her dress.

"The Fairy Folk," she murmured, so low that Kate could hardly catch the words. "Those that rule over the Well. The People of the Hill."

Then, as if she were afraid that she had said too much, she drew back again and bent over the child in her arms. He had fallen asleep while they were talking, worn out with shock and exhaustion, his head cuddled into the hollow of her neck and his fingers closed determinedly on a sticky curl of apple peel.

Kate hesitated. Somewhere at the back of her mind, she

could hear Master Roger's voice discoursing gravely about folly
and superstition ("I saw myself what the country people can
believe in with no more than old rumors and idle tongues to
set them going"); but out under the oaks at the edge of the
Elvenwood, with that quick terrified murmur in her ears, Master
Roger's voice no longer spoke with the same authority it had
had in the Princess Elizabeth's little parlor. The Lady in the
Green was at least a real person — Kate had seen her with her
own eyes — and the redheaded woman was certainly very much
frightened of something.

"Where do the People of the Hill live?" she asked cautiously.

The redheaded woman flinched back and then edged nearer
again, like a panicky horse coming up sideways towards a tempt-
ing handful of oats. Frightened though she was, she was
apparently half-fascinated too. "In the Hill," she whispered.
"Down in caves under the Hill. Wonderful they are, the walls
all covered with gold, and the Fairy Folk with crowns on their
heads, drinking out of magical cups and dancing to the music
of harps and pipes; and they do say that any mortal man who
drinks from one of those cups will dance to that music for the
rest of his days, and never find his way out of the Hill again."

Kate disregarded the gold and the harps and the crowns; that
was the sort of stuff people used to trim up a tale when they
were telling stories by the fire on a winter night. But the caves
— they had been one of the few things about Derbyshire she
had heard of even in London, the caves in Derbyshire, the
quarries, the chasms, the lead mines. The lead for repairing the
windows at Hatfield that spring had come from Derby, and she
remembered Master Roger nodding as if he were pleased and
telling them that there was lead mining in Derby as far back
as the days of the old Romans. Caves — mines — all sorts of
passages under the ground: abandoned workings and forgotten

shafts and undiscovered caverns; and if anybody wanted to hide —

She put the thought away for a minute, and came back to what the redheaded woman had actually said. "But the Lady in the Green wouldn't be one of that kind, surely?" she suggested. "I've heard that the fairies were little wee folk, no larger than puppets."

"Never believe it. Not when they're in their true shapes, and that's the size of men and women like ourselves."

"Do you mean," Kate ventured, "that they *are* men and women like ourselves?"

"Like ourselves?" The redheaded woman seemed puzzled by the question. "How could they be like ourselves? They cannot abide cold iron or the sound of church bells, and they cannot be moved by pity because they have no hearts in their bodies. They were here in the land for many and many a hundred years before us — yes, and ruled over it; but when the cold iron came into the kingdom their power failed them, and wherever a church was built they fled and hid in the caves and woods for fear they should hear the sound of the bells and be withered away." Her voice died out, and for a long moment they sat together in silence, the redheaded woman cuddling the little boy, and Kate looking down at the swirling brown water of the river.

She had not understood what the woman meant by the cold iron, but the talk of building churches and the sound of their bells was different. It sounded as though she were trying, vaguely and fumblingly, to speak of something which had been driven out by the coming of Christianity; and what had been driven out by the coming of Christianity? The old pagan deities of the land, the heathen gods. Kate remembered Master Roger speculating whether stories of the heathen gods might not be handed down the years, becoming more and more confused and distorted with the passing of time, until in the end the gods themselves would be remembered only as a race of strange beings, the Fairy Folk, the People of the Hill. There was nothing so very unlikely about that. It would explain everything: the redheaded woman's dread of "the Fairy Folk," her insistence that they were not "like ourselves," her wild tales of their magical powers, everything except —

Everything except the one thing that Kate was actually sure of.

The Lady in the Green had been real.

She might be a great lady — and Kate had always known at the root of her heart that nobody with that face and bearing could be a gypsy tinker or a charcoal burner's wife — but she was not a forgotten goddess out of heathen antiquity. Forgotten heathen goddesses did not stand about under trees; or if they did, it was not Katherine Sutton who would see them.

And then suddenly the old nightmare sense that there was something she had missed, something she should understand, something urgent, something she ought to be doing, was back on her, stronger than ever — and it was concerned in some way with the Lady in the Green. The redheaded woman had started chattering again about golden crowns and magical cups, but Kate did not really hear what she was saying. Her mind seemed full of other voices, all crying confusedly together, just as they had in her dream: Randal's voice singing "Down in the stone O, but not in the stone," maddeningly, over and over; Dorothy's voice asking, "Why should we trouble ourselves with the saints? Those that rule over the Well were here in the land many and many a hundred years before them"; Master Roger's voice still talking gravely of the heathen gods: "The stories of the Fairy Folk are only memories of the old heathen gods, overlaid with fantasies and superstitions"; and then — suddenly, cutting through the confusion — a stillness without word or sound, like a thought taking shape in the depths of her own mind.

Not heathen gods, she thought. There were never any heathen gods. There were only heathen people who believed in them.

Not heathen gods: people.

That was it. People. Heathen people.

But what difference would that make? The heathen people were gone too, long ago.

And yet — and yet — surely in the beginning there must have been heathen people who wanted to keep on worshipping the old gods. Not common heathen people. True believers, lore masters, priests and priestesses, great folk who hated the New Faith, with followers and friends in high places who could help to hide them from the power of the Church. Why should they not go on meeting in secret, passing down the old knowledge and the old arts to their children? Half their cults had been secret and mysterious even in their own day; it would not seem strange to them. They might dwindle and diminish more and more as time went on, but perhaps always remembering the old worship, lingering about the old holy places, carrying on the old rites and ceremonies as well as they could. And if they kept themselves to wild solitary caves and woods, living off the land or on what their secret followers gave them —

Kate turned back to the redheaded woman.

"Tell me," she said, "does anybody in the village ever leave out food for the Fairy Folk?"

The redheaded woman shrugged. "They do some places, but they've no need of that here," she replied. "The castle feeds them. Na, na, if they come about the village it's not food they want. It's a child to take away with them."

"But why should they?" Master Roger had said something about the Fairy Folk taking children too, but Kate could not recall exactly what it was.

"Some will tell you it's for to have servants and slaves down there in the golden halls, and some will tell you it's for worse than that, and either way the child's gone," said the redheaded woman. "My own grandmother had a cousin put her baby down under an elder tree while she went to the hedge for a berry and never laid eyes on it again. The trouble is, there's no proper ring of bells to the church, and not likely to be, while Master John has the ordering of things at the castle. Some times are better than others. They do say that when there's been a bad harvest you had ought to keep watching every minute." Her arm closed fiercely about the little boy. "But there!" she added, recovering herself. "That's one tale I don't set any store by. It was this spring when they took the Big Lord's daughter, and that was long before the harvest failed us."

All the voices and thoughts in Kate's mind suddenly stopped at the same moment, and there was a dead silence.

"The —" she had to pause before she could go on. "The Big Lord?"

"The Big Lord who came out of the sea lands to the east and wedded the castle lady," explained the redheaded woman impatiently. "Him they call Sir Geoffrey."

"Sir Geoffrey's daughter was drowned in the Holy Well."

"I've heard that story," said the redheaded woman, "and who but a fool would believe it?"

"They found her slipper on the curbstone, torn off."

"Torn off when she was taken," said the redheaded woman. "You're never going to tell me she climbed up on that curbstone by herself. It's nearly a grown woman's height off the ground."

"Yes," said Kate slowly. "I know it is. I know it is, but —"

"There, then!" said the redheaded woman. "And who saw her fall, answer me that! You're never going to tell me —"

"Sir Geoffrey's brother was with her."

"The Young Lord? I've heard that story too. And I've heard he had his eye off her for a minute, like my grandmother's cousin."

"He'd been in the cave, and there was nobody there. He sat watching outside, and says nobody could have slipped past him."

The redheaded woman looked at her almost contemptuously.

"Could he see what was deep in the Well?" she demanded. "That's where they lurk, to catch up the gold and the precious things that the pilgrims throw into the water. I'm not saying the child didn't go down the Well, mind you. I'm saying there was something come up out of the Well, and it took her."

Kate saw a sudden and intolerably vivid picture of the high carved curbstone at the Holy Well, with a long, thin, dripping arm beginning to reach over the rim.

"But how could anyone lurk down in the Well?" she protested. "It goes into a cavern below the rocks, and there's an underground river that carries everything away."

"Caverns and rivers under the ground are no more than houses and halls to some folk," said redheaded woman darkly; "and you mark my words, that's where she is now, poor little lass, a-sitting on a golden chair. They know it well enough up at the castle — and a wicked shame it is to them, too, never saying a word of the truth and letting the Young Lord break his heart with thinking he killed her. — There, there, be still now, my honey."

The little boy had stirred in her arms, and was beginning to cry fretfully. The redheaded woman bent over him. "There, there," she said.

Kate scrambled to her feet.

"I have to go," she said in an odd, breathless voice. "I have to get back to the castle."

The little boy stopped crying and stared at her fixedly.

"Apple," he said.

"Hush love, be a good boy, mother will give you an apple tomorrow," said the redheaded woman. "Sit up, my honey. Let the lady have her cloak again."

"No, no, never mind the cloak," said Kate, over her shoulder. "His own clothes are still drying. I can't wait. Keep it till I come for it."

"Anybody in the village can tell you my house," said the woman. "And —" she paused, coloring, "you needn't fear for your welcome from this day on, my lady, seeing as what you've done for —"

"Very well then," said Kate quickly. "Take it to your house for me. I have to get back to the castle now. I have to go and see — I have to tell — there's something I ought to be doing."

She had almost reached the path when she heard another cry of "My lady!" and swinging around, saw that the redheaded woman had come up behind her and was drawing something out of the bosom of her dress.

"I — I —" she stammered. "If you would take a gift from me, my lady? I can't rightly thank you, and — and it's an ill thing, living up at the castle. I'd feel easier to know you had a bit of the cold iron about you."

It was a little cross strung on a chain, such as peddlers sold to country women, and remarkable only because it appeared to be made of steel rather than the usual brass or silver. The workmanship was of the crudest kind, and the righthand bar was so skewed and bent that it looked ready to snap off at a touch.

"Thank you," murmured Kate, feeling a little as she had on the day that Alicia had come running out after Sir Geoffrey's horses, all in tears, and holding up her own most precious possession — a feather fan with a mirror set in it — for Kate to take on her journey. Then, seeing the anxious question in the woman's eyes, she added impulsively: "I shall wear it always. I promise you that I will. See!" She put the chain around her neck and thrust the cross down safe under her bodice.

The redheaded woman drew a long breath of relief and satisfaction.

"And you'll be sure to lay your hand upon it if the Lady in the Green ever comes nigh you again?" she begged. "There's a great virtue in the holy sign and the cold iron, and my grandmother always said —"

"Yes, I want to hear all about your grandmother when I come for the cloak," Kate interrupted her. "I have to get back to the castle now. There's —" and she too drew a long breath of relief and satisfaction, "there's something I ought to be doing."

VI ᡒ
The Leper's Hut

Kate had somehow expected that Christopher Heron would be standing and looking at the dark entrance to the Holy Well, exactly as she had left him, but he was not there. Half an hour later, much discouraged and painfully aware of her feet, she was still searching the valley for some trace of him. He was not in the Well cave or by the spring or anywhere near the Standing Stone, and it was only when she left the path and began threading her way through the masses of tumbled stone along the cliff wall that a distant flicker of white caught her eye.

It was the napkin-wrapped bundle she had seen swinging from the page's hand earlier that morning; but the page was gone and the bundle was lying in a hollow on the top of a broad flat slab of rock. Just beyond, a little way up the valley, more rocks had been dragged against the cliff face to form low walls which had been roofed over with rough-cut stone. A wooden door had been fitted into one of the walls, but it was so gray and weather-beaten that even near at hand the leper's hut could easily have been mistaken for a broken fold in the cliff itself.

The door was open, and there was nobody inside. Along the back cliff wall ran a long low shelf of rock which in Henry Warden's time had probably been softened by cushions and blankets from the castle; but there was nothing on it now, only the bare rock. In the right-hand wall was a crude fireplace of blackened stones with not even the ashes of a fire on the hearth. The only sign that the place was still inhabited was an ironbound chest set against the left-hand wall, with Christopher's gold-hilted hunting knife flung down carelessly on the closed lid. Otherwise, a cell or a tomb could hardly have been more desolate; and after one quick look Kate turned aside and went back to wait in the sun on the flat rock beside the bundle of food. He would certainly come for it sooner or later; meanwhile she could only hope that he had not been watching the path and was deliberately keeping out of her way.

The knot that secured the napkin was loose, and without lowering herself so far as to pry into the bundle she was able to see that it contained nothing except a half-loaf of coarse kitchen bread, at least a week old and harder than a billet of wood. She turned it over with one distasteful finger.

"Hungry?"

Kate swung around, too taken up with the loaf of bread even to be annoyed by the tone of the voice. "Is this all you get to eat?" she demanded accusingly.

"I might have known that that would be the first question you'd ask me," said Christopher Heron, standing over her. He had certainly been tramping about in the rain, just as she had thought he would; the old tattered blue smock was now hardly more than a sodden mass of rags. His face was set in the mask of contemptuous amusement which of all his masks was the one she disliked the most.

"What's the matter?" he inquired. "You're smirking like somebody with a sweet for a child: 'which will you have, the right hand or the left one?' Stop hovering, can't you? I don't care which hand it's in; and whatever it is, I don't want it."

Kate hesitated, and then made up her mind to tell him the whole story of the morning, step by step, exactly as it had happened. She wanted to see his face change while she told it.

"I was walking down by the river today —" she began.

Christopher listened without interrupting until she came to the end. His set face did not change at all as she went on. It only became slightly more set and contemptuous.

"And what made you trouble yourself with that old wives' tale?" he demanded curtly.

Kate flushed. She felt as if one of the splendid racing clouds overhead had suddenly begun to dissolve into a shower of cold rain. "But I saw the Lady in the Green," she protested. "I saw her with my own eyes."

"You saw a woman standing on the bank," Christopher corrected her. "She didn't have to be the Queen of the Fairies to look down at my brother's men as they went by on the road. Be reasonable, can't you?"

"I am being reasonable," Kate insisted. "And the curbstone of the Well is nearly five feet off the ground."

"O Lord!" said Christopher wearily. "Do we have to go over all of that again? I know, I know, you don't believe Cecily could have climbed up there; but it's a deal easier to believe in than a pack of bogles lurking down in a cavern to steal children! And I thought you had such a good clear mind!"

"You didn't see her fall. You said yourself you couldn't find out what became of her. Haven't *you* ever thought that she might still be alive somewhere?"

"Oh yes, often," said Christopher. "Very often. When I was a boy in Norfolk we had an old serving man who'd lost one of his hands. He told me that for a long time afterwards he kept thinking the hand was still there, he could feel all the fingers, it was so real to him that sometimes he'd wake on a cold winter morning and start trying to light the fire with it — before he remembered."

"I don't see what that has to do with Cecily," said Kate stubbornly.

"It was by way of being a parable or fable," said Christopher. "Now in *my* case —" He broke off in the middle of his sentence and said: "Listen! What's that?"

Somewhere above them, on the path that led down from the Standing Stone, a voice was singing. It was a high, familiar voice, curiously piercing and sweet:

> *It fell about the winter time,*
> *A cold day and a snell,*
> *That as I to the hunting rode*
> *That from my horse I fell —*

The tune suddenly curved over, sweeping down on a sort of low mournful cry:

> *And the Queen of the Fairies took me,*
> *In yon green hill to dwell.*

"Randal," said Christopher, with a jerk of his head. They could see the small brown figure now, flitting along the path between the rocks. "Have you ever heard *him* talking of the Fairy Folk? He says they took his wits away from him. That's what comes of meddling in such foolery. You'll end wandering about the country too, with a harp over your shoulder, looking for the way in again, if you're not careful."

"The way in where?" asked Kate.

"God knows," said Christopher. "I was only repeating the words after him. The way back into his right mind again, perhaps, poor soul."

Randal had seen them. He had left the path and was making his way towards them down the slope, pausing as he approached to bow and flourish the battered cap. The feather had now broken off altogether, and only a small crimson tuft remained in the band.

"That was the ballad of *Tam Lin* I was singing down there, but it was wrong of me," he remarked a little anxiously, as if apologizing for some carelessness. Then he looked at Kate, and his whole face lit up like a delighted child's. "I know you well; the lady who gave me the bread from her hand one day in the forest. There are words for you from Sir Geoffrey. He came safely to his home in Norfolk, and said I was to carry him news of your doings when I went back again. To his brother," he added, in a rather puzzled voice, "Sir Geoffrey sent no word."

"Why was it wrong of you to sing the ballad of *Tam Lin?*" Kate cut in. She cared nothing for the ballad of *Tam Lin* — Alicia was the one who liked ballads — but any question was better than letting Randal talk any more about Sir Geoffrey's feelings for his brother.

"It's not a song to sing so close to the Queen's hall," said Randal, shaking his head. "Surely they'd never show me the way in again if they heard me. For it tells of the lady who rescued her lover out of the fairy land, and that's a story they wouldn't care to remember; and in it the teind is openly spoken of, and that's a thing they would choose to have for a secret."

"Teind?" asked Kate. She had never heard of a "teind" before: it might be a treasure, or a hiding place, or even a ceremony of some sort, for all she knew.

"It's a word they use in the north country," said Christopher's voice from behind her. "Meaning a tax — the sort of tax you pay to the Church. Like tithes."

"Yes, yes," Randal nodded eagerly. "That was the very same as Tam Lin said to the lady in the ballad." He began to sing again, softly this time, almost under his breath:

> *And pleasant is that fairy land,*
>   *To them that in it dwell,*
> *But aye at the end of seven years*
>   *They pay a teind to hell:*
> *And I'm so fair and fu' of flesh,*
>   *I fear 'twill be mysel'.*

"He means," said Christopher's voice behind her, "that the gentleman feared that he was to be put to death as a kind of sacrifice because he was tall and handsome. Don't ask me why."

"They would always take a man for it if they could," said Randal. "A young man of high degree, strong and with no blemish about him, like Tam Lin in the ballad — for he would be the one to have the greatest power in his spirit and his blood. I've heard it said that there was a time once when they might take the king of the land himself if it pleased them. But that was in the old days, a long time past, a long, long while ago. The king is beyond their reach now, and it's been many and many a year since they could lay their hands even on a man. I never saw a man in keeping for the teind among them, not any of the nights I've been in the Queen's hall."

"Where?" asked Kate sharply.

It was a mistake; she knew it before the word was even out of her mouth. Randal drew back as if she had struck him, and gave her a vague, confused look. The sudden question had been too much for him. "Yes, my lady?" he mumbled. "What did you say?"

"Nothing," said Kate. She settled herself on the flat rock again, and stretched out one casual foot to study the tip of her shoe. "I only wanted to know how you came to be in the Queen's hall."

Randal twisted his cap nervously between his hands.

"I-I found the way in once," he stammered, "and by their law they can never use a singer to pay for the teind, so — so they took my wits away, to keep me from telling their secrets, and then they turned me out into this world again. But some nights . . ."

"Some nights?"

"Some nights they let me come back to them."

"To see the teind paid, no doubt," murmured Christopher's voice behind Kate's shoulder.

"I never saw the teind paid," said Randal. "It's not a thing they do except when the seven years are past, or else during a time of great need, when the harvest fails or an enemy has broken into the land. No, no, if they let me come back, it's only to play my harp for them on a night when they are dancing." His whole face suddenly lit up again, and when he spoke it was as though he were lost in some dream. "O the dancing!" he whispered. "The cup that I drink from, and the singing and the gold! I've seen them strip the crowns from their heads and the jewels from their hands and throw them to me like pennies at a fair for a tune that pleased them; and then I think sure they will keep me forever, but they never do, they never do." He shook his head mournfully. "For at the last I always fall asleep, and when I awake I am lying out on the cold hillside again, and all that I have in my hand —"

He knelt down with one of his quick, fantastic movements, and taking the leather pouch from his belt, emptied something out over the stones at Kate's feet. It was a cluster of brown oak leaves and a little circlet of dead wildflowers, the blossoms so withered and dry that they had begun to fall from the stems. One or two were caught by the air and went floating away on the wind.

Randal watched them go with miserable, bewildered eyes.

"Did you ever see the like of that?" he said.

"No." Kate had never heard Christopher use that voice before. She would not have believed that he could speak so gently. "No."

"But, Randal —" she began.

Christopher dropped one hand warningly on her shoulder. *"No,"* he repeated. Randal had picked up the cluster of oak leaves and was looking at it doubtfully.

"I keep thinking maybe they'll turn back to the gold some day, but they never do, they never do," he said with a long sigh, putting the cluster down and fumbling in the pouch again. "It's always so when I wake. There was a little yellow-haired girl who gave me the slipper from her own foot, all made of butterfly wings it was, but when I awoke all that I had in my hand —"

He drew the hand from the pouch and held something else out to them. It was a child's slipper which had once been fine leather, bright crimson, with a lace at the ankle, exactly like its mate that Christopher had found on the curbstone of the Holy Well — but this one was stained and faded and worn almost to rags.

The hand on Kate's shoulder closed suddenly and gripped it to the bone. "What little girl?" said Christopher in a harsh, tearing whisper.

Randal was busy gathering his treasures back into the pouch, and did not even glance at him.

"A little girl," he said vaguely. "A little yellow-haired girl dancing in a ring with the others. On a dancing night they make no difference between their own kind and those they have taken. It's not as it was in the old days. I've heard it said that in the old days they might take the king of the land himself to pay the teind if it pleased them; but now the best they can

hope for is to find a child that's run away or been left to roam, and steal it away with them."

Kate felt Christopher behind her draw a deep, gasping breath; and for an instant she thought her shoulder would break as the hand that gripped it suddenly took the whole weight of his body. Then, just as suddenly, the hand was gone; and she heard his feet stumbling away blindly among the rocks.

"Where is he going?" asked Randal, getting up and turning his head to look.

Kate lunged to her own feet and swung him around by the arm. "There's a matter he has to see to," she gabbled, improvising wildly. "We've all of us been talking too long, look at the sun, it must be almost time for dinner, you ought to get back to the castle, Sir Geoffrey won't like it if he finds out you aren't having any food or rest. Don't you remember what he told you?"

"He told me to carry him news of your doings," said Randal conscientiously, "and also that I was to play on my harp for you."

"Yes, yes, that was very kind of him," said Kate. "I'll tell you what we'll do now. You go down to the castle and have your rest, and tonight when everyone's asleep you come up on the terrace by the great hall and I'll whisper you the news of my doings out of a window. That way it will be like having a secret. None of the others will know. No one will know but you and me."

"No one but you and me," said Randal, nodding and putting his finger to his lips. He slung his cloak around him with a great air of secrecy, as pleased as a child with a new game, and then stood hesitating. "There's somebody weeping up there in the little house," he said. "Can't you hear him?"

"No," said Kate. "That's only the water from the spring by the Well, running over the rock."

"The water springing out of the rock, and a man weeping for joy up there in the little house," said Randal. "I can hear him. Don't you want to go over and see?"

"No!" said Kate. "It's nothing to trouble for. Show me now how you can go away very quietly without his catching you. Remember that no one must know you're coming up on the terrace tonight but you and me."

Randal nodded again. "Nobody but you and me," he agreed happily and went tiptoeing off up the path with all the stealth of a Robin Hood.

Kate, taking care not even to glance at the door of the leper's hut, went back to the flat rock and fixed her eyes and her mind deliberately on the walls and towers that rose into the sky at the far end of the valley. She remembered the redheaded woman saying, "They know it well enough up at the castle," and old Dorothy on the battlement walk telling her how Lord Richard's wife had taught him the ways of the land, "and he reared his sons according to the custom at the Gard; and for many and many a hundred years they held the Elvenwood and kept it free and safe from all the world." She had thought at the time that Dorothy was only boasting of the family's dignity, but now —

There was a sound as if a door had slammed open somewhere behind her, and then feet among the rocks again — very quick feet this time: running. Christopher had come out of the leper's hut and was hurtling like a comet up the slope to the pathway.

Kate caught at his hand as he shot by her.

"Where are you going?" she demanded.

The comet paused for an instant in its burning flight through heaven.

"To get her back," said Christopher, in a dangerously reasonable voice. His eyes were still wet, but they looked as though they had seen the Resurrection itself, and his whole face was dazed and radiant. "Kate, did you hear him? Did you hear what he said? She's alive in there somewhere. O merciful God, Kate, she's *alive!*"

"Of course she's alive!" said Kate. "What did I tell you! But as for getting her back —"

"Kate, I can't stay." He was throwing the words over his shoulder now, straining against her hold. "I have to go find Master John. We never really searched that chasm under the Well. There must be a hidden way into it somewhere, and with every man from the castle and the village —"

"Have you gone mad?" Kate interrupted him. "Look at the castle! How much help can we get from there? Christopher, don't you see? Whatever it is, they're all in it together — Master John and old Dorothy and the others."

Christopher's eyes followed hers up to the line of walls and towers stretched like a protecting arm across the entrance to the valley, with the great blackened hulk of Lord Richard's keep shouldering over the rest. Then, slowly and reluctantly, the straining grip on her hand slackened.

"Yes, you're right: I must have gone mad," he said. "I wasn't thinking. What do we do now?"

"Talk," said Kate. "And would you mind if we sat down and ate a bit of your bread while we're talking? I don't know about you, but it must be almost noon by the sun, and *I* haven't had any breakfast."

"I might have known that would be the first thing you'd say," murmured Christopher; but he went over to the hut for his knife, and they hacked the loaf into shares and settled down together on the edge of the flat rock to eat it. The sun was now nearly overhead, and the whole valley lay in clear light from the archway in the distant wall to the dark mouth of the cave among the rocks.

"Master John is the one to reckon with," said Kate.

"I can't see Master John as the King of the Fairy Folk," remarked Christopher dryly.

"Neither can I, but he must be working for them, the way he did for the old lords. I wonder if even the old lords ever did anything but work for them. All they seem to have done for hundreds of years is stick to this place as if they were stewards or bailiffs or —"

"Wardens," said Christopher. "Guard the valley, get in the food, keep the world out of here, hold off the Church — and take their pay for it. Oh yes, it hasn't been just a matter of putting out a bowl of milk on the doorstep every night for the Little People. Or believing in the heathen gods either, perhaps. If there *is* anyone lurking down in that chasm to catch up the gold and the precious things the pilgrims throw into the Well, the creatures must be able to pay a fortune for whatever help or protection the castle gives them. Geoffrey never could understand where Anne's father got *all* the money he had to spend on long galleries and Italian paintings and tapestries and other gear. I'm glad she didn't tell him."

"I think she must have wanted to break away from them," said Kate, remembering the book she had found in the long gallery, and some of the other things she had learned about Lady Heron.

Christopher paused a moment before he answered.

"Yes, poor Anne," he said. "God forgive me, no wonder she was so set on getting Geoffrey out of the country! Can you imagine telling Geoffrey that your family belonged to a heathen cult that paid teinds to hell, and he would have to connive at it? Geoffrey, of all men?"

Kate thought of Sir Geoffrey's stern face, the iron mouth, the level implacable gray eyes. She shook her head. "Even old

Dorothy told me you could never teach *him* the way of the land," she said, and added: "I suppose that was why they had to steal Cecily."

"Why they had to steal Cecily?"

"They'd want her for a hostage."

"Hostage?"

"To bargain with." It seemed to Kate that it was taking him a long time to see something so simple and obvious. "How could they know that you'd shut yourself up here and he'd go off and leave the place to Master John again?" she asked impatiently. "They must have had some other plan when they took her. Tell me, what would Sir Geoffrey give them to keep her safe?"

"Geoffrey," said Sir Geoffrey's brother, "would give them the castle and the Elvenwood and the last drop of blood in his body before he'd let them harm a hair of her head."

"There, then!" said Kate. "What did I tell you! It would be the first thing they'd think of."

"Yes," said Christopher slowly. "It would certainly be the first thing they'd think of, if —"

"If?"

Christopher's eyes went from the archway in the castle wall back to the dark entrance of the well cave.

"If they think of it as we would."

In spite of the noonday sun and the warm rock Kate suddenly felt as if a cold finger had reached out and touched her.

"What do you mean?" she asked sharply.

"I mean we're not dealing with just Master John or old Dorothy," said Christopher. "They're only on the edge of the circle; they're people like ourselves. But we can't be sure about Those in the Well. I'm not saying they're gods or anything of the kind. It's that we don't know how their minds work. We can't judge them by ourselves. Whatever they are, they're dif-

ferent. They live by another rule. *We* may think that the only
way they could use Cecily would be as a hostage, to give them
power over Geoffrey. *They* may think they could get far more
power by using her for something else."

"But what else?" cried Kate, almost angrily, because she was
so frightened. "What else could it be?"

"You heard what Randal told us," said Christopher grimly.
"I don't know whether the seven years are past or not, but surely
they must have come to 'the time of great need' that he was
speaking of? They've lost the Wardens; Anne never even tried
to teach Geoffrey the way of the land; everything's turning
against them. And now this last week the harvest has failed too.
You and I may say that it was only the chance of a bad storm
coming after a wet summer. But don't you understand how it
must seem to *them?*"

Kate gripped her hands together.

"Randal said they would always take a man to pay the teind
when they could," she protested.

"Yes — when they could," retorted Christopher. "He also
said that they've had to be satisfied with a child for a long while
now."

"I don't believe it. I don't believe it, I tell you. They must
be keeping her for a hostage. I'm sure they only want her for a
hostage."

"We can hope so, certainly. But how much would you be
willing to risk on the chance?"

"She was still alive when Randal saw her. They hadn't done
her any harm."

"That means nothing. They may be waiting for some particular time or feast day. In the tales they're supposed to be
very scrupulous about forms and observances and keep to the
exact letter of any bargain they make." He paused, frowning.

"That ballad about Tam Lin," he said abruptly. "The one Randal was singing. How does it go on? What night did he tell his sweetheart that he would have to pay the teind?"

"I never heard *Tam Lin* before. I don't know."

"It was All Hallows' Eve," said Christopher. "I remember now.

> *The night is Hallow'een, my love,*
> *The morn is Hallows' Day —*

All Hallows' Eve. That's the night before All Saints' Day, the very end of October. So if they follow the same rule here, it would mean that we still have a little time."

"More than two months," said Kate, the blood coming back to her heart. She had been thinking of the very next night, or the night after that. By comparison, the end of October seemed blessedly far away.

"Yes," said Christopher. "The trouble is, we can't be sure they follow the same rule here. We can't even be sure that All Hallows' Eve is the right time. Two lines from a ballad aren't much to go by. Ballad singers are always changing verses about and forgetting them and putting in new ones." He slipped to his feet and walked restlessly away from her to the verge of the path, where it began to climb up steeply towards the Standing Stone.

"What we ought to be thinking of," said Kate, "is how to get hold of Sir Geoffrey."

"Geoffrey?" Christopher had his back to her now, and was looking down the path in the direction of the Holy Well.

"That's the one thing we *can* be sure of," said Kate, a little impatiently. All this hazy discussion of uncertainties and possibilities was beginning to grate on her nerves. It made her feel as though she were moving about in a fog, through which dim shapes kept looming up only to disappear or shred away into cloud when she tried to grasp at them. She wanted to see a line of good, solid, heavily armed men who had soldiered in Ireland ride down the road from Norfolk with Sir Geoffrey at their head. Then at least they would have something to rely on. "How much time would it take you to get to your home and fetch him here again?" she demanded eagerly.

"That would depend on what this storm's done to the roads and the fords," said Christopher, without turning to face her. His voice sounded troubled and uncertain. "And if the floods are out in the fen country too — call it a week at the very best. Two, more likely."

"What's the matter?" asked Kate. "Wouldn't that be enough? If we have until All Hallows' Eve —"

"I may be wrong about All Hallows' Eve."

"You don't know you're wrong."

"And I don't know I'm right either. That's what the matter is. Neither of us *knows*. I'd only be gambling on my own convictions, and — and it isn't even my own money I'd be playing games with, if you want to put it that way. I can't risk Cecily's life for this kind of chance. Suppose I'm wrong, and something happens to her while I'm God knows where looking for Geoffrey? He may not even *be* at home when I get back."

"Well, I don't see what good you can do by just staying here," Kate pointed out tartly. "Do you think you can fight your way into the Queen's hall and save Cecily with your single arm, like King Arthur in a romance?"

There was a long pause, while Christopher went on gazing down the path and Kate at his unresponsive back. She could not tell what he was thinking. She had never met anyone like him before, not in her own world, the London world of trade and law and merchant-adventuring and the fire-new court of the Tudor kings and queens, who had (when all was said and done) been nothing but adventurers themselves only eighty or ninety years ago. The Herons, she reflected bitterly, had probably been knights and ladies when the Suttons were still hauling up nets on a fishing smack. She wished nevertheless that she had not said what she had about King Arthur. It came to her suddenly and a little frighteningly that perhaps King Arthur *had* looked like that once — not the great King, the Lord of the Round Table, but the young Arthur, standing troubled and uncertain with his head lifted to read his fate written in the carved letters over the sword in the stone.

Then Christopher swung around to face her, and she saw to her relief that he was simply looking resigned, even a little amused. "Very well, madam," he said. "Your gentle words have touched me to the heart."

Kate let this piece of deliberate provocation go by her; she would have put up with much worse in return for winning the argument. "Master John won't stop you from leaving, will he?" she asked eagerly.

"Stop me? He'd give me a golden horse with a silver bridle and ten trumpeters to play me down the road if he thought there was the least hope of getting rid of me," said Christopher. "I'll tell you how we'll manage it. You go back to the Hall now and have your dinner before he and old Dorothy start wondering what's become of you; and afterwards you find a hidden corner in some obscure room and write me out a full account of this whole matter to take to Geoffrey."

"What!" It was so unexpected that for a moment Kate could only stare at him. "But Christopher, I can't do that! Suppose they catch me at it!"

"Surely you won't let them catch you at it? A clever girl like you."

"But why do it at all? Your word must be just as good as mine. Don't you think Sir Geoffrey's going to believe you?"

"I may fall sick or be thrown from my horse somewhere along the road," said Christopher persuasively. "We ought to get all the evidence down in writing, as soon as we can. I'd do it myself, but I've no ink or paper here at the hut; and if I start asking for them about the house, Master John may get wind of it."

Kate hesitated. Hovering uneasily at the back of her mind was an odd and remarkably clear recollection of herself sending Randal off up the same path only a short while before, inventing a little plan to keep him happy, a little secret business that he was to carry out for her, a little something she had scrambled together to get him out of her way so that she could turn her thoughts to quite another matter which she had no intention of confiding to him.

She looked at Christopher very hard, but there was no protest she could reasonably make. She could see that the letter might be very useful. She did have to get back to the house. Master John or old Dorothy would certainly be wondering what had become of her by this time.

"Christopher," she said, almost appealingly. "Christopher, what are you going to do while I'm up at the Hall?"

"What do you think I'm going to do?" asked Christopher. "Throw another penny into the Holy Well and tell them that I didn't really mean what I said the first time? You run away to the Hall now like a good girl and have your dinner and write that letter for me."

VII ❧

The Evidence Room

To eat dinner and write a letter afterwards should have been easy enough. In actual practice it turned out to be surprisingly difficult. When Kate got back to the house — inconspicuously, by way of the stairs up to the battlement walk that ran around the old curtain wall — the dinner hour was past; and as she emerged from the long gallery, she was pounced on by old Dorothy, in a very bad temper after her attack of rheumatism, scolding and wanting to know where she had been, why she was so late, and what, Those in the Well be good to us! had she done to her clothes? — the second dress she had ruined in a week, covered with mud, Mistress Katherine, covered with mud the whole front of the skirt, and half the sleeve ripped out at the elbow.

Kate tried to placate her by explaining what had happened to the little boy, but Dorothy refused to be placated. She merely observed that it would not be a great matter if all the village brats were drowned together like kittens in a sack; that was no reason why castle folk should miss their meals and destroy good gowns playing about on the banks of dirty rivers. She then marched the culprit down to the great hall, and flounced out to the buttery to get her a plate of fruit and cheese with her own hands, pointedly remarking that she did not like to give the servants trouble on a day when everyone had so much work to do after the storm. By way of emphasis she limped about the table on her poor aching feet throughout the meal, with unnecessary dishes and paring knives, muttering under her breath about fine London manners. When Kate had finished, she drove her upstairs again, and fetching the sewing basket, sat faithfully beside her while the muddy skirt was sponged and brushed and the sleeve mended as well as it could be. Kate, always clumsy, had never been deft with her needle like Alicia, and she was obliged to pull out her stitches and reset the sleeve and sew it up again more than once before the task was completed to Dorothy's satisfaction. Her only answer to any protest was to purse up her lips and inquire ominously whether Mistress Katherine would like her to put the matter before Master John?

The huge and inordinately expensive new castle clock which the late Lord Warden had installed over the main archway to the outer courtyard was striking four when she finally closed the sewing basket and grumbled herself out of the room.

The next problem was to get ink and paper to write with. There was plenty of ink and paper in the little whitewashed chamber off the great hall, the "evidence room" where Master John did the business of the estate; but the last thing Kate wanted to do at that moment was to attract Master John's attention to herself or give him any reason to wonder why she needed ink and paper at all. In the end she returned to the long gallery, where she came at last upon a quill pen and an inkhorn covered with gold filigree work among the curiosities in one of the cabinets. The ink in the horn was dried hard and had to be thinned with water, and the only paper she could discover was a blank page at the end of Anne Warden's old *Lives of the Saints*.

The sun was dangerously low in the sky by the time she finished the last of the letter, folded it up, and hid it under the

bodice of her dress, catching her finger on the crooked bar of
the redheaded woman's cross in her hurry. She shook it free
with an exclamation of annoyance. Five o'clock supper would
soon be on the table, and with old Dorothy in her present mood,
it would never do to be late for that as well. She thrust the
cross hastily down again among the folds of the letter, and made
her way back to the great hall just as Master John took his place
by the cupboard and the serving men began to file into the
room.

Supper was a less ceremonial meal than dinner, but it took
a great many dishes to feed the entire household on what was
left over from the high table, and courtesy required that all the
dishes should at least be offered to the high table first, even
when there was only one girl sitting there to pick and choose
between them. Kate did not dare to choose less or even to eat
a little more quickly than usual, though the food choked her
and she felt as if the procession of venison pies, stewed pigeons,
hot mutton with caper sauce, grilled chicken, roasted plums,
sallets, custards, and sweet cakes was never going to come to an
end. Christopher would be waiting for the letter to Sir Geoffrey;
if it did not reach him soon he might not be able to set out with
it until morning, a whole night wasted; and all she could do
was sit in the great hall with Humphrey bending over her
shoulder to offer her cream for her roasted plums. The only
blessing was that Master John seemed thoughtful and pre-
occupied, and scarcely glanced in her direction after he had
bowed her into her customary seat. When the supper was
over he went straight back to the evidence room, taking old
Dorothy with him.

Kate rose from her chair and sauntered over to the doorway.
The evening was a fine one, with a brilliant sunset, and it was
only natural to stroll out on the terrace and then wander quietly

down the steps into the courtyard. She did not even have to wait for a loitering groom or page to get out of her way; there was nobody in sight. She turned the corner by Lord Richard's tower and melted thankfully into the shadows of the passage.

Christopher was waiting for her by the Standing Stone. She had just crossed the flat wide stretch of rough grass beyond the archway when she heard a low voice say, "Kate!" and looking around, saw him leaning against the great rock on the side away from the castle. He reached out his hand and pulled her over to him.

"Keep your voice down," he murmured in her ear. "Where have you been? I thought you were coming hours ago."

"I couldn't get away sooner," Kate whispered back. "It's all well. I have the letter for you. Why are we hiding here? Is anything wrong?"

"Nothing," said Christopher. "But there's another matter I want you to see to for me. Listen carefully: we haven't much time. I can't set out tonight. Go back to the house this instant, and give that letter to Randal. Don't let anyone see you. Tell him to take it to Geoffrey. He'll understand. You can always trust him with a message to carry if it's easy enough. The trick is not to confuse him. Be very simple and plain. Don't use many words. Only make sure he knows exactly where he's to go and how soon he has to get there. Do you have that straight? Are you sure?"

"Yes, but —"

"Good. The rest is easy. No, don't start talking. Listen to me. With any luck at all, Geoffrey should be back here in another two weeks at the most. When he comes, you can say anything you please to him. Until then, I want you to keep inside the house and put all this business entirely out of your mind. You hear me? *Out* of your mind, as though it had never happened.

Whatever Master John and old Dorothy tell you, believe them. Don't come near this place. You know far too much for your own good as it is. Forget it. Stay in your room and spend your time taming a spider or teaching yourself Greek. You won't be safe otherwise. Do you understand that?"

"But I *don't* understand," Kate protested unhappily. "Why are you sending Randal to Sir Geoffrey? It would be much surer if you went yourself, you know it would. What do you think you can do if you stay here?"

"Kate," said Christopher. "Dear Kate, kind Kate, clever Kate, will you for the love of heaven go away without asking any more questions?"

"No," said Kate flatly. "You're planning something. What is it that you're —"

But Christopher had not waited for an answer. He was gone, dropping down the steep slope towards the lower valley and the Holy Well, without so much as a backward glance to see whether she had obeyed his orders. He was moving very quickly, almost at a run, cutting across the winding turns of the path and the tumbled rocks between them in long, sure-footed strides.

Kate, however, had to keep to the path, hampered by her skirts, stumbling on her awkward feet, slithering over pebbles. She did not dare to call out, and he was too far ahead to hear her coming. It was not until he had reached the little bay of grass and flowers at the far end of the valley that she finally saw him stop short and turn sharply to see who was following him.

"Oh, Lord!" he said. *"No!"*

"What —" Kate began again, gasping, "what is — it you're —"

Christopher took her by the shoulder without another word and forced her over towards the spring. The falling water had at some time centuries past seeped into a fault in the face of the cliff there; and as the stone weathered, part of it had split away. Two huge shards, as tall as houses, were still standing, one almost touching the living rock, the second half-fallen like a great slab against the first. Between this slab and the cliff itself was perhaps a foot or two of space thick with fern and long spears of grass. Christopher thrust her down into it.

"*Will* you be quiet!" he whispered savagely.

"How can I be quiet when I don't even know what it is I'm supposed to be quiet about?" Kate hissed back.

"I had a dog in Norfolk once that trusted me."

"I'm not a dog," Kate informed him fiercely, "and I'm not completely blind or witless either. What did you go and do this afternoon when you'd sent me back to the house?"

"Do?" said Christopher. "Why, what the other pilgrims do. I went up to the Holy Well and threw my gold ring into the water, speaking my troubles aloud, so that Those who rule over the Well could hear me."

"I don't believe you."

"You tell me what I did, then. After a time, a voice spoke out of the Well, and it answered me."

"It didn't. You couldn't have done anything so lunatic. And even if you did, it was probably only an echo in the shaft."

"Then it knew its own mind remarkably well for an echo. It said I was to go and come back here again in the evening, as soon as the sun was down. Not being one to argue and dispute over every word of command, like some people, I went. I wanted the time myself, to see you and be sure you were safely out of the way before —"

"But, Christopher!" Kate broke in uncontrollably. "I don't understand. Why should they want you to come back here? What did you say to them? Why in the name of heaven did you say anything at all?"

"I told you this afternoon, I like to play games with my own money."

"What do you mean?"

"Never you mind," said Christopher. He had turned his head and was looking away up the valley in the direction of the castle. "Be still," he murmured under his breath. "Don't move. Keep behind that rock. You'll know soon enough; it's coming." Then he was gone.

Kate had no idea what was coming. She could see only the curve of the cliff wall to her right; and straight ahead of her, through the narrow jagged crevice between the two great stones, only a strip of grass and flowers with the pathway winding through them to the dark entrance of the cave on the other side of the little bay. The next instant even this was blotted out. Christopher had moved around to the front of the crevice, and was standing with his back against it.

Then in the silence Kate heard a faint scutter of pebbles and the creak of a boot. Somebody was coming down the path from the castle.

"Stop where you are," said Christopher.

"Very well, sir." It was Master John's voice, speaking composedly. He might have been any steward acknowledging an order from his master's brother. The creak stopped.

There was a long pause. Then, quite suddenly, Kate was aware that Christopher was moving again. The crevice opened; the strip of grass and flowers swung slowly back into view. She could see the shadowy wall of cliff opposite — it was already shadowy in the deep gorge — and Master John over to her left, waiting at the last dip of the path. Christopher was beside him. Neither of them had said another word; but as if in some common understanding, they had both turned and were looking intently at the dark opening of the cave among the rocks.

In the shadows of the cave something was coming up out of the Well. Kate was too far away to see exactly what it was. It appeared flickering for a second on the lip of the curbstone, heaving itself up on two long thin crooked arms like a spider's; then it had a knee on the ledge, and sliding over to the ground. It seemed to be a tall figure dressed in gray, a shifting gray like the shadows around it, and it moved as silently as a shadow. It drifted over to the dark entrance of the cave and hovered there, waiting.

Kate thought afterwards that she must have shut her eyes for an instant, like a child hoping against hope that it was all only a bad dream. When she opened them, everything was still there, Master John at the head of the path, the gray creature at the mouth of the cave. Christopher was walking across the grass to meet it. The creature was advancing a step or so to meet him. They stood together and spoke in very low voices to one another. Kate could not hear what they said.

The parley, or whatever it was, did not last very long. It ended with the creature reaching into the draperies at its breast and drawing something out, a small object, like a phial or a flasket. Christopher took the thing and drank what was in it. Then he knelt down, and the creature bent over him, putting its shadowy hands on his shoulders and murmuring to him in a soft, rhythmical whisper. Presently it nodded, as though satisfied, drew Christopher to his feet, and went back into the shadows of the cave. Christopher remained standing exactly where it had left him. He was so still that he might have been turned to stone.

The creature came out of the cave again. This time it was carrying a child in its arms. She was a little girl — Kate could see the long yellow hair curling and tangling against the gray shoulder — motionless, evidently asleep.

The creature went to Christopher and gave the child to him,

saying a few words as it did so. Christopher turned and began to cross the grass, moving stiffly, as though he were walking in a dream or trying to make his way step by step through deep water. His eyes were wide open, staring straight ahead of him, and his face was completely blank. Every vestige of understanding and will had been wiped out of it. He did not appear to know what he was doing, only to be going through a set of motions that had been laid down for him, like a piece of clockwork. He plodded to the head of the path and put the little girl into Master John's arms. Then he said, spacing it out like the clock striking, one thick, clogged word at a time:

"Take — her — back — to — my — brother."

"Very well, sir," replied Master John imperturbably.

Christopher said again in that strange voice: "Take — her — back — to — my — brother." Then he swung around as if obeying an order and went plodding over to his master.

The creature put its hand on his shoulder again, and drew him with it into the shadows of the cave. Kate could not see what became of them after that. In the bluish twilight the entrance to the cave was only a black hole among the rocks.

Master John shifted the sleeping Cecily to a more comfortable position against his shoulder, and said very quietly:

"You can come out now, Mistress Katherine."

Kate's heart lurched sickeningly into her throat.

"Come out," Master John repeated. "I know where you are."

Kate cowered back against the kind cliff as if she could somehow flatten herself into it and vanish.

"Mistress Katherine," said Master John patiently. "You can come out of your own accord, or I can send a couple of serving men up from the castle to fetch you. Take your choice. It makes no particular difference to me."

Kate took her choice. Anything was better than to be

dragged out kicking and struggling like a rabbit from a hole. Master John stood aside courteously to let her go down the path to the castle ahead of him.

Old Dorothy was waiting on the terrace in front of the great hall. She came hurrying down the steps to meet them, her hands stretched out and the tears pouring down her wrinkled face. "Oh my lamb! my lamb!" she sobbed, reaching for Cecily. "Come to old Dorothy! Oh, my lady's own child! Mistress Katherine, if I ever spoke ill of the Young Lord I take it back! I take it all back!"

Master John merely put Cecily into her arms with a curt: "See to her!" and went on past her up the steps.

The evidence room had a door on the terrace, so that carters and grooms and gardeners with business to do could get to him without trailing their muddy boots in and out of the great hall. He pulled open the door and bowed. "In here, Mistress Katherine," he said.

The little room was very plump and clean and commonplace, rather like Master John himself. There was a big table covered with papers and account books; more account books were ranged tidily on a shelf against the smooth whitewashed wall. Under the shelf was a great iron-bound chest. The floor had been polished and strewn with fragrant herbs — meadowsweet, rosemary, thyme. A pleasant handful of fire burned on the hearth (for the summer nights were growing chilly), and Master John's after supper morsel, a platter of cheese and ripe pears, was laid ready for him on a joint stool beside the modest wooden armchair.

Master John turned the key in the lock and glanced around him with the air of a man who finds himself at home again after a long day. He put another log on the fire and lit the new wax candles in the seven-branch stick on the mantelpiece. Then he sat down in the armchair, leisurely crossing his legs, and beckoned Kate to come over to the hearth.

"I want to have a little talk with you," he said. "You're shivering, Mistress Katherine. Shall I stir the fire? Or would you care for a glass of wine?"

Kate shook her head, but she came over to the hearth and knelt down to warm herself as close to the flames as she could. Her hands felt icy cold, and she was shivering uncontrollably.

"Just a little talk," said Master John, leaning back in the armchair. "To make our positions plain to one another, like two reasonable human beings. Do you know, I have always thought well of you, very well indeed? You and I are two reasonable human beings, Mistress Katherine. We are, if you do not mind my saying so, the only two reasonable human beings anywhere about Elvenwood Hall. The People of the Hill are *not* (to speak between ourselves) reasonable human beings, and as for Christopher Heron —"

"What did they do to him?" Kate cried out before she could stop herself.

"Oh, that?" said Master John. "That was nothing — merely to quiet him for a little, until they were sure of him. He'll be over it in another hour or two: believe me. They have no intention of actually taking his wits away from him, or doing anything else that might weaken or spoil him for the —" he paused to select the exact word he wanted: "ceremony."

"What ceremony?"

"They have a great many ceremonies," explained Master John. "This is the one on All Hallows' Eve."

"Are they going to use him to pay the teind? For the human sacrifice? Is that what you mean?"

"What *I* mean?" asked Master John. "You can't have understood me, Mistress Katherine. I'm not one of Those in the Well.

The teind means nothing to me. I only supply certain goods and certain services to certain people and am paid a certain reasonable price for it; your own grandfather did the same every day of his life. Do you think he ever asked whether the buyers would make a good use of the wine or the corn or the wool before he'd strike a bargain with them? Why should he? It was no concern of his. Neither is it any concern of mine. And if Christopher Heron chose to strike a bargain with them on his own account, that is no concern of mine either."

"What bargain?"

"I should think it would be clear to you by this time."

"Did he tell them that they could have him instead if they gave Cecily back?"

"I believe it was something of the sort," said Master John. "He seems to have assumed — rightly — that if they were given the choice, they would prefer to have him. As well as I can judge (for I know very little of such matters) the whole purpose of this ceremony we were speaking of is to get for oneself the force and power of the —" he paused again: "participant. Now it stands to reason (if one reasons as they do) that Christopher Heron would serve their ends much better than a child like Cecily. You and I may think him deplorably reckless and passionate and foolish, but neither of us can with justice deny that for the purpose of this ceremony he would be a young man of extraordinary power. It is partly a question of his mere strength, breeding, vigor, and comeliness, and partly (I am arguing as they might) the fact that he would be doing the thing of his own free will. I have been given to understand that when the participant in the ceremony is terrified or reluctant — as a small child is likely to be — there is always some risk that a portion of the power may be lost or kept back. With Christopher Heron, on the other hand — but I am sure that you see what I mean."

"Yes," said Kate helplessly. "I see what you mean."

"I thought you would." Master John reached out and chose a pear from the platter at his side. "However," he went on briskly, "as I told you before, all this is no concern of ours. What you and I have to consider —"

He took a small silver knife from the pouch at his belt, and weighed the pear in his hand for a moment. Then he began to cut it delicately into thin slivers, all precisely the same size.

"I am sure," he said, "that you must see that my position at this time is a very trying and painful one for me."

"I can see that it may well be." Kate straightened up and sat back on the floor, cautiously regarding him, trying to assess the exact meaning of that last sentence. She had stopped shivering. The talk was finally moving in a direction where she felt herself to be to some extent on her own ground, away from the dark, alien, mysterious world of the Fairy Folk. She knew better than to take Master John's word that he was an honest trader, like her grandfather, but he was at least a dishonest trader, not a heathen magician dealing in spells and charms and human sacrifice. A dishonest trader would be concerned first and foremost with his own profits and his own safety. He would not be the sort of man to stick by a bad bargain out of pure loyalty to his partners, and if he could be convinced that his position was trying and painful enough —

"Wouldn't it be better to cut loose from them entirely, before it's too late?" she inquired, doing her best to sound lightly assured, almost indifferent. "You'll never be able to explain to Sir Geoffrey how all this has happened."

"The ceremony should be safely over long before Sir Geoffrey

comes back. He isn't returning until some time after All Saints' Day. Randal brought me word this morning that he may even put it off to the Christmas season."

"But when he does come, Cecily will still be back here at the castle, and Christopher will have gone instead. How do you think you can possibly account for that?"

"Be reasonable, Mistress Katherine. You know — and I know — that it would be easy enough to account for it. Don't you remember old Dorothy saying over and over again that he'd killed the child to get the whole inheritance for himself? These reckless and high-spirited young men are sometimes sadly ambitious. He didn't kill her; when the time came, he couldn't bring himself to do that. He gave her to a band of wandering tinkers — or was it gypsies? Yes, on the whole, I think it had better be gypsies — and bribed them to take her out of the way and see to it that she stayed lost for the rest of her life. Fortunately, his miserable confederates became panic-stricken — or did they quarrel with him over their pay? No, that won't do; they became stricken with panic and remorse at what they had done, and decided instead to bring the child to me and break away from him entirely, before they were caught. Christopher Heron broke away when I accused him of it, and fled rather than face Sir Geoffrey once the truth was known. What else could he do? Sir Geoffrey is a stern man at the best of times, and he was harsh enough with his brother even when he thought it was only a question of his being foolishly careless with Cecily."

Kate stared at him, her wits scattering like sheep. Dishonest trading of this scope and quality was something she had never met with before. It had simply not occurred to her it was possible. "That's a very unlikely story," she said, but her voice only came out as a sort of whisper because her throat was so dry.

"Not altogether likely, perhaps," Master John admitted, shaking his head. "In my opinion, it would be far more reasonable to take the child straight back to the Hill tonight (she can always be used for a hostage if the worst comes to the worst) and tell Sir Geoffrey that his brother had grown weary of his coldness and gone off to seek his fortune in the Indies. Unhappily, Those in the Well are very strict about keeping to the exact letter of any bargain they make, and the exact letter of this bargain was that the child should go safely back to her father. Still, such as it is, the story should do well enough. Certainly it should do."

"Sir Geoffrey won't believe it."

"Why won't he believe it?" inquired Master John, cutting another slice from the pear.

"Nobody could believe it — nobody who knows Christopher, He almost tore himself to pieces over what happened to Cecily."

"I wonder just how well Geoffrey did know his brother?" asked Master John softly. "I judge that he was at one time deeply attached to him, but he's been away from him in Ireland for the past five years, and as for knowing him — it isn't so easy to know Christopher Heron, not with all his fine talk and his tongue like a skinning knife: haven't you seen that for yourself? He might tear himself to pieces, if you choose to put it so extravagantly, but it would go very hard with him to make a display of the pieces: haven't you seen that too? He used to come back to the house when Sir Geoffrey was here and stand about the great hall looking as if he'd never seen the inside of a leper's hut in his life; and his appearance was so cold and callous that Sir Geoffrey must be to some extent prepared to believe he never truly cared for the child at all. I'm not saying it won't be a blow to Sir Geoffrey, mind you. He was, as I told you, deeply attached to his brother. Indeed, he still is so deeply attached to him that in the future he may find Elvenwood Hall even more unbearable than he does now. When the Herons find anything

unbearable, Mistress Katherine, their way is to repudiate it —
withdraw themselves from it — leave it — go."

"Why hasn't Christopher gone, then?"

"Because to stay was the worst punishment he could lay on
himself," Master John pointed out unanswerably. "Sir Geoffrey
won't feel called upon to do that. Why should he? No, Mistress
Katherine, I don't think we'll see much of Sir Geoffrey at
Elvenwood Hall after this. It isn't as though he needed to be
here, or trouble himself over the estate — not while he can trust
it to me. Bless you, I don't intend to rob him. I've never
touched a penny from the farms or the rents or the woolpack or
anything else that could rightly be called his. The Queen's
Lord Treasurer himself would be welcome to go over my account
books."

"You're still running a great risk," Kate argued stubbornly.

"What risk?"

"The village is suspicious already. They know there's something wrong with the castle."

"A pack of country folk full of old wives' tales, and a poor
unlettered priest who can hardly read the words in his mass
book? Who'd listen to them? Oh no, Mistress Katherine, I can
deal with the village."

"There must be at least fifty people up here at the castle, too.
That's a good many to be in on a secret."

"Mistress Katherine! Mistress Katherine!" said Master John,
almost affectionately. "What makes you think that more than
one or two of them *are* in the secret? The old lords were no
fools, and neither am I. There was a serving man once who
started prying about Lord Richard's tower, and sneaking off to
walk in the Elvenwood; but —" said Master John, peeling
another slice of his pear, "he was lost there on a dark night, and
he never found his way out again. That was twenty years ago,

and I don't remember anyone trying it since. They know better."

"Dorothy —"

"Dorothy doesn't know the whole of the truth; and if she tried to tell Sir Geoffrey the little she does know, he'd soon find out that she's nothing but a silly babbling old woman. And she won't tell him. I can make her keep her mouth shut."

"Randal —"

"Randal's mad."

"Cecily —"

"Cecily is only four years old. By the time she sees her father again, in three months or more, she won't remember much about Fairy Folk. No, Mistress Katherine, you and I will have to come to the point. There is only one person in this whole house who is likely to put the slightest difficulty in the way of Sir Geoffrey believing anything I may choose to tell him. Surely you agree with me?"

Kate looked around her at the quiet room, the big table with its inkhorn and papers, the account books standing in line on their shelf, the one window thoughtfully provided with a grille of iron bars, the closed door leading to the terrace, the closed door leading into the great hall. Then she lifted her chin and surveyed Master John in her stoniest manner. She knew it was ridiculous — a mouse driven into a corner might just as well have tried to stand on its dignity with the cat — but it was all she could do. "Yes," she said. "That's true."

Master John ate the slice of pear.

"I take it," he remarked gently, "that Christopher Heron was depending on you to give Sir Geoffrey a true account of the matter? Or even to get him word so that he could come back in time to make trouble before the ceremony? Yes, I thought so. It was a very fortunate chance that I saw you following him up to the Holy Well as I came through the archway."

"That wasn't a chance," said Kate bitterly. "It was a judgment on me for behaving like a fool. If I'd done what he told me —"

"Don't blame yourself overmuch," said Master John in the kindest way. "These things happen, you know. It's of no importance, no importance at all — except, as I was telling you, that it puts *me* in a very trying and painful position."

"Not your conscience grieving you, surely?" asked Kate, deciding that it was all the same whether she was eaten for a shrew or for a mouse.

"I can't afford to keep a conscience," said Master John, looking rather taken aback, as though she had asked him why he did not keep a coach or ten horses. "Who do you take me for — Christopher Heron? And considering what that one of his has cost him —! No, Mistress Katherine. My conscience wasn't what I was thinking of."

"Yes," said Kate. "Were you by any chance thinking that I *am* one of the Princess Elizabeth's ladies, and that Sir Geoffrey made you answerable for my safe keeping until he comes back again?"

"That *is* what makes it so trying," confessed Master John. "What am I to say when he asks for you? I suppose I might put you under some sort of oath or vow never to reveal the truth to him, but I couldn't trust you to keep to it, and I should think you were an idiot if you did. You must understand: there's nothing I can do but take the risk and dispose of you somehow. I put it to you, as one reasonable human being to another, that I haven't any choice in the matter."

He paused to remove an infinitesimal brown speck from another slice of pear with the point of his knife. There was very little left of the pear now, only enough for about two more good mouthfuls.

"After all," he remarked thoughtfully, "when everything is said and done, Sir Geoffrey's a just man. He won't hold me accountable for more than flesh and blood can be expected to do. How was I to know that you'd fall secretly in love with Christopher Heron and run away with him when he fled from the castle?"

"What!" Kate jerked bolt upright, her wits scattering again.

"I shall, of course, conduct the most rigorous search for you both," Master John assured her. "But no one will care if it comes to nothing. Sir Geoffrey will be glad in his heart to have his brother escape the blow of the law; and do you think Queen Mary is likely to make any great stir over losing you? I understand you have never been what might be called a favorite of hers."

"B-b-but —" Kate stuttered furiously, "I'm not in love with Christopher Heron! How could I be in love with Christopher Heron? I've only talked to him twice in my life!"

"In this sad age," said Master John, "a young and ignorant girl like you can go astray very quickly: everybody knows that. Don't you trouble yourself, Mistress Katherine. The blame of it is sure to be laid chiefly on Christopher Heron, not on you or on me; and he is going to have so much to answer for by that time that a trifle more here and there should hardly make any difference to him — and in any case, what's a good name to the dead? You must perceive that I could never tell Sir Geoffrey that you had simply died of an illness or disappeared of your own accord. It would be entirely too strange and remarkable to have the both of you vanishing separately for different reasons at one and the same time. As it is, the only problem will be why I failed to discover what was happening, but that would have meant keeping my eye on you every minute of the day and —"

"Never mind," Kate interrupted him. She did not want to

hear any more about Master John's difficulties. "Just answer me this, will you? You said you were going to dispose of me. How are you planning to do it?"

Master John finished the last thin delicious slice of his pear in a leisurely manner.

"I can't tell you," he replied. "That isn't altogether for me to decide. There are various ways to dispose of you. Some you may have thought of already. Others will no doubt occur to you." He strolled over to the door leading into the great hall and opened it. "If you won't mind being left alone for a little, Mistress Katherine?" he inquired courteously. "I will come back as soon as my associates and I have considered the matter."

VIII ॐ
The Lady in the Green

The door closed demurely behind Master John, the latch
clicked and Kate was left staring at the neat little pile of peelings
and seed that lay among the pears and cheese on the dish by the
armchair. From the dish her eyes went again, slowly, almost
unbelievingly, to the account books, the money chest, the
polished candlesticks, the quiet walls and shelves and windows
of Master John's private room.

She had had a nightmare once when she was a child. She
could still remember it, a nightmare in which solid, familiar
objects — like walls and shelves and windows — had begun to
slide and blur, to dissolve, to lose their true shape and turn into
something else, the same and yet not the same as they were in
reality. It was like that now. Master John's room was the
kind of place she had known all her life. It was part of her own
world, the world she had always lived in, her father's world
and her grandfather's — and yet suddenly it seemed stranger and
more terrifying than even the dark world of the Fairy Folk. At
least the Fairy Folk wanted the reality of Christopher Heron, to
get for themselves the qualities of spirit and body which he
actually had. Master John did not so much as want that. In his
world, Christopher also would lose his true shape and be turned
into something else, the blurred distorted figure of a thief and a
coward, entirely unreal; but to Master John that would not

matter one way or the other: "What's a good name to the dead?"

She rose to her feet in a sort of bewildered outrage, her eyes going back to the dish of fruit by the armchair; and more than anything else on earth at that moment she wanted to snatch it up and fling the whole tidy abominable platter with a great satisfying crash down the smooth whitewashed wall over the pens and papers and the account books spread out on the work table. The platter would be broken to pieces; the fat pears would burst and spurt, and —

And Master John, quite unperturbed by such childishness, would send for Tom or Dick or Humphrey; the fragments would be swept away and the walls covered with more whitewash, the stained pages of the account book would be copied out fresh, the table scrubbed clean. By the time Sir Geoffrey saw the room again, the little difficulty would be completely disposed of.

Disposed of.

The good, hot, comforting wave of fury that had swept over her broke and drained away, leaving her empty.

If Christopher was caught in the nightmare, so was she. She could not break out of it, any more than he could. It was useless to pretend that anyone who was capable of destroying a Christopher Heron without a second thought would hesitate for an instant to dispose of a Katherine Sutton. That at least she could be absolutely sure of.

She looked at the closed door leading to the great hall. In a little while it would open again, and Master John would come through it with a knife, a small silver knife like the one he had used to cut the pear to pieces, and then he would kill her.

No, he would not. She might be frightened, but there was no need to be foolish. Master John was the last man on earth to commit a murder with his own hands, particularly a murder in his own private room, overturning the furniture, making a nasty mess of the sweet smelling, herb strewn floor. That would be too "trying" and "painful" even for him. It was much more likely that he would have the castle people take her and do whatever had to be done out of his sight and a long way off.

No, not that either. Not the castle people. The castle people — or at least the "one or two" who were in on the secret — could be trusted to support Master John against the outside world on any ordinary occasion; but he would never trust them with anything like this. Master John was not, after all, one of the old Wardens, the lords of the manor. Sir Geoffrey was coming back after All Saints' Day, and then Master John would have enough trouble on his hands without taking chances on any possible carelessness or disloyalty or panic. Master John was not the sort of person to take chances except when he had to; and this was certainly one chance that he did not have to take. If all he wanted was somebody who would dispose of her out of his sight and a long way off —

It was a long way down the black, echoing shaft of the Holy Well, into the unknown caverns and passages and hidden places that lay under the Hill and the dark interlaced trees of the Elvenwood. Anyone who escaped from the creatures who lived there might perhaps wander until he dropped and died without ever finding his way out again. And even if he did find his way out, he might no longer be in a state where it would make very much difference whether he did or not.

She caught her breath sharply. In Master John's world, there were only two possible ways to protect oneself from an enemy, by fraud or by violence; but in the dark world of the Fairy Folk, there was another. She thought of Randal, with his wits shattered into fragments, and Christopher Heron's blind, enchanted eyes turning to his master; and her heart failed her utterly. There were some things she might perhaps bring herself to face, scraping a little courage together in her last need, but not that. She could not bear to have her mind taken away from her. The mere possibility of it was unendurable. She could not bear it. She would rather die.

— And that, she told herself savagely, was ridiculous. What was the use of proclaiming in a lordly way that she would rather die? Nobody was going to give her any choice in the matter. When the moment came, they would do exactly as they pleased; and she would have to endure it whether it was unendurable or not. What she ought to be thinking of, while she had the time, was how to get out of the evidence room and away from the castle.

She knew that the door to the terrace was locked. She remembered Master John turning the key and putting it into the pouch at his side. She tried the door leading into the great hall. It had been locked too, from the other side.

That left the window.

The window itself was simply a common window, with two latticed leaves opening outward on the terrace. The protecting grille of iron bars had been fitted over it, cage fashion, on the inner wall of the evidence room. Like all the rest of Master John's possessions, the grille was in excellent repair, freshly painted and firmly secured: not even a speck of dust fell when she shook it. The most she could do, by thrusting her hand between the bars, was to push one leaf back a few inches and look out at the courtyard. The moon had risen, and the courtyard was swimming in dim silvery light, except where the great black hulk of Lord Richard's tower threw everything into darkness.

In the light a shadowy figure was coming up the steps to the terrace.

For one dreadful moment Kate thought that the gray creature

from the Holy Well had trailed them up to the castle, and was hovering about the door. Then she realized that the figure coming up the steps was singing softly to itself, another part of the ballad about the minstrel who had met the fairy lady under the elder tree, the same ballad that she had once heard him singing in the forest:

> So they fared on, and further on,
>   The steed went swifter than the wind;
> Until they came to a desert place,
>   And living land was left behind.
> For forty days and forty nights,
>   They wade through red blood to the knee;
> And they saw neither sun nor moon,
>   But heard the roaring of the sea.

He broke off as he emerged on the terrace, and paused to look about him, his shadowy head turning from side to side. "Where are you?" he whispered.

"Randal," said Kate. In the strain and excitement of the long day, she had entirely forgotten her flurried arrangements to meet him on the terrace that night, when it was dark, and give him the news of her doings that he was to carry to Sir Geoffrey.

Randal took an uncertain step towards the window.

"That's not your own room you're in," he said doubtfully.

"No, but I'm staying here for a little," Kate answered, deciding that it would only waste time and confuse him if she tried to explain any further. She must not waste time, and she must not confuse him — that was what Christopher had told her to remember, it was very important not to confuse him. "See what I have for you, Randal."

She drew the folded paper out of her bodice and shook it free from the coils of the redheaded woman's chain. (What else was it that Christopher had said? Don't use many words. Be very simple and plain. Make sure he knows exactly where he's to go and how soon he has to get there.) "Look! I've written down all the news of my doings for you to carry to Sir Geoffrey. It's a letter."

"A letter?" Randal seemed pleased. "A true letter with a seal on it?"

"No, there isn't any seal on it, but it's a letter, a true letter, and Sir Geoffrey will be very glad to get it," said Kate carefully. "I want you to take it to him at his house in Norfolk. Now. Tonight. See, I'll reach it out to you through the bars just as if I were a prisoner in a dungeon and you were trying to help me. And," she added, "don't show it to anybody else, because it's a secret letter, and that would spoil the secret."

"You forgot to say I was to put it into his own hand," Randal pointed out, like a child insisting that a story should be told in the exact words to which he was accustomed. But he took the letter without any more dispute and tucked it away into the breast of his doublet. Apparently, all her other instructions had been familiar and acceptable to him.

"Yes, yes, that's right, you put it into his own hand," Kate hurried to assure him. "And, Randal — there's one thing more I want you to tell him. It's not in the letter. It's a spoken word from me. Tell Sir Geoffrey that something else had happened here" — better not say what the "something" was; it would be too much for Randal to grapple with — "and tell him that he *must* be back on All Hallows' Eve at the latest. At the very latest. Do you understand that?"

"I can say it all over by heart," Randal informed her proudly.

"It's a secret letter for Sir Geoffrey. And I'm to carry it to him at his house in Norfolk. And I'm to put it into his own hand. And I'm to tell him to be back here on All Hallows' Eve."

"By All Hallows' Eve."

"Isn't it the same?"

Kate could have kicked herself. She had been a fool. She ought to have said simply that Sir Geoffrey must come back at once.

"Isn't it the same?" Randal repeated. His voice had begun to waver again.

"Yes, it's the same," Kate answered quickly, terrified that he might become completely bewildered if she argued about the message any longer. And after all, she reflected, it did not make very much difference. Sir Geoffrey would be sure to start back as soon as he had the letter, no matter what Randal told him. "Don't worry your head over the word from me: you have it all fine and clear. Now, go before anyone sees you, and — O heavens! I didn't think! The gates will be locked by this time."

"I don't like having gates locked on me," said Randal, shaking his head disapprovingly. "One night when they were locked on me here, I found a way of my own over the castle wall down back of the stables, for it's an ill thing to stay in a place you can't get out of. That's the way I go now if I don't want anyone to see me. Watch!" and with one of his sudden, fantastic movements he turned and was gone down the steps so quickly and lightly that Kate did not even hear the sound of his feet on the stones.

What she did hear was Master John's voice speaking to someone outside the closed door that led to the great hall.

She had barely time to get back to her old place, kneeling down by the fire, when a key rattled in the lock, the latch was lifted, and Master John appeared on the threshold. Kate had not, after her first moment of panic, really thought that he would swoop down on her with a knife in his hand; but she was entirely unprepared for what followed. He did not even glance about to see where she was. He was half turned away, looking back towards the great hall, his shoulders a little bent in the tag end of a deferential bow. He swung the door open obsequiously, sidling along with it until it stopped against the wall; and then, to Kate's amazement, he went down on one knee and lowered his head, like a court gentleman waiting for the Queen to go by.

The Lady in the Green came quietly past him into the room and stood still, looking down at them both, very much as she had stood that evening on the forest road. She had not changed at all — rather, it was the walls and shelves and windows of Master John's room that suddenly looked changed, unreal and grotesque, as if a young disdainful living tree had sprung up by magic through the flat boards of the floor. The mingled light of the fire and the candles flickered over the long, cloudy dark hair, the glinting bracelet on her wrist, the shadowy greens of her cloak. The cloak was woven in varying shades of leaf color that wavered and shifted continually under the light, oak leaf, willow leaf, holly leaf, ash leaf, thorn leaf, elder and hazel, ivy and moss and fern. The dress under the cloak had been made of the same stuff; and both were cut in strange patterns, the dress all soft flowing lines that clung to the body, the cloak turned back at the throat into great curving folds that were caught on the left shoulder with a long pin of dark bronze. The fluctuating shapes and tints baffled the eye like the interlaced branches and foliage of a thicket. The only thing Kate could really see was the face with its hard delicate bones and faintly amused, disdainful mouth.

"Is that the girl?" said the Lady.

Her voice was lilting and musical like Randal's, but it was not Randal's that sprang into Kate's mind the instant she heard it. It was the royal voice of the Princess Elizabeth. They both spoke with the same clarity, the same inborn, almost unconscious power to command.

Only they were not altogether the same. The Princess Elizabeth's voice could cut like a knife when she was impatient or angry with a maid of honor — but when she called anyone "girl," it had never sounded exactly as though she were saying: "the dog" or "the horse."

"That is the girl, madam," said Master John, with another deferential bend of his head. Master John actually confronting the Lady in the Green was a very different man from Master John talking of reasonable human beings while he sat cross-legged in his armchair. Kate could hear his steward's chain give a faint nervous chink as he shifted the weight on his knee against the hard boards of the floor.

She suddenly realized that she too was still down on her knees by the fire and scrambled awkwardly to her feet. At least she did not have to stay groveling on the hearth like one of the enchanted pigs in a story about Ulysses and Circe that Master Roger had read to them in the old days at Hatfield.

"Is she always so clumsy?" inquired the Lady.

There was no malice in the question. She was merely running her eye over the lines of the dog or the horse.

"Always, madam," said Master John.

The Lady glanced at Kate's set face.

"And stubborn?" she asked.

"Very stubborn," agreed Master John. "Even if her mind were to be taken away from her —"

"I won't have my mind taken away from me," Kate interrupted

him, forgetting that she did not have any choice in the matter.

The disdainful curve of the beautiful mouth became slightly — only very slightly — more pronounced; but when the Lady spoke again, it was still to Master John. "Do you want me to take her mind away from her?" she said.

"Well, madam," replied Master John, "for my own part — so far as I may judge, since you ask it of me — I do not see why you should put yourself to the trouble. I have always been one to hold by the old proverb, 'Stone dead hath no fellow,' and so please you, I would rather it were that."

The Lady glanced at Kate again. It was impossible to tell what she thought of Master John's suggestion. Her face was entirely unchanged. Kate could only stand there and wait for the answer, suddenly and agonizingly conscious of her own living body, the feel of her foot on the floor, the pounding of her heart against her side.

"I see no need of her death," said the Lady indifferently. "She does not appear to me to be of any great value, and in my land she will be worth even less than she is here; but there are certain mortal women that we keep in the Hill for our servants and scrubbers, and if she is taken and trained I think some use may be made of her. Fetch me a —"

Kate did not hear the rest of the sentence. Her foot had lost the feel of the floor; the walls and shelves and windows were all sliding and blurring together, just as they had in her dream. She caught at the back of Master John's armchair and clung to it while the room reeled around her.

When it steadied, Master John had disappeared and the Lady was no longer watching her. She had moved closer to the fire and was unclasping the bracelet from her left arm. On the inner side, where the turn of the wrist had hidden it, was a huge rounded stone, green like an emerald, set in the gold. The Lady touched one of the little claws that held the stone down, and it sprang erect as if it were the lid of a box.

Master John scurried back through the door to the great hall. This time he had a cup in his hand; when he knelt again and offered it to the Lady, Kate could see that there was wine in it. The Lady struck the edge of her bracelet very lightly against the rim. A tiny stream of white powder poured out from under the green jewel and fell over the wine. Then she took the cup from Master John and beckoned Kate to come to her.

"No," said Kate, gripping the back of the armchair. It was as though she were at the Holy Well again, pressed against the sheltering stone, watching the gray creature lean over Christopher with the phial in its hand, seeing once more the blank face and the blind witless eyes. "No," she said breathlessly. "Please. I will go without it. Quietly. Truly I will."

"This drink is not what we gave to the Young Lord, if that is what you fear," said the Lady calmly. "That was something else. This is only what we mingle with the water in the rich pilgrim's cup, to free him from sorrow and pain or the grief of a wound. The mortal women we keep in the Hill drink it every day. It takes away the heaviness of their minds, and makes them peaceful and content."

Kate ran her tongue over her dry lips. "I do not want my mind to be taken away," she said.

"It will not take away your mind," said the Lady, "only the part of your mind which sees what is harsh or unpleasing. And who would not be glad to lose that?"

"Well —" Kate ran her tongue over her lips again. "Are you?"

"I?" said the Lady, almost sharply.

"You and the others. Your people. T-the Fairy Folk," Kate stammered. "Do you also drink it every day?"

"We do not need to be eased so," said the Lady. "But you will not be able to endure the nature of my land without it. We do not ask that except of a teind-payer, and even then only if he is a young man strong enough to serve his nine weeks' death-time, as the kings of the land did in the old days."

"*You* live without it," Kate insisted.

"We are not of your kind," said the Lady. "Do you think *you* could live as we do?"

Kate stiffened. She did not mind the question: it was the tone of the voice that stung her past bearing.

"I don't know how you live," she retorted. "But why should your land be any more dreadful to me than it is to you?"

"You would find that out soon enough if you tried it," said the Lady. "And then you would come to me crying and begging for what I have offered you freely."

"Well, couldn't I have till then?" asked Kate doggedly.

"Do not be impudent, girl!" said Master John. "Madam, if you want her to drink it, I can easily —"

The Lady did not even glance at him. Her eyes were still on Kate's face, and they as well as her mouth now looked very faintly amused.

"You may have till you please," she replied. "It will all be the same in the end." She set the cup down on the little table beside the platter of fruit and drew a narrow strip of green silk from somewhere under her cloak.

"What is that for?" inquired Kate, apprehensively.

"To tie over your eyes," said the Lady. "And in this I can give you no choice, for you must not see the way that we are going."

The last thing that Kate actually did see, with curious distinctness, was the cup standing on the little table and gleaming softly in the light of the fire. It was a plain silver cup, one of a

set that were used every day at the high table. The next instant
it disappeared as the silk closed over her face. A breath of cold
air from the terrace door blew against her cheek.

"Take hold of my cloak," said the Lady's voice.

Kate clutched at the fold of cloth that was put into her hand,
and feeling ridiculously like a puppy on a lead, stumbled behind
the Lady down the terrace steps and across the familiar paving
stones of the courtyard. Presently they paused; there was a
creak of hinges, and when they began to move again it was
over a rough board floor. The air was suddenly close and
heavy with the dry sweet smell of stored grain.

For a moment Kate could not tell where they had gone; then
she remembered all the times she had seen carters unloading
sacks of corn at the dark arch across the courtyard from her
window, and understood. They were in Lord Richard's tower.
The secret way that they were to follow must begin there.

She took a quick, excited step forward, and was told to keep
herself further back.

Kate fell back obediently. It did not matter. She had the
answer now to a number of questions that had been puzzling
her — why Master John sent so many household supplies to
the old tower, instead of the cellars in the new wing; why there
was never any other outward evidence of his trade with the
Fairy Folk. A secret entrance to the castle storerooms would
allow them to come and go and take what they chose even at
times when they could not show themselves openly.

"There is a stair here," said the Lady's voice. "Put your free
hand on the wall to your left, and stay as close to it as you can."

Kate would have fallen otherwise. The stair was a spiral one,
very steep, its stone treads uneven and worn hollow from
centuries of use. She had to struggle and fumble for almost
every step, lurching on her awkward feet and clinging helplessly

to the wall. The spiral swung around and turned and swung around on itself again, coiling down and down, until she felt as if her brains were beginning to turn with it by the time they reached a level place and there was another pause. The air was still very close, but it had become bitterly cold and she thought they must be a long way under the ground. Then there was the faintest possible touch of warmth on her right cheek, as though the Lady had lighted some sort of lamp or a candle.

"Walk slowly now," said the voice. "Keep your head and your shoulders down, or you will hurt yourself. It is all stone here, and the way in is narrow and low."

They went twenty steps and turned sharply to the left; then thirty-four steps and turned right; ninety-five and then left again; a hundred and two —

"A hundred and three, and a hundred and four, *left*," Kate whispered to herself, hanging desperately to the count. It was at least no worse than the terrible games of blindfold chess her father had once made her play with him, as a way of training her mind and memory. If she could only keep the exact pattern of turns and the number of steps between them clear in her head, there was a chance — a very faint chance — that she might be able to find the way out again to Lord Richard's tower when the time came.

It was her own physical clumsiness that defeated her. Everything was going well when the Lady's voice said: "Take care; there is slime on the path here," and for the next five minutes she was too occupied with keeping her feet under her to mark the turns or make an accurate count of the steps they had taken. When they got to better ground at last, she was lost.

Once she noticed that the air was growing much warmer and very damp, almost steamy; but she could not tell what had caused the change, and after a while it was cold again. Later still, she began to hear a sound in the distance. At first she thought it was thunder, and then realized that it could not be: they were too far under the ground. It was the roar and crash of water, a cataract or a river in flood, booming and echoing through the depths of a chasm. In the beginning it came from a long way off, but as the path twisted and turned, it drew nearer, rising louder and louder, until she could feel even the wall of the passage quiver with it under her hand.

Then suddenly the wall was gone and they were walking straight into the noise — into it, over it, as though they had come out and were making their way along a ledge or a bridge somewhere high above the chasm, and the pealing echoes were all around them, splitting, shivering, reverberating from rock to rock over the hiss of driven spray and the insufferable clamor of the water plunging down coigns and archways and masses of fallen stone far below. Then, just as suddenly, they seemed to be in a passage again. The rock closed down over her head, brushing against her hair, and the noise from the chasm dwindled and died away behind them like light at the end of a tunnel.

The new passage was straight and very smooth, and grew rapidly higher and wider; in a few minutes she could no longer touch the wall with her free hand or feel the rock pressing down above her. But after the uproar in the chasm its stillness was unnerving. The uproar had at least given Kate some idea of space and location, by which to judge the direction in which they were moving and the distance they had come. Here she had nothing to go by, only her hold on the Lady's cloak and the whisper of the Lady's feet on the path ahead of her.

They went on and on and on, one slow, monotonous step after another, through the smooth unbroken dark.

Kate never knew just how long they went on; it seemed like hours. The dark and the sense of her own blind helplessness became more and more painful. In spite of the constricting bandage around her eyes, she found that she was making frantic efforts to see. "I can't bear any more of this," she thought, "I can't bear it," and then realized that the feet ahead of her had stopped moving and the cloak was being pulled out of her hand.

"You will stay here," said the Lady's voice. "There is a place for you to sleep on the floor behind you."

"Can I take this thing off now?" asked Kate. She plucked at the band of green silk over her eyes. "I want to see."

It was a moment before the Lady answered; and when she did, her voice was soft and very faintly amused, as it had been when she let Kate have her own way in the matter of the cup.

"Do as you please," she said. The next sound was the murmuring rustle of her feet moving away again over the stones.

The strip of silk was too tight for Kate to pull over her head, the knot that tied it too subtle for her clumsy fingers. It was only after a bungling struggle that she finally felt the thing come loose and drop away in her hand.

It did not make the slightest difference. There was no flicker of light anywhere, no faintest outline of wall or roof or door, nothing but the same black darkness, unbroken, impenetrable, and absolute. Somewhere in the distance she could hear water running, a spring? a brook? a little stream of water? — but she could not see. All she could do was stand still, the strip of silk in her hand, gazing blindly and helplessly around her.

Then, out of the darkness, not very far away, there came the last sound in the world that she had expected to hear. It was a comfortable wallowing heave, like the flop of a heavy body turning over, followed by a drowsy contented animal grunt.

Kate straightened up with a jerk, her mind stammering indignantly. Not pigs. She would not, she would *not*, be sent to sleep with the pigs. It was bad enough to be regarded as a dog or a horse.

And then the absurdity of trying to make fine distinctions of rank between pigs and horses and dogs suddenly struck her, and she found herself grinning wryly in the dark. What did it matter? To the Lady, one beast was probably very much like another.

And furthermore, stable or kennel or sty, she could not go on standing on her feet the rest of the night.

She stooped down and felt cautiously for the floor behind her. The pigs must have something to sleep on, straw or dead leaves perhaps — but there had been no rustle of straw when she had heard the creature turn over; it had sounded more as though it were wallowing in mud. The skin on the tips of her searching fingers began to crawl a little at the thought. Straw or dead leaves she thought she could bear with, but if it came to mud —

She tried to shift back a step, stumbled, and fell forward, her hands sinking to the wrist as they went down into a hideous softness of —

Velvet. Not straw or mud or dead leaves, but velvet. Quilted velvet (as she discovered when she collected her wits enough to kneel and grope over it), a great coverlet of quilted velvet luxuriously lined with fur and spread on a very wide, low couch with a square carved chest at its head. There was a pillow, two pillows, both down; and sheets of some fine stuff that might have been linen, but felt more as if it were silk. The inner coverlets were wool, lighter than feathers to the touch and smelling deliciously of lavender when she dragged the velvet quilt back.

Kate drew a fold of the velvet through her hand, almost unbelievingly. She did not know what to make of it. She had heard the pigs wallowing and grunting in the darkness. Surely she had heard the pigs?

She got to her feet, still holding fast to the velvet, and stood for a moment, listening intently for some further sound. The water was still running in the distance, but the animal noises had stopped. All she could hear was a faint echoing sough like some chance murmur of wind among the stones.

She stooped down again and passed her hand over the fine carved surface of the chest at the head of the bed, and the yielding delicacy of the pillows, and the sweetness of the fur. The noises might easily have been a trick of her overwrought nerves misinterpreting an echo; but the bed was unquestionably real: solid, comforting, and warm. And wherever she was, she could not stand up weighing uncertainties and possibilities any longer. Her whole body felt numb with cold and strain, and the chill of the rock floor was cutting through her feet to the bone. She would have to lie down and rest.

Without a candle or a comb or proper nightgear or even a drop of water for washing — she did not dare to try to find the stream in the dark — there was very little she could do to get ready for bed, only say her prayers and slip out of her gown and her shoes. The gown she folded up and laid on the top of the chest, setting the shoes beside it. The prayer she hesitated over a little, and then fell back on the steadying familiarity of her ordinary evening paternoster. She hesitated again for a moment when she came to "Deliver us from evil," but decided in the end not to add anything more to that. "All you'll do nine times out of ten is start trying to teach the Lord His own business," was what her father had said to her once. The redheaded woman's cross she took off and slid under her pillow, to keep the skewed bar from snapping if she flung herself about in the night. In the morning, she thought vaguely, she must try to find something she could twist about the bar to protect it, but not tonight, she could not do any more tonight. She turned her head over on the pillow with a sigh and was almost instantly asleep. She was so weary that she did not even hear another snuffling grunt and then a slow, heavy flop as another body turned over again in the darkness, not very far away.

IX ๛

The People of the Hill

Kate was awakened by a light shining in her eyes. It was so sharp after the long darkness that for an instant all she could see was a wheeling dazzle of fire. Then, as her sight cleared, she became aware that another girl was standing beside her bed with a branch of lighted candles in her hand.

"Is it morning?" asked Kate drowsily.

The girl stood looking down at her gravely. She was dressed in green like the Lady, and carried herself with the same air of remote, delicate grace.

"We do not go by mornings or evenings here," she said.

Kate blinked and sat up, the room taking shape around her. The candles did not do much to illuminate it even now; but they gave enough light to show that the place had once been a natural cave of some kind, all brownish-gray rock. The floor and the walls had been squared off and hewn smooth; but above the walls the rock was wholly untouched and the low roof hung in great laps and folds and waves and pendulous bulges of stone. It was not high enough to suggest the carved arches of a hall or cathedral; rather, it appeared as if the stone were sagging under the pressure of some enormous weight that might bring it down at any moment. Kate took one look at it and then fixed her eyes on the girl's face again.

"My name is Katherine," she said. "Katherine Sutton."

"Oh?" said the girl, without any particular interest. She stepped back a pace and lifted her branch of candles so that Kate could see beyond her down the length of the cave. "Those are Joan and Betty and Marian," she said.

Set at intervals along the wall were three more couches like Kate's own, each with its carved chest at the head of its coverlet of velvet, brownish-gray velvet, the same color as the rock. Out from under the coverlets shadowy figures were crawling. In the uncertain light she could just make out one of them rummaging vaguely for the lid of her chest, another stooping to shake down her long fair hair. First one and then another began to utter sleepy grunts of complaint as the chill of the air struck them, murmurs and squeals that even now sounded extraordinarily like the snorting of animals. Kate drew back. "Who are they?" she asked sharply.

"The mortal women that we keep in the Hill," said the girl. "Did not the Lady tell you?"

"Yes, but —" Kate hesitated. "Do they always make noises like that?"

"No," said the girl. "They will be peaceful and content as soon as they have seen the Lady and are fed and warm again." She set her branch of candles on a ledge in the wall and stooped to pick up Kate's dress, fingering it with a dissatisfied shake of her head. "You cannot wear that here," she said. "This place is too cold for your kind. Put it away. I will give you another." And opening the chest, she drew out a dark folded garment and laid it at the foot of the couch.

"You will find the belt and your other gear in the chest also," she said. "Dress yourself now, and be ready to come when I call you. What did you say your name was?"

"Katherine," Kate repeated. "What is yours?"

"Mine?" The girl straightened up, her brows lifting very

slightly. For some reason, she seemed to be surprised and even offended by the question.

Kate flushed, and straightened up in her turn. She had told the girl her own name; it was only right that there should be a proper return of the courtesy. "Yes," she said. "Your name."

"We do not tell our names to your kind."

"But what am I to call you, then?"

"You may call me Gwenhyfara, if you choose," said the girl. "That name will do as well as any." She walked away to the arched entrance of the cave and stood there, waiting. "Dress yourself," she said over her shoulder.

The dress she had left at the foot of the couch was a long straight robe with wide sleeves. The fair-haired woman by the next bed was huddling into one too, and so was the fat dark woman just beyond her. The robe was made of what appeared to be cured deerskin or some other kind of animal hide, but it was sumptuously lined with fur like the coverlets, and the broad leather belt which went with it was clasped and studded with gold.

There was nothing else in the chest except a pile of clean linen towels and a bag of oddments: hair-ribbons, tooth-cloths, sponges, a ball of fine Spanish soap, and a comb. The back of the cave, beyond the last bed, had been fitted up as a sort of washing place, and the other women were clustering about it. A jet of water, like a fountain spray, spurted from a crack in the wall, fell into a stone basin, and then poured down into a deep drain that ran across the floor under a stone close-stool, to carry the waste away. It was all very clean — as clean as Kate's own garderobe at Elvenwood Hall — but there was no more privacy or dignity than there would have been in a stable. Apart from the fact that the mortal women appeared to be still capable of washing and grooming themselves, it seemed to Kate

— jostled about as she waited for her turn at the drain and the water — that "stable" was exactly the right word for the place.

When they had all dressed, braiding their hair in plaits down their backs and pulling one towel through their belts at the waist, Gwenhyfara rounded them up and led them single file through the archway out into a passage. She went first to light the path, Kate after her, and the others trotting behind them like a string of packponies. The passage was the same one down which the Lady had brought Kate the night before — she recognized the smooth feel of the stones underfoot — but in a few moments they turned off it and began to make their way along another passage, much rougher and with an occasional step here and there, always a step up. Presently they went by two doors on the right, both closed; and then a narrow dark opening to the left, apparently the entrance to still another passage. Just beyond it, on the same side, was a third door, through which came light and the sound of voices; and beyond that, at the end, closing the passage, one last door, so low that Kate had to stoop her head as she went through it.

When she lifted her eyes again, her first confused impression was only of height and space; then Gwenhyfara took nine steps forward — slow, ceremonial steps — drew herself erect, and stood still.

They had come out into a cavern, a huge shadowy place like a great hall. At the far end, set on a dais three steps above the level of the floor, was a stone chair with a high, leaf-shaped back. The Lady was sitting in this chair, so quiet that she looked as though she also were made of stone, a gold cup in her hand and clusters of candles burning on the wall behind her. The wall appeared to be one sheet of ore, threaded with crystal or spar that shone in the light, points of green and blue fire darting and flickering over the rock like the play of colors in an opal.

The rest of the cavern was nearly dark and almost entirely bare. Kate could just make out another door in the back wall to her left, matching the door on her right through which they had entered; but apart from that there was nothing to be seen except a sort of ledge like a bench running all the way around the cavern from one end of the dais to the other — and even this might easily have been nothing but the natural formation of the rock.

Then, suddenly, she was pushed aside and the place was full of sound and movement. The mortal women had broken out of line and all three of them were running towards the Lady in an excited pack, with whimpering cries of supplication and joy. She uttered a sharp command and they fell away, two crouching on the steps of the dais while the third crept up and knelt beside the stone chair.

The Lady held her gold cup to the lips of the kneeling woman for a moment, and then, looking into her eyes, began to speak, though Kate was too far away to hear what she said. Presently the woman rose and came back down the hall, gracefully now, with a curiously light, feathery step that made her seem almost to be floating. She went by Kate, smiling at her blissfully as she passed, and sank down in back of her on the bench-ledge against the wall. One by one, the second woman and the third were in their turn called to the dais, given the cup to sip, and sent drifting across the cavern to join the others.

When she had done with all three, the Lady bent forward in her chair and sat for a long moment gazing down the length of the hall in silence. Kate drew a little further back into the shadows behind Gwenhyfara. At that distance, she could not see the Lady's face very clearly, but she had an uneasy feeling that the Lady could see hers and was deliberating over what she saw. Then the gaze was withdrawn. The Lady nodded;

Gwenhyfara ran to the dais, took the cup from her hand, and bore it ceremonially off through the door in the wall to Kate's left.

As she disappeared, there was a murmur of steps and voices; and a line of slender, green-clad figures carrying lights began to file into the cavern from the other door to her right. Kate, still standing where Gwenhyfara had left her, was directly in their way; she had only just time to get to a place on the back bench-ledge alongside Joan and Betty and Marian before they came sweeping past.

Thirteen women, in long green gowns and cloaks like the Lady and Gwenhyfara. And after them, thirteen men in short green tunics, with bare feet and garlands of oak leaves on their heads. Kate, who was not really warm even under the thick fur-lined robe, shivered as she looked at them, wondering how they could endure the cold. The gray creature she had seen at the mouth of the Holy Well was not among them, and neither was Christopher Heron. Both men and women had dark hair and very pale, exquisitely cut faces: severe, remote, and as quiet as stone.

They circled around the cavern one by one in a beautiful curving line — all their movements were beautiful — and finally came to rest ranged in two exactly spaced rows down the walls along the whole length of the room. When the last to enter had taken his place, they turned before they seated themselves and all together lifted their candles to look first at the single motionless figure erect in the stone chair at the head of the hall, and then down at the huddle of mortal women slumped on the bench-ledge at the foot.

Joan and Betty and Marian did not appear to know that anything was happening. They went on sitting in the sudden glare as if lost in some happy dream, each staring straight ahead of her, and each of them smiling, three identical smiles.

Then the lights were lowered; the People of the Hill swung about and sat down in two long lines facing one another. At the same moment, Gwenhyfara returned through the left-hand door, this time together with a young man of her own age, she carrying a small wooden spoon and a round wooden bowl full of something hot that steamed and smoked on the cold air, he an ox's horn hollowed and polished into a kind of primitive cup. They paused side by side as they entered, so close to Kate that she could see the horn contained only clear water, and the bowl only a handful of boiled grain, like a frumenty, sodden with milk and a little honey. These they bore up the cavern and offered to the Lady; and behind them followed a second couple, much younger, and finally four children, two boys and two girls, all similarly laden. They went to and fro, up the hall and down again, out the left-hand door and in again, between the lines of seated figures, serving them in order, a horn and a bowl to each.

Nobody spoke. The seated figures were too far apart to talk to one another, spaced out very widely along the walls, as if to fill room that had once been taken up by a much larger assembly. The young people waited on them in grave silence, coming and going with ceremonial dignity, even the children, though the two youngest were hardly more than babies and, in Kate's opinion, should not have been out of their beds at that hour of the night. — Or was it night? The word had slipped almost unconsciously off the tip of her mind because the shadows and the candles made the place look so much like a lighted hall at evening; but how did she know? The place would look the same no matter when she saw it. For all she could tell, it might really be noon, or only a few hours after sunrise. She did not know how long she had slept, except that it must have been a

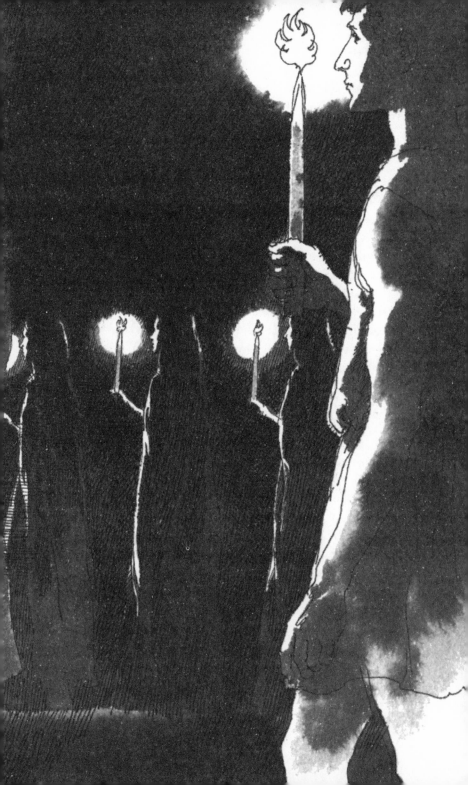

considerable time. She was no longer exhausted. She was also beginning to feel ravenously hungry.

Her eyes went to the last of the wooden bowls as they were carried past her, wondering whether she and the other mortal women would be allowed a share after the People of the Hill had done with it. Boiled grain with a spoonful of milk and honey on it was not her notion of what to eat for dinner; still, even boiled grain would be better than nothing at all.

When all the men and women had been served, the two youths and the two maidens gathered in the center of the floor, facing the Lady. One of the youths took out a reed pipe like a shepherd's flute and started to play, a thin, crystal air that seemed to come from a long way off. The four children went back through the left-hand door and returned carrying four more bowls which they set down on the floor in front of Joan and Betty and Marian and Kate. These bowls were about the same size as the wooden ones, but were made of beaten gold, very heavy, and had silver spoons and handles shaped like animal heads: geese and asses and swine. They were heaped almost to overflowing with fragments of some rich dark meat in a sauce that smelt delectably of wine and sweet herbs.

Joan and Betty and Marian roused up at the sight of the food. They flung themselves on the bowls with little cries of delight, tossing away the spoons, snatching, gobbling, slavering as they tore at the meat with their fingers and stuffed great chunks of it into their mouths. The four children stood looking at them. They did not point or whisper or nudge one another, only stood there looking, gravely and dispassionately, as though at some page in a book that they had been told to learn by heart.

Kate felt she could have borne it better if she had only been able to think that they were deliberately trying to insult her; but clearly they were not. She glanced away from the mortal women to the line of austere, delicate figures seated on either side of the cavern, and a furious wave of color began to flood over her face. Then she picked up her silver spoon and began to eat: slowly and with attention to her manners. There was no sense letting good food go to waste; that was what her father had always said to her.

The music ended; the horns and dishes were ceremonially carried away. The People of the Hill rose and stood in silence while the Lady went out of the hall, the two youths carrying branches of candles before her. The men remained motionless, standing erect, but as she passed the women sank down to the floor, one hand lifted and the other laid across their breasts, in a sweeping, magnificent bow. They held it flawlessly until she had disappeared through the doorway; then they rose again as lightly as leaves in the wind and followed her out. The men went next, and last of all the children. Only Gwenhyfara and the second girl were left in the cavern with Kate and Joan and Betty and Marian.

The second girl rounded up the three women and took them off by the door to the right. Gwenhyfara beckoned to Kate and led the way back through the one on the left, into the room beyond.

This was a large chamber in the form of an L, with the door at the end of the long stroke and another door at the end of the short one. It was evidently the place where the food had been dished and prepared, though anything less like the kitchens or buttery in her father's house Kate could hardly imagine. There was no fireplace, no proper salting trough or log box or chopping block, no pots or cleavers or spits hung up on hooks, no baskets for vegetables or poultry, no hams or strings of onions dangling from rafters, no stir or bustle or smoke or confusion, no pages or kittens running about underfoot. Here everything was fastidiously ordered and very bare. In the longer arm of the room were two charcoal braziers that held burnished copper pots; and opposite them, a fountain of hot bluish water gushing from the wall into a wide carved basin of stone. In the shorter arm of the room, the used horns and bowls had been set in careful rows down a stone table, the four golden ones at the far end, some distance from the rest. Underneath the table was a rack carrying a line of swabs and copper basins.

Gwenhyfara told Kate to stand still by the door at the foot of the table, and then went out of the room, only to return almost at once carrying a last food bowl made of bronze, which she put down between the lowest of the wood and the highest of the gold. Then, under her direction, Kate brought water from the fountain in one of the copper basins and washed all the cups and dishes clean, drying them with the towel at her belt and laying them out again along the table in readiness for the next meal. The bronze bowl still held a few flakes of the sodden grain that the Fairy Folk ate; and Kate rinsed the stuff out hurriedly, thinking of the gray creature she had seen at the mouth of the Well cave. Apparently it took its food alone by itself, for which she was thankful: not even in the solemn assemblies of that underworld would it have seemed right for anyone to sit down and eat in its company.

By the time she had finished her work, the second girl was back with Joan and Betty and Marian. They too were supplied with swabs and basins of water; and then all of them went into the great cavern, where Gwenhyfara and the second girl stood ceremonially at the doors holding lights while the others washed down the candle stains from the walls, and after that scrubbed the bench-ledges, the steps of the dais, and finally every inch of the floor.

It was long and tedious work, all reaching, stooping, kneeling, dragging the swabs over interminable stretches of stone, breathing the damp chill of the wet rock, running back to rinse out and refill the basins the instant the water grew cold or dirty — why in the name of heaven, Kate reflected bitterly, could they not at least supply the servants and scrubbers with proper brushes and pails and mops! But Joan and Betty and Marian did not seem to care. They were now in the highest spirits, fairly crowing and giggling with happiness, dabbling their fingers through the water as if it were perfume, and sloshing away at the floor with great exhilarated sweeps of their arms. From time to time they would raise their heads one after another and gaze blissfully about them, though as far as Kate could tell, there was very little to see. The clusters of candles were still burning on the dais wall behind the stone chair; but without the Lady, even the dais appeared bleak and empty. She edged closer to the fair-haired woman and said in a whisper: "What are you looking at?"

The woman stared at her and then broke into a peal of joyful laughter.

"Isn't it wonderful?" she answered, pointing towards the echoing darkness over her head. "O wonderful, wonderful, wonderful, wonderful, wonderful!"

"What's so wonderful?" asked Kate.

"Be silent," said Gwenhyfara.

They scrubbed down the rest of the floor in silence, and afterwards the floor and walls of the food place (for kitchen Kate could not bring herself to call it); and when that was done, Gwenhyfara bowed gravely to the second girl and led her four charges out through the door at the short end of the room. This brought them back into the passage down which they had come earlier; Kate recognized the dark narrow opening in the wall to her right, and the two closed doors where the steps began further on.

The three women were more subdued now, and seemed to be growing drowsy. There were yawns and stumbles behind her all the way along the passage; and by the time they reached the stable, it was as much as they could do to huddle out of their clothes and collapse wallowing into the down and velvet of the beds. The wallowing passed into heaves and gurgles, and the gurgles into loud contented snores. Gwenhyfara lifted her branch of candles and turned to go.

"Why are you standing there?" she asked.

"Can I come with you?" Kate inquired hopefully. She did not want to be left shut up in the dark listening to Joan and Betty and Marian.

"No," said Gwenhyfara. "Take off your dress and lie down."

"When do we get up?" asked Kate, unclasping the gold-studded belt reluctantly.

"When I call you."

"When will that be?"

"When we have need of you."

Kate folded the skin robe away and lay down, wishing that she did not feel so much like a horse being backed into a stall until it was time for her to be harnessed and fed and watered and worked again. "Can I have one of your candles to keep by me?" she asked, adding hastily, "Just for the light."

"No," said Gwenhyfara. "Light is precious here, and we do not use it except when we must have it for our work or to find our way by the signs through the secret passages, or to honor the Lady and the gods. Also, the weight may be coming upon you, and that is a thing which it is easier to bear in the dark."

"What do you mean?" Kate asked, caught by the word

"signs." It had sounded as if the passages must be marked somehow so that anyone who had the secret could move freely about in the Hill — but if that was true, Gwenhyfara would certainly not tell her the secret for the asking, and it might be better to keep her from knowing that Kate even thought there was a secret at all. She changed the question hurriedly to: "What do you mean by the weight?"

"That is our name for it," said Gwenhyfara. "I do not know if it has a name in your world."

"But what is it?" Kate insisted. "Where does it come from?"

"There," said Gwenhyfara, and lifted her candle to let the light pour along the mass of rock over their heads. Then she turned without another word and went out through the archway, the darkness closing in behind her as she disappeared down the passage.

Kate, for the first time, was almost glad of the darkness. When she had asked Gwenhyfara to let her have one of the candles, she had not been looking up at the rock. Even now, she could not get that last glimpse of it out of her mind, the great mass hanging in huge pendulous folds which had appeared more than ever to be sagging and bulging as if under the pressure of some enormous weight.

She told herself not to be a fool, and fumbled under the lid of her bed-chest for a loose ribbon from her own old gown. Then she drew the redheaded woman's cross from its hiding place, and, settling back doggedly against her pillows, began to twist the ribbon around it. That would serve both to protect the weakened crossbar and keep Gwenhyfara from finding out that Kate had a bit of the cold iron about her. A bit of the cold iron —! She thought of the redheaded woman's eager, anxious voice saying, "I'd feel easier to know you had a bit of the cold iron about you," and hunched one shoulder ruefully in the dark. It would need more than a bit of the cold iron to get her safely away from the Fairy Folk, but the little gift was at least a friendly thing to have in her hand as she lay there under the weight of the rock, the great mass hanging in —

She told herself again, furiously this time, not to be a fool.

The huge pendulous folds were nothing but flow-patterns left by the water that had cut the cave out of the rock, centuries ago. She knew that.

The dead weight of the earth and the stone lying above was not forcing them down. She knew that too. If she would only think clearly of the place as it really was —

And then suddenly all that she knew of the place as it really was came rushing over her. The earth and the stone; the blind passages worming their way under the ground; the slippery paths with the slime underfoot; the cold air and the darkness; and always, everywhere, pressing about pit and cavern and passage, the incalculable weight of the rock. Her breath was coming quickly now, in light shallow gasps, as if she had no room to draw it. The fear that the cave roof was bulging and collapsing had been a fear of appearances, something she could argue away. The agonised horror she felt now was of the reality of the Hill itself — the tons and tons of actual earth and stone lying above her, closing down on her, shutting her in. It was like some suffocating dream of being buried alive; or rather it was like the moment of awakening from that dream to find that it was true.

At last, very slowly, the horror receded; the sense of the weight lifted; and she sat up dizzily, pushing back the wet hair matted against her forehead. Joan and Betty and Marian were still grunting and flopping in the darkness, but the redheaded woman's cross had slipped from her hand and was gone. She groped about for it uncertainly — her fingers seemed to have no strength in them — and somehow or other found it on the floor and pulled the chain over her head. She was too spent even to think why she wanted it: she only felt empty and worn out, as if from a long fit of vomiting. Her last hazy recollection was simply of shutting her eyes and drifting off into an exhausted sleep.

When she awoke, Gwenhyfara was bending over her again with the branch of candles in her hand.

"Did you feel it?" she inquired composedly.

Kate nodded. "Yes," she said: and then: "Do you ever feel it too?" she asked. "The weight?"

"It comes from knowing the nature of this land," said Gwenhyfara. "How should we not feel it? But our kind can endure that knowledge without easing. Your kind are too weak. Even for us it is not a light matter. Be wise, and do not seek for your own sorrow. Entreat the Lady, and she will take it from you."

Kate thought of herself kneeling on the floor of the great cavern and grinning blissfully up at the rock over her head, the wonderful, wonderful, wonderful, wonderful, wonderful rock.

"No need," she said. "It has passed by."

"It will return," said Gwenhyfara.

"When?"

"At its own time," said Gwenhyfara. "Get up and dress yourself now. We must go."

"Go to do what?"

"What you have done already."

This proved to be literally true. The new day — Kate could not stop herself from thinking of it as the "day" — was exactly like the one before it. She followed Gwenhyfara down the same passage to the great cavern, stood in the same place while the Lady dealt with Joan and Betty and Marian, watched the same line of figures enter the door, ate from the same golden bowl, cleaned the same dishes afterwards, scrubbed down the same interminable stretches of stone, and was finally led back to lie in the same stable with the same company under the same overhanging rock, only to get up when Gwenhyfara called her and go through the same business the next "day," and the next "day," and the next "day," and the next. At first she tried to keep a count of them, but after a while she gave up trying. What was the use? Even supposing that the "days" and the "nights" never varied in length (which was by no means certain), it would still be impossible to say how much earthly time had gone by without some way of telling the exact number of "days" and "nights" it took to make up twenty-four hours according to the heavens. Down in the enclosed world of the Fairy Folk, life was only a timeless, endless, monotonous round that was broken by nothing but the attacks of the weight.

These alone were completely unpredictable. They never came except during the "nights" — the time she spent lying in the stable under the rock — but apart from that she never knew when they would strike her. Sometimes for whole "nights" running she would be free of them; on others, the horror would suddenly descend without warning and batter her to pieces. It was as if her misery and revulsion against the land piled up in some inaccessible region of her mind until the accumulated pressure became too great for it to bear any longer; but she never learned just when the attacks would break out nor how long they would last when they did. The discovery that her mind was not wholly under her own control frightened her more than anything else, but it also made her cling with furious stubbornness to the one moment of independent choice that was left her: the moment when she stood behind Gwenhyfara in the cavern every "morning" without following Joan and Betty and Marian up to the Lady's chair. Whether the Fairy Folk were similarly tormented she could not tell. Gwenhyfara had not spoken of the matter again, and Kate knew better than to ask her. Gwenhyfara did not waste words on the mortal women. She would answer questions, but always briefly, and only when she thought that it was necessary. She would say very little about the Fairy Folk, and nothing at all about Christopher Heron.

Christopher had to be somewhere in the Hill — that much Kate was sure of — but she could not find out where he was kept or what was being done with him. He was never at the gatherings in the great cavern, and she was never close enough to the Fairy Folk to hear any talk concerning him. The Lady she saw only at a distance, from the far end of the hall; and the Lady in her turn did no more than glance at her every "day" after she had finished with Joan and Betty and Marian. The four children who brought the mortal prisoners their food only stood and watched her as they did the others; and the rest of the Fairy Folk ignored her completely. Joan and Betty and Marian could give her no help. During the "days" they were always deep in enchantment, and they spent the "nights" sleeping so heavily that she could not rouse them.

It was sometimes possible to get a few coherent words out of them at their first waking, before Gwenhyfara came in; but then they were invariably dazed and stupid, and for the most part would only whimper and complain of the cold. With Betty and Marian she could make no headway of any kind. Joan — the fair-haired woman — was quicker and more talkative, but very vague. She once spoke of a house where she had had a fire on the hearth and a baby in a cradle, but not as though they were real things she had lost, only fleetingly, almost indifferently, like someone remembering a pleasant dream. It was the same with the life that she lived in the Hill. She did not know exactly where she went every day after she left the great cavern; it was all lovely white linen towels that she washed and hung up to dry, lovely white linen towels, lovely. She could not say if she had seen a tall young man with yellow hair who did not look like one of the Fairy Folk. She might have. Or then again, she might not. There was so much to see, and all of it wonderful.

"Yes, but what do you see?" Kate insisted desperately one "morning." Compared to Joan, even Randal, with his shattered wits, had begun to seem to her like a miracle of wisdom and understanding. "Do you ever see anyone go by you carrying a bowl of food? A gold bowl with meat in it, like ours? He must eat somehow. They can't be letting him starve."

"Oh yes," said Joan. "They carry the gold bowls out of the room with the beautiful warm blue water, and then they carry them back again. I have a gold bowl, and you have a gold bowl, and Betty has a —"

"No, no, not those," Kate interrupted her. She knew all the bowls that were carried into that room: the four for the mortal women, the twenty-seven for the Lady and the Fairy Folk, and the one bronze bowl for the creature in the Well.

"Gold for the maids, and wood for the masters," said Joan dreamily, "and one bronze bowl for the King of the land, at his death-time."

"Who told you that?"

"I don't know," said Joan, yawning. "But isn't it a beautiful saying? Beautiful, beautiful, beauti —"

"There's no King of the land now," said Kate. "That bowl is for someone else."

"Then isn't the saying true?"

"It can't be."

Nevertheless, when she did the washing that "day," she rinsed out the bronze bowl slowly, turning it in her hands and looking at it carefully for the first time. It had certainly been used to hold the boiled grain and milk and honey that was reserved for the People of the Hill. Neither was it made of gold, like the mortal prisoners' dishes; nor was it ornamented with animal heads, but only with an intricate embossed design of bird shapes falling and rising in and out of a circle of flames.

"It can't be," she repeated to herself. "It can't —"

Then suddenly the answer came to her. Joan had been right. Contempt for ordinary human comfort and delight was drilled into the People of the Hill from the time they were children, old enough to stand in the great cavern and watch the mortal women making pigs of themselves out of riches and art. All their kind, even the Lady, ate from plain wood. No member of that community, however strange, could possible count it a privilege to have his food served to him in a splendidly ornamented bowl of metal, any more than if it had been a swill pail or a chamber pot. A bowl like that would be given only to a mortal prisoner.

A mortal prisoner — Kate set the bronze bowl in its place on the table and went to fill her basin at the fountain — but not a common mortal prisoner, one of the servants and scrubbers? This one was fed on what the Fairy Folk surely regarded as worthier food; and the bowl was finer too, less precious and not so heavily or scornfully decorated. Gwenhyfara always went to fetch it herself, as she did the Lady's own dish, and put it down carefully separate from the others: below the wooden ones, to be sure, but well above all four of the gold. Evidently, then, the mortal prisoner was someone of dignity, set apart from the rest, almost as if — in Joan's words — he were the King of the land at his death-time. She could think of only one mortal prisoner that the People of the Hill might treat like that, only one. And that one could not be very far away. It never took Gwenhyfara more than a few moments to go and bring back the bowl through the door at the short end of the food place.

The trouble was that once she was out of the room, there was no telling in what direction she went — left to the great cavern, or right to the dark narrow opening in the wall and the two closed doors further down the passage.

Kate did not dare to follow her when she went out the next morning. The most she could do was fall back on the trick of counting to see exactly how long she was away. It was no longer than it took Kate to reach thirty: say, roughly, fifteen counts to get to her destination and fifteen to come back again.

Later, when the day's work was over and the scrubbers were returning to their stable, Kate made another count, this time in the passage.

That settled it. The nearest of the two closed doors was forty-one counts down the passage from the food place, even without doubling the number to allow for the return. Fifteen would carry Gwenhyfara only as far as the dark narrow opening in one direction, or else the great cavern in the other. And she could not have gone to the cavern, not possibly. Kate herself would have seen anybody who was kept there. It was the dark narrow opening, then. There was nothing else left for it to be.

Fortunately, Gwenhyfara never lingered in the stable after she had seen Joan and Betty and Marian and Kate safe in their velvet stalls. Kate watched the flaming points of her candle-branch dwindle to sparks and vanish as they moved off down the passage; then, with a sigh of relief, she slipped back into her fur-lined robe and crept from the room, feeling her way along the wall in the darkness.

She was by now so familiar with the path to the cavern that she was not afraid of getting lost; the chief danger was that she might encounter one of the Fairy Folk or be taken by a sudden attack of the weight. But for once the luck seemed to be with her. The weight held off and nobody appeared to question or send her back, not even when she stumbled over a step that she could not see and loosed a shower of echoes from the hollow rock all around her. She crept by the two closed doors and then moved across to the opposite wall, groping for the narrow opening on the left.

The narrow opening was, as she had thought, the entrance to another passage. After three or four steps, it turned sharply to the left again; and she was just feeling her way cautiously around the corner when she heard a sound that brought her up short, frozen to the wall. Somewhere in the darkness ahead of her a voice was speaking.

The voice was very low, and so stumbling and broken that it was unrecognizable. It was an instant before she even caught the words and realized that it was not speaking to her.

"Help me," it said in an agonized whisper. "Help me. O my dear Lord Christ, make me able to bear it."

Then it died away, and there was a complete silence.

Kate flattened herself against the rock, hardly daring to breathe. She felt as if she had broken unforgivably into somebody's private room and did not know how to get out again. Her first thought was simply to keep him from finding out that she was there at all. She did not want him even to wonder if by some chance she might have overheard him.

It was not until the silence had gone on for a long while that she finally took a step forward, bringing her foot down hard and dragging the hem of her robe rustlingly along the wall to warn him.

Christopher said, steadily now but more grimly than she had ever heard him speak:

"Have you come back again? This isn't your time."

"Christopher?" said Kate, wondering who he thought she was. "It's Kate, Christopher. Where are you?"

"Kate?"

"Kate Sutton."

There was a cry from the darkness.

"No!" said Christopher — and then, like a man driven beyond all endurance: "Oh, good Lord! What are *you* doing here?"

X ॐ
"Neither Sun nor Moon"

Kate stood still. She had sometimes, lying in her bed or washing down the floor of the cavern, comforted herself with the thought of this meeting; but on those occasions, the first words Christopher spoke had always been entirely different. "Master John caught me at the Holy Well, and the Lady brought me here to be one of the scrubbers," she informed him, in her stiffest manner. "I couldn't find out where they were keeping you until now. And I do think," she added, "that you might at the least say you were happy to see me."

"Happy!" retorted Christopher. "What would you do if you met your best friend in hell? Say you were happy to know he was there too, and isn't the pitch hot? Stop nattering and come here to me. I can't get any nearer to you because of the mesh."

"What mesh?" Kate demanded, groping her way forward. The next instant she was brought to a halt as if by a solid wall.

A row of thick wooden stakes had been set across the whole width of the passage, blocking it from floor to roof. The stakes were sunk in the rock, and the spaces between them were filled with a closely woven net of tough bark strips or withy, interlaced like basket work. Kate ran a dismayed hand along the intricate knots that lashed the mesh to the bars. "Isn't there any way through?" she asked.

"There must be a door in it somewhere, but I've never found

it," said Christopher. "And a sort of little window to the left where they give me my food. I don't know if you can open it."

Kate tried, but there seemed to be no bolt or latch or handle anywhere and the window had been so cunningly fitted that she could not even feel the joins in the stakes and the basket work.

"One of their tricks," said Christopher briefly. "No matter. We can talk well enough as it is. Stay low to the floor and keep your voice down."

"Are they likely to hear us?"

"Not very likely. There's never anyone moving about this hour of the night — by 'night' meaning the time when they're quiet and I don't see lights going back and forth in the outer passage so I call it 'night' in a manner of speaking, but heaven alone can tell what it really is. This place is worse than the one in the ballad, where they had neither sun nor moon and had to go by the roaring of the sea."

"I know," said Kate, settling herself on the stone of the floor as close to the mesh as she could. She heard Christopher move in the darkness on the other side, and then felt the mesh stir a little at her shoulder as if he had leaned his own shoulder against it.

"Where are you?" he whispered.

"Here," said Kate.

"Good. Now! Tell me. What's been happening? Where's Cecily? Have you seen her? Did they send her to Geoffrey?"

"No, but she's safe at the Hall. They're planning to give her to Sir Geoffrey with some tale or other when he comes back after All Saints' Day. But never mind that. I'll tell you later, after we're out of here. This door in the mesh, Christopher. Couldn't you break it down if you tried?"

"Now who's talking as though I were King Arthur in a romance?"

"But couldn't you?" Kate insisted, remembering the grip of the hands that had dragged her away from the Holy Well. "This thing is only made of wood, not iron or steel; and as soon as I find out how the passages are marked so that we won't get lost, couldn't you —"

"No," said Christopher flatly. "Stop it, Kate. They'd only take Cecily again if I did."

"They won't be able to, once Sir Geoffrey comes back."

"Everything will be over and done with long before Geoffrey comes back."

"No, it won't. Christopher, listen. You don't understand. There's something else. I saw Randal."

She heard him catch his breath.

"Ah!" he said very softly; and then: "Did you? How? I thought you said Master John and the Lady had you."

Kate told him about the window in Master John's evidence room.

"— and I'm still not certain that Randal knows just what I meant by All Hallows' Eve," she ended apologetically. "But it can't have done any harm. Sir Geoffrey's sure to come as soon as he has the letter. I thought it was safer to gamble on it than to argue with him."

"Don't fash yourself over that," said Christopher. "What else can you call this whole business but a gamble from start to finish? I seem to have been playing pretty freely with *your* money too, haven't I? O Lord, I wish I'd never dragged you into this coil, Kate! I'm sorry."

"Why should you be? You tried hard enough to keep me out of it," said Kate tartly. "You and your conscience! One of these days you're going to start trying to carry the whole world on your own back, and then God won't have any more work to do."

"One of these days your husband is going to beat you," said Christopher between his teeth. "And if I could only get out of this foul hole, how gladly I would save that poor unfortunate man the trouble!"

"Is it really a foul hole?" asked Kate anxiously.

"No, except in a manner of speaking. There's a bed and another little room at the back for washing and a rush mat on the floor that I'm sitting on now, and once a day — if 'day' you can call it — a pretty girl brings me my porridge and leaves a light out there in the passage for as long as it takes me to eat and clean myself up."

"Gwenhyfara," said Kate.

"Is that her name? I didn't know. She's never said a word to me because I'm dead."

"What?"

"Dead."

"Oh, don't be so silly, Christopher! You're not dead."

"Thank you: I was beginning to wonder myself. I only wish the People of the Hill agreed with you."

"What *do* you mean?"

"Didn't the Lady tell you? In the old days, once they chose a man to pay the teind, they shut him in here for the last nine weeks before All Hallows' Eve to be trained and prepared, so that when the time came he would go freely — even willingly — without trying to hold any part of himself back. The 'death service' was what they called it long ago, when the King of the land did it. To their way of thinking, he *was* dead from the moment he entered this place, or at least couldn't be treated as if he were even in the world any longer. Everyone was strictly forbidden to touch him, and nobody was allowed to speak to him except the Guardian of the Well."

"Is that another name for the Lady?"

"No. The Guardian is the one you saw at the Well that night, the one who took me. When I came to my senses, I was lying on my bed in this place, and he was over somewhere beyond the mesh — like you, only on the other side of the passage — and whispering to me in the dark. He was telling me about the old days, and what it was that had to be done to a teind-payer while he was practising death. He comes back on some of the nights, as soon as that girl takes the light away, and sits over there in the dark again."

"But what for? What is it that he does to you?"

"Nothing much." She knew from the tone of his voice that he was not going to tell her anything else. "What it is that has to be done to a teind-payer. But that's why they've never liked to use a child to pay the teind — no child can go through with a nine weeks' death service, and so the power gets lost or wasted. The Fairy Folk think —"

"I don't care what the Fairy Folk think!" Kate broke in on him indignantly. "*I* think it's abominable! Just as if you were a goose in a cage being fattened for a dinner!"

Christopher gave a sudden gasp and then burst out into helpless laughter. He laughed and laughed, and went on laughing wildly.

"It *is* like that, isn't it?" he choked. "I never thought of it before."

"I wasn't trying to jeer at you," Kate protested, horrified at what she had done.

"I know you weren't, sweetheart," said Christopher. "But when it comes to the day of judgment, I only hope I can get somewhere near you in the crowd."

"Why?"

"I want to know how you'll describe the proceedings."

"That isn't the point." Kate was in no mood to laugh, and she did not see that there was anything to laugh at. "They *are* using you abominably."

"They don't see it as the goose would." Christopher was still laughing. "Didn't I tell you they were using me like a King of the land in the old days? Though why anyone should have *wanted* to be a King of the land in the old days I cannot conceive."

"Christopher."

"Yes?"

"Will you tell me one thing? I wouldn't ask you, only — I — it's worse in a way. Not knowing."

There was a moment's pause. Then Christopher said:

"What is it?"

"Did they say how they were going to do it — on All Hallows' Eve?"

"Up at the Standing Stone. You remember, that big rock on the path to the Holy Well? That's where it was always done in the old days. They use the ashes afterwards for spells and charms. It's one of their four great yearly festivals. The other three —"

"Ashes?" Kate interrupted him sharply. "What ashes?"

"From the burning."

"What burning?"

"When I was a boy at home in Norfolk," said Christopher, "we young folk always lit a great fire in the fields on All Hallows' Eve, and then threw in a figure of a man made of the last harvest's straw. The chaplain didn't like us to do it, but it was a very old custom and he was never able to stop us. We called it 'burning the payer.' None of us thought that in the old days the man might not have been made out of straw."

There was another long pause, and then Kate said, with her voice sticking in her throat: "Not — not — made out of —"

"Randal must be well on his way to Geoffrey by this time," said Christopher. "Keep that clearly in your mind, will you? And as for the burning: well, it seems to have been the customary manner of offering a sacrifice to the gods among the heathen British that the Romans found here when they first came to England. I remember reading about it at school. It's in Caesar somewhere."

"But that —" said Kate numbly, "that was almost sixteen hundred years ago."

"What's sixteen hundred years to them? There must be ice lying in some northern caves that's older yet — and why should it ever melt as long as it keeps to a cold hidden place where the sun can't reach it? They don't have to go by our time here, Kate. They can go by a time of their own, as the ice does."

From somewhere in the distance there came a sharp silvery sound, like a bell striking once. It was followed, almost instantly, by a dull rumbling roar that rushed along the outer passage and then died away. Kate rose to her knees, startled. "What's that?" she asked.

"I don't know," said Christopher. "If we were at home in Norfolk, I'd say someone was sending water over a spillway to ease the pressure on a dam, but down here God alone knows what it may be. The Guardian won't tell me. It does sound like the roaring of the sea, doesn't it?"

"Yes," said Kate.

"I hear it every night. Afterwards, they're always quiet for a little longer, and then I begin to see the lights moving back and forth again. You'd best go now, Kate. They mustn't find you running about where you have no business to be."

Kate scrambled to her feet.

"I can come tomorrow," she said.

"What's the risk to you?"

"You're a fine one to talk of taking risks," Kate retorted. "And anyway, there's no risk. I can come easily. Every night, if you want me."

"Men dying of thirst have often been known to want a drink of water," said Christopher. "Very well, then. Get back safe to your bed, Kate, and rest well."

Kate got back safe to her bed, but she did not rest well. It was a long time before she slept at all, and when she did, the sleep was broken and restless, filled with confused dreams of bird shapes rising and falling through circles of flame. The next morning she could not seem to take her eyes away from the lighted candles ranged against the wall behind the Lady's stone chair, or the lighted candles circling around the cavern as the Fairy Folk entered it. Watching the beautiful procession sweep in and then out was ordinarily the only pleasure of her day; but on this particular day, she was unable to see anything clearly except the little points of flame streaming up from the blazing wicks to lose themselves in the shadows cast by the rock overhead.

She was standing in her usual place at the door when the Lady finally came down the hall, the two youths with their branches of candles before her, the People of the Hill forming in order behind. The points of fire lifted and wheeled like birds in flight and began, very slowly, to move forward.

Kate stood watching the long burning line come down on her, one flame after another, all burning — the word went tearing through her brain like a scream: burning, burning, burning, burning — and then suddenly the points of fire blurred and ran staggeringly together, and with a cry she lurched back against the wall in such a blind rush of suffocated horror as she had until now felt only during her worst attacks of the weight.

"Not here, you fool!" she thought frantically, as another wave of thundering darkness broke over her and went by. "Not *here!*" She would have to stay on her feet at least until the Lady had gone by; she would have to. The mist was beginning to clear from her eyes. She drew a deep shivering breath and forced herself to look up.

The Lady was standing within a yard of her, very erect and still, the two youths on either side lifting their branches of candles to let the lights fall on Kate's face.

"Why have you broken the order of my hall with this confusion?" said the Lady.

Kate did not answer. It was as much as she could do to hang where she was, limp as a scarecrow, propped against the wall.

"Can you hear what I say?"

Kate nodded.

"Then listen to me," said the Lady. "I have told you before, and I tell you now again, that it is not given to your kind to live as we do. Why should you torment yourself to no purpose? With the Young Lord I can understand it, for he is not in the common run of men, and he would have been a King of the land in the old days. But you I do not understand. He has only a short time of pain to endure, and by enduring it he will give power to many and save the child that is dear to him. But your time will not be short, and you will get nothing from it. You cannot hope to escape, for without light and the signs not even we can find our way among the passages of the Hill; and you cannot hope to be rescued, for I tell you plainly that if Geoffrey Heron or any mortal man comes into this place to take it by force, I will destroy you and every other prisoner I hold before I will give them up to him. All you can look for — the rest of your days — is to serve and to drudge, to scrub stone on your knees, to live like a beast, to toil and be weary and in the end to die. Is not that the truth of the matter?"

"It may be," said Kate.

"It is," said the Lady. "But the knowledge of truth is only a shape in the mind, and that much I can change to ease you. You have borne it already longer than I thought it was possible that you could; and there would be no shame in your asking me to take it away from you now, nothing but wisdom, to lay down a load that is too great for you to carry. And so: answer my question. Why did you do what you did?"

Kate looked from the inexorable face to the blazing lights, and back again.

"I slipped," she said. Even in her own ears this did not sound particularly convincing, but it was the best she could do. "I caught my heel and slipped and I fell against the wall."

The Lady merely lifted her hand and glanced down at the empty palm as if she were waiting for something to be put into it.

"I — I'm very clumsy," Kate stammered desperately. "You know how it is with me. You spoke of it yourself, and it's true."

The Lady closed her hand and dropped it.

"With my kind it is a matter of pride always to speak the truth," she observed calmly. "The most that can be said for your kind is that they will sometimes tell a good lie instead of a bad one. But let that pass. I will take what you have said to me. You are not in pain, you need no easing, you stumbled in your clumsiness, and you fell against the wall. Is that as you would have it?"

"Yes," said Kate thankfully.

"Very well," said the Lady. "But I think you would have been wiser if you had told me it was only the weight."

It would have been wiser: Kate knew that before the Lady had even done speaking. The Fairy Folk might have forgiven her for a fleeting attack of the weight — anybody, even the Folk themselves, could have a fleeting attack of the weight. Habitual bungling awkwardness would seem by far the greater offence to them.

"I couldn't help myself," was all she could say.

"And is that a good reason why the order of my hall should be broken by your clumsiness?"

"No," said Kate, adding despairingly: "I only meant that I would help it if I could."

"There are ways of doing that," said the Lady. "Have you ever looked well at the mortal women we keep here in the Hill?"

A quick cold stab of terror went through Kate's heart like ice, but there was nothing she could do except answer, and only one answer she could give.

"Yes," she said.

"Would they be clumsy if they were left to themselves?"

"Yes."

"But are they clumsy now?"

"No."

"Why not?"

Kate's eyes went helplessly to the Lady's right hand. It was empty but she could see the golden cup in it as clearly as if she were already crouching on the steps of the dais, waiting her turn along with Joan and Betty and Marian. "Because of what you gave them," she said.

"Then can you think of one way that I might rid you of your clumsiness, since you wish it so much?"

"Yes," said Kate. There was nothing else she could say.

"And if you were in my place," asked the Lady softly, "would you take that one way to do it?"

Kate lifted her head. She was sick of being run up and down for the Lady's entertainment like the last forlorn piece on a chessboard.

"Yes," she replied deliberately. "In your place I think it very likely that I should."

The Lady stood for a moment regarding her with a smile so faint that it could hardly even be called malicious.

"You must learn to attend more carefully to what I say to you," she observed at last. "I said: one way, not that it was the only one. Gwenhyfara!"

"Madam?"

"Take this clumsy girl somewhere out of my sight and teach her to move as our kind are taught to do."

"Gwenhyfara's going to teach me how to move," said Kate.

"Is she?" asked Christopher; and then, after a pause, "Why? What's the matter with the way you move now?"

"The Lady doesn't like it," Kate answered vaguely, thinking not of Christopher's question, but of his voice when he asked it. She had not talked with him very often, and when she did, her mind was taken up with other concerns, but surely his voice as she remembered it had never been so — so — what was the word she wanted? Lifeless? Colorless? Empty? Remote? It sounded almost frighteningly like her grandfather's during his last illness, when he was so far gone that it was only by a great effort of will that he could attend to what was said to him, or even hear what was said.

"Christopher —" she began tentatively, wondering what the gray creature had done to him while she had been away. Certainly it had done something.

"Christopher," she began again and then broke off, drawing back a little as she had drawn back the night she had come upon him praying in the darkness.

"Yes?" said Christopher. "What is it?"

"Nothing," said Kate, wishing passionately — not for the first time — that she were only somebody else. Her father, with his wisdom, would have known what to say: the right words to comfort and hearten him; or Master Roger, with his calm authority; or the Lady Elizabeth, with her royal spirit. She even had a momentary vision of Alicia, laying her velvet cheek against the mesh and crying: "O Christopher! how dreadful it must be for you! O I wish I could help you! Truly I do!" But when she thought of herself, all she could see was herself, Kate Sutton, that first day up at the Holy Well, making stupid demands, pelting him with questions and arguments, rummaging with her great clumsy hands through his pride and his grief and his dignity until he had finally ordered her off, because — she remembered exactly how he had put it — he could not otherwise end a stupid and profitless conversation. Stupid. Profitless. Enough to drive any man mad.

"You're not talking," said Christopher. "Go on talking."

"What do you want me to talk of?" asked Kate helplessly.

"I don't care," said Christopher. "Whatever you like. Anything. Only talk."

Kate cast wildly around in her mind for the "anything," wishing more than ever that it was her father who was sitting there, her father or Master Roger or the Lady Elizabeth or Alicia. Surely that was the least God could have done for him, the very least.

"Christopher," she blurted out, "do you ever think about food?"

"Food?" The heartbreaking control of the voice flickered a little, as if in surprise, and the next question was a real one. "What do you mean?"

"J-j-just food," Kate stammered. "Things to eat. I mean, they don't feed the mortal women on boiled grain and milk, like you, but with us it's always meat in wine and spices, every single day, richer than Christmas, and I'm so tired of it. I keep thinking all the time what it would be like to have a loaf of bread, a new loaf out of the oven, with the crust on it, and clotted cream and strawberries."

"I might have known that would be what you'd think of," said Christopher.

"Well, it's better than thinking about nothing," Kate retorted defensively.

"Very true," said Christopher. "Much better than thinking about nothing, especially the nothing. That wasn't what you meant, was it?"

"I don't know what you're talking about."

"Thank God for that," said Christopher. "What else do you think of, when you're thinking of food?"

"Well — apples," Kate floundered on. "Those hard greenish apples, the kind you get in October, that taste cold when you bite into them."

"Yes," said Christopher. "I remember. There was a whole orchard of those apples on my manor once."

"Is the manor your home in Norfolk?"

"No," said Christopher curtly. "It's an old deserted house with some land around it on the other side of the marsh. I used to go there sometimes when I was a boy. It must have been a very fine manor once — a hundred years ago." His voice was still colorless, but it did not sound empty now, only shy, as though he were speaking of something he cared for very much.

"Why was it deserted, then?" asked Kate cautiously.

"The family let it go to ruin. They were all fools." The voice quickened furiously. "Our old bailiff told me that they were cutting off the woods and grazing the pastures bare in *his* father's time, and the last man was a miser who starved the place and himself to death. Now it belongs to some cousin in London who's been try to sell it off ever since I was born, not that he ever will. Nobody but a lunatic would buy it: Geoffrey says it would cost a fortune to set it to rights by this time. And you needn't tell me that I'm a younger son with no fortune to speak of. I know that as well as you do. But I always wanted — I did think — if I could only clean the scrub out of the water meadows and had the money for ditching and draining the fen land —"

"What?"

Kate had thought she knew Christopher fairly well by that time — but now she realized, in a sort of bewilderment, that she did not know this side of him at all. She had always somehow, in her secret heart, never thought of him except in a world of knights and ladies, the sort of world that one read about in the old romances, where hermits knelt praying among the gray rocks and champions rode out to slay dragons from high turreted castles — not the sort of castles that could ever go to ruin because the scrub had not been cleaned out of the water meadows and there was no money for the ditching and the drainage.

"But why should you care so much about ditching and d-drainage?" she stumbled. "My father says that trying to drain land in the fens is only a waste of good money."

"Much he knows!" Christopher retorted rudely. "Fen land is the richest in England — if you know how to keep the water out of it. It's too heavy, and it lies too low, so the dead water backs up in it, and then it goes sick. What do you mean — a waste of good money? Your father sounds like old Martin to me."

"Old Martin?"

"The bailiff at home. He does say that I'm crazed in my wits over drainage," Christopher admitted. "But that's only because he thinks it's the will of God to go on ditching the same way we've been ditching for the last thousand years, and the world can't ever be otherwise! You might as well argue with a stone wall. I'd try liming too, of course, and marling, and some of the new root crops; but when it comes to sick land, there are two things you have to do before you do anything else — and one of them is *drain*." He drove his fist against the mesh by way of emphasis, forgetting to keep his voice down.

Very slowly and carefully, Kate settled back on the floor. "O be careful!" she thought incoherently. "Be careful! Don't let me spoil it! . . . And what's the other thing you have to do first?" she asked him. She knew nothing whatsoever about tending sick land, or any kind of land for that matter, but it seemed like a safe question.

"Manure," said Christopher. "Good plain dung. You take those water meadows at the manor. What I had in my mind —"

The next morning Gwenhyfara came into the stable some time earlier than usual, while Joan and Betty and Marian were still asleep, and took Kate back with her to her own room. This proved to be a little bare cell some distance down the "smooth passage," with nothing in it but a chest and a thin pallet of woven straw that had been rolled up and laid against the wall. Gwenhyfara sat on the chest and made Kate walk up and down the floor by the light of three candles, studying every movement she made much as the Queen's Master of the Horse might have observed the gait of an unpromising colt.

"Who in the name of the gods trained you to carry yourself?" she demanded.

"Nobody," said Kate, flushing. "My mother said it was no use, I was always too clumsy. Blanche Parry used to try to teach me how to curtsy sometimes when I was with the Lady Elizabeth at Hatfield, but I could never seem to learn the way of it."

"And small wonder," said Gwenhyfara. "How did she think you could learn the way of anything when your backbone is as stiff as a stake and you hold yourself as if you were strapped to it? That is what she should have begun with. Stand where you are."

"Yes," said Kate apprehensively.

"Now: stretch your arms out before you — so — and let your hands drop. No. *Drop,* stop holding them, let them drop from your wrists and hang. Now let your arms drop and hang from your shoulders. Now drop your head forward and let the cords in your neck go loose. Do you have that? Now — slowly — slowly — try to feel that same loosening all down your back, one link after another, slowly, as though they were melting — no, no, don't stoop." She came over to Kate and made a little light gesture with her hand. "Here is where you want it, and here, and here. You must know how to let your whole body go before you can fall without hurting yourself."

"Fall?" Kate jerked bolt upright again, making a wild plunge to recover her balance.

"Fall," said Gwenhyfara calmly. "It is easy enough."

"Couldn't you —" said Kate, "couldn't you teach me how to move some other way? Without falling?"

"Not I," said Gwenhyfara. "For there is no better way to learn the flow and the manage of your body. I will teach you other things in time, but that will be the first. Start over, now. Stretch your arms before you — so —"

"No, no, no," said Christopher. "The sheep folds at the manor were on the other side of the barn, *across* from the stables. Start over."

"You turn right off the road at the bridge and go up a deep lane to the gate," Kate recited. "The gate leads into an outer yard with a well and a dovecote, where they used to have a watering trough and a pond for the ducks. The farm buildings ran around another yard to the left of the well. First the kennels, and then the stables, and then the forge, the toolshed, the workshop, the storerooms, the pigsty, the sheepfolds — I'm sorry, that's wrong, it was the hen yard — the hen yard, the sheepfolds, the barn, and the wall of the orchard. On your right as you come in from the outer yard is another wall with a door in it and some steps down to the rose garden and the house. You never told me about the house."

"The house?"

"Yes," said Kate. "The house."

"The house is a wreck, like everything else."

"What do you mean by a wreck? How much of a wreck?"

"Well —" Kate could not see Christopher's shrug, but she could feel it in his voice. "The roof was still on, the last time I saw it, but even that may be done by now. The steward lived there for a time after the old miser died, but he got drunk one night and started a fire that burned out the kitchens and the dairy and about half of the north wing. Then after the fire, the place was shut up, and thieves and strollers tore out most of what was left of it. One of the doors at the back had rotted clean off its hinges. Anybody could go in."

"Did you ever go in yourself?"

"Anybody could go in."

"Then what are you planning to do with it?"

"Do with it?"

"Well, you can't spend *all* your time down in the orchard or the water meadows or the stables," said Kate impatiently. "What are you planning to do with the house?"

"No, no, no," said Gwenhyfara. "Lightly, lightly, I tell you.

You must learn to walk lightly, just as you learned to fall. *Walk,* not put your feet down on the floor dump, dump, as if they were two great logs of wood. Think that your body is hanging from the roof by one single hair drawn up from your head, and you can't let yourself break it."

Kate thought obediently, taking two or three tentative steps, but picturing herself strung up by her hair like Absolom in a church window did her no good at all: it only distracted and confused her.

"No," said Gwenhyfara. "You have not caught the way of it. Think of something else. If you can once get the shape of your need alive in your mind, your body will follow it. Suppose that you had to pass an enemy in the dark, and so you want feet made out of velvet, light, so light that there would not even be the fall of an echo to warn him. Would that image speak to you more than the other? Try it, then . . . Softly now, softly, more lightly still . . . There! what did I tell you?"

Christopher was having what Kate had come to think of as "one of his bad nights." A "bad night" — and the "bad nights" were growing more and more frequent as the weeks went on — always meant that the gray creature had been at him again. He had never yet told her exactly what it did to him. Once, on a particularly bad night, he had said to her, with curious intensity: "Don't let them into your mind, Kate! Whatever else you do, *don't* let them into your mind!" — but that was all. On another night, when she had spoken to him about her attacks of the weight, he had seemed almost surprised to hear that they troubled her so much, because he himself rather liked to feel the hard walls and the rock pressing about him, especially after he had gone away.

"Gone away?" Kate had said, startled. "I didn't think they ever let you out of this place."

"They don't. It isn't that kind of being 'gone.' "

He had said nothing more about the "going away," and Kate had not pressed the matter further. It was much more important that he should feel there was one person at least under the Hill who would treat him as a living individual with a right to keep his mind to himself if he chose to. When the bad nights came, she asked no questions and merely brought the talk as quickly as she could around to the never exhausted topic of the manor. They had walked over it, ditched it, drained it, rebuilt it, and argued about it for so long now that Kate sometimes felt as though she had lived there all her life.

But on this particular night even the manor seemed to have failed them.

"— and the new dairy could fit into the far corner of the yard," Christopher was saying. "Along the old orchard wall."

"What do you mean?" Kate demanded, more sharply than she meant to. She had come to know every tone and shade of his voice by that time, and what she heard in it now troubled her. It was empty again, empty and oddly remote, as if he were speaking from somewhere a long way off; and never before had he made the smallest mistake when it was a question of anything to do with the manor. She pulled herself up. "Not straight across the wall, surely?" she asked, treading as lightly as she could. "Didn't you tell me that the gate to the orchard was there?"

"Did I?" said Christopher, in that far, indifferent voice. "Yes, I did. The gate to the orchard. What does it matter where the gate to the orchard is?"

"The new dairy will block it."

"Cut a new gate in from the other side, then."

"How much would that cost?"

"Cost?" Christopher was trying to speak lightly too, but Kate was startled by the bitterness of the question. "It won't cost us a penny. None of this is real. Go on, spend as much as you please. Why trouble yourself? What does it matter? We're only dreaming like Joan and Betty and Marian."

"Then we may as well begin with a palace straight off, on a golden cloud, all hung with diamonds and rubies, and be done with it," Kate retorted. "We're not talking about a place like that. We're talking about the farmyard at the manor."

"With the new dairy and the new barn and the new stables and sheepfolds and gardens?" Christopher inquired grimly. "If you want to talk of palaces on golden clouds — dear heart, do you know what *is* there? Nothing. Half an acre of ruins knee-deep in stinging nettles, and the old gate in the orchard wall is rusted so stiff you couldn't even open it."

"Yes, but it's still a real wall, isn't it?" Kate argued. "And if you build the new dairy there, after we get out of here, you'll still have to cut a new gate in it for real money, won't you? When my father put the new gates in down at the counting house, it cost him fifty shillings for the labor alone."

There was a moment's silence; and then, to her bewilderment, Christopher suddenly went off into one of his wild gusts of laughter. "F-f-fifty shillings?" he gasped. "Oh, Kate! Here I am, the King of the land at his death-time, and you won't even let me spend fifty shillings!"

Kate stiffened furiously. It was bad enough never to be told exactly what it was that the gray creature did to him (for though she honored his privacy, she resented it very much, always to be shut out, treated like a child, kept at a distance), but if he thought he was going to laugh at her too —

"I don't see why —" she began.

"What don't you see?"

Kate checked herself. Anything — even being laughed at — was better than having him sit there on the other side of the mesh, sounding as if he were a thousand miles away.

"I don't see why you want to spend fifty shillings for nothing," she said. "It's foolish."

"Very foolish," Christopher agreed with her gravely. "Fifty shillings — and all for nothing! Very well, then. Where else can we build the new dairy?"

"You are learning the way of it," said Gwenhyfara. "Make the great bow to the Queen now, as the women of our kind do."

Kate obeyed a little anxiously. The exquisite, long drawn out sweep of the Queen's bow had to be done perfectly, if it was to be done at all. The smallest failure of grace or balance sent the performer toppling over into a dreadful sprawl on the floor.

"Good," said Gwenhyfara. "That will be enough. You may rest."

Her voice, if not exactly warm, was perceptibly less cold than usual, and as she sat back, she made — for the first time in Kate's experience of her — an unnecessary remark. "A little longer, and I will tell you to bow to the Lady with the others, when she passes out of the hall. It would be good to see you do it, before I go."

"Before you *go?*" said Kate, startled. Gwenhyfara had always seemed to her as much a part of the Hill as the passageways and the caverns and the rock. "Go where?"

"South on a journey to gather herbs which do not grow in these woods, but not as you see me now." Gwenhyfara smiled faintly. "If you met me on the roads of your world, you would take me for a tinker or a gypsy woman, and you would not know me again."

"I thought your kind never went out of the Elvenwood."

"No," said Gwenhyfara. "Only the Lady and the Guardian of the Well may stay forever in the holy place. The rest must come and go. And yet we are more fortunate than most of our kind, for they are a wandering folk, with no holy place to return to; and when they meet, it is only for a dancing night. Not even our kind can form a true circle of power or pay the teind to the gods in a holy place that has once been defeated or broken, and they were all driven out of their holy places long ago. But here in the Elvenwood it is otherwise. For of old this Hill was the highest and the most holy of all the holy places: it alone remains as it was, and here alone the true way of the land has never been lost or forgotten. So much the Lady said that I was to tell you."

"T-t-tell me?" Kate stammered. "But why? Why should she want to tell *me?*"

"I did not ask her that," said Gwenhyfara. "Our kind do not question the Lady, nor dispute with her. It is for her to command the people, and to keep them. We have come upon a very evil time, and the weather of the world is blowing against us; but when she has paid the teind to the gods, she will obtain the power to master it, and then you will be as you have been again."

"I?"

"No — the others of your kind," said Gwenhyfara. "The warden and his servants who keep the valley safe for us, and the rich pilgrims who come up through the forest to bring offerings to the Well. One of our passageways opens far down the shaft, over the water; and there the Guardian sits, to catch their offerings in his net and listen to their foolish cries, so that he can judge and choose those who need easing the most, who will come

again and again once they have tasted the stuff that we put in
their cups, and will pay any price and keep any secret to have
more of it. You must not think that we choose all who come.
We take only a few, those who can be of the greatest use to
us; and even to those few we do not reveal ourselves. We are
not like the priests of your faith, to make holy things common,
and tell our mysteries about the streets, and waste our lore on
any poor man who will ask us. Why should we trouble ourselves with your kind? Or give them more than we must?
When have I ever given *you* more than I was bidden to? Even
though —" she added, "if I could choose, I — I —"

Kate waited for the rest of the sentence, but it did not come.
Gwenhyfara was looking at her and frowning. She appeared to
be turning over some problem in her mind.

"The Lady did not speak of that," she said, almost reluctantly.
"But I might ask her."

"Ask her what?"

Gwenhyfara picked up a strand of her long dark hair and sat
twisting it between her fingers. It was the first time Kate had
ever seen her make a restless or an unnecessary movement.

"You would not have a bad voice," she said, "if somebody
taught you how to use it."

"Do you know, Christopher," said Kate, "I think I must be
rising in the world?"

"Are you?" inquired Christopher. It was one of his "good"
nights, and until that moment the talk had been running easily.
"How's that?"

"Gwenhyfara," said Kate. "She wants to ask the Lady to
make me speak properly. Would you believe it? She used
to treat me like a workhorse on the farm. Now it's more like
a dog that she thinks she can train for the house."

She heard Christopher come to his feet on the other side of the mesh.

"Oh, is it?" he asked between his teeth; and then, in a voice that was fire-hot with fury: "I don't see that's anything to laugh at."

"B-b-but I was only trying —" Kate stuttered. She had thought that he was going to enjoy Gwenhyfara's nonsense as much as she had. "Why shouldn't I laugh? You laugh at yourself all the time. You laugh at me, too."

"That's different," said Christopher shortly. "And what's more, I won't have any of this making you speak properly, either. Good Lord, do you want to start lilting and fluting as if you were one of the Fairy Folk? There's nothing wrong with your voice. Leave your voice alone. I like it as it is."

"You might remember," said Kate, "that it's *my* voice."

"Did you hear me?"

"It's my voice."

"Did you hear me?"

"Yes," said Kate coldly. "And they can probably hear you all the way up at the castle."

"Then what were we talking of before you began on this foolishness?"

Kate let the question of her voice go by. There were times to argue with Christopher, and other times when she had learned that it was very much better not to.

"You were talking of clearing the wasteland at the manor, down by the village," she said, "and whether it would hurt the village if you did. But would it hurt them so much? They're only using it to feed a few hens or sheep, and pick up a stick or two of wood for the fire."

Christopher laughed suddenly, and then dropped down into his usual place, with his shoulder against the mesh beside hers.

"When you're as poor as they are," he said, "a hen or a stick or two of firewood can seem like a great matter. That is, if you're *starving* poor, like me."

"Like *you?*" Kate demanded. "What do you mean?"

"Only that I'm as bad as they are. Why should I care what becomes of *you* as long as I have my bit of fire and my hen to comfort me?"

"I'm not a hen," said Kate indignantly. "I thought you wouldn't have Gwenhyfara even treat me like a dog or a horse."

"Perhaps we'd better not pursue the question," said Christopher. "Now about that wasteland on the manor —"

XI ১৯
The Cold Iron

From the question of clearing wasteland they had gone on
to the whole problem of the village people's rights and privileges,
and Christopher was giving Kate a long description of the
ordinary proceedings at a manorial court of justice when he
broke off in the middle of a sentence, and said: "Listen!"

"What is it?" asked Kate. "Has the bell rung? I didn't hear
anything."

"No," said Christopher. "But I thought — listen! There it is
again."

This time Kate heard it too — floating from somewhere away
down the outer passage, very faint and clear, the sound of a high
sweet voice singing.

"O where is the Queen, and where is her throne?" it sang,
just as it had sung that first evening long ago on the forest road.

"Randal!" thought Kate incredulously. "It's Randal!" but
even as the name shot through her head, she knew she was
wrong: not Randal himself had a voice so high or so sweet as
that. And then there was an outbreak of laughing cries, and a
chorus of other voices answered the first, singing together,
dancingly light: "Down in the stone O, but not in the stone."

Kate sprang to her feet, the manorial court, the wasteland,
the orchard, the house, and the water meadows all vanishing as

if a light had been blown out behind a painted glass window. The dark fear that was never very far from the surface of her mind rose and poured over it.

"Are they coming for you?" she cried, before she could stop herself. "Are they coming for you?"

"Is that your idea of a teind hymn?" inquired Christopher dryly. "No, they're not coming for me: when they do, it isn't going to sound like all join hands and dance singing to the maypole! But get back where you belong, and be quick about it! They mustn't find you out of your bed if they're wandering around at this hour of the night."

Kate went as quickly as she could, but it was not quickly enough. She had only just reached the two closed doors halfway down the outer passage when there was a rush of feet and torchlight behind her, and a whole troop of the Fairy Folk came running through the archway from the great cavern. The leader was on her before she could even look about for a hole to hide in.

It was the grave youth with the pipe who usually played at the gatherings in the hall, but the pipe was gone now: his head was thrown back and he was laughing as he ran, the flame from his torch streaming on the air behind him. He checked in his stride for an instant as he saw Kate cowering against the door.

"What are you doing there?" he shouted hilariously. "Come out! come out! don't stand in the way! We'll be late!" and taking her by the shoulder, he swung her back into the crowd, thrust the door open, and was gone. Somebody caught her hand, a child, one of the little boys. "Come out!" he cried, tugging at the hand impatiently. "Come out!"

"Where?" Kate gasped, completely bewildered, straining against his hold.

There was another burst of laughter. "Out!" and "Out!" and "Out!" called a dozen voices at once. "Out! It's a dancing night!

The Lady has given us a dancing night!" and then they were all singing again:

> *O where is the Queen, and where is she now?*
> *Go out by the oak leaf, with never a bough!*

— singing and racing through the open door after the leader, sweeping Kate along with them.

They ran on and on, down passageways and around turns and through arches of stone, so fast that Kate could not tell which way they were going: it was all she could do to keep up with them. She was still dazed with the shock of relief from the terror of the last few minutes, and the insistent rhythm of the music was driving everything else out of her mind. "O where is the Queen, and where is she now?" the voices sang around her, the leader's torch dancing and tossing in the darkness ahead, the words dancing and beating through her ears: go out by the oak leaf, with never a bough — go out by the oak leaf, with never a bough — "O where is the Queen, and where is she now?" — go out by the oak leaf — and then the light was flashing on something thin and silvery like glass — not glass, water, a sheet of water falling over an opening in the rock, and then they were running through it, and plashing among the pebbles of a shallow pool and up the bank, and then they were all standing still and the night air was blowing against their faces, alive with wind and the scent of grass and the rustle of falling leaves.

They had come out into a wide level space like a glade in the forest, walled around by dark masses of trees, and with one enormous oak alone in the center of the clearing. The sky was gleaming with stars, and a great globe of a moon, almost full, was just beginning to swing free from the branches that entangled it. But at that first instant all that Kate could feel was the air, the shock of the air after the stillness and the stifling confinement of the Hill. She lifted her face and looked up into it, up and up and up into the sudden incredible heights and vastnesses over her head.

The little boy at her side shivered and caught at her hand. His face was lifted too, very white in the moonlight.

"Oh, look!" he whispered. "Look at it! Look!"

And then another wave of the Fairy Folk came plunging through the waterfall, and the stillness melted into a happy confusion of voices and laughter, blowing about the glade like the leaves on the wind. A cup was going from hand to hand. Somebody passed it on to her, laughing, and she laughed and drank and passed it on in her turn; a cool, spicy liquid, smelling of flowers. A ring of dancers had begun to circle the oak tree. The song broke out again, call and answer:

> O where is the Queen, and where is her hall?
> Over the wall O, with never a wall!

The quick, driving rhythm was setting the measure for the dance; and one of the flying figures — she thought it was Gwenhyfara — reached out and drew her into the line. That was the last thing she remembered clearly. Then she was dancing too, round and round the tree, lightly and more lightly still, the new sweet sureness in her own feet catching the beat of the music, faster and faster, dancing around the tree with the Fairy Folk — out of her body — racing on the air —

She opened her eyes to find that she was lying on the couch back in the stable, with the mortal women whimpering beside her. Gwenhyfara was just stooping down to rouse them, the branch of candles in her hand and her severe delicate face locked and remote again. The glade, the stars, the oak tree, and the dancers were all gone like a dream.

"Lord!" said Christopher that night, when she told him about it. "What *did* they give you to drink?"

"Nothing but what they drank themselves," Kate protested. "It wasn't that."

"No? What was it, then? One of their tricks?"

Kate shook her head. She did not know how to explain it to him. Now that the enchantment was over, she could hardly explain it even to herself. "It was the air," she said lamely, "the air, and everybody laughing, and the leaves blowing, and — and —"

"Leaves?" Christopher's voice cut across the halting phrases, suddenly quick and hard. "How do you mean? Leaves on the trees?"

"No, not on the trees," said Kate, struggling to remember. "Well, some on the trees — the branches weren't bare — but all over the ground too, and blowing on the wind —"

She stopped short, realizing just where the answer was leading her, but it was too late: Christopher had reached it already.

"We must be nearly into the autumn, then," he said. "Randal seems to have gone blowing off on the wind too, doesn't he?"

Kate found that she had closed her eyes as if to shut out something that she could not bear to look at, even though it made no difference at all in the blind darkness of the little passage.

"He may be having a hard time getting to Sir Geoffrey," she pointed out. "With the rivers in flood, and the roads — you said yourself that it might take you over a week, even riding. Randal's on foot."

"Creeping like a snail?" inquired Christopher. "All this while? Kate, it's *autumn.*"

"But I may have been wrong about the leaves," Kate argued

imploringly. "I may have been clean out of my head; I may have been having a dream. Or the leaves may be falling early this year, such a cold, ailing summer, it would never surprise me if they were. The time can't be up yet, not possibly. It's too soon."

"How do you know?"

Kate thought of pretending that she had kept a count of the "days" and "nights" they had spent in the Hill; but then he would only ask her what the count was in earthly time, and to that she had no possible answer.

"I don't know," she said.

"Well, then? Who's to say?"

Kate tugged at her braid for a moment in silence.

"Gwenhyfara might," she suggested. "If she begins to talk to me again tomorrow, I could ask her how long —"

"I won't have you sit on your hind legs to beg scraps from Gwenhyfara," Christopher interrupted her.

"We have to find out somehow."

"We'll find out soon enough. What difference would it make if we *did* know? Licking the time out of Gwenhyfara's hand isn't going to stop it from — oh, curse that bell! Kate, listen. I mean it. I will *not* have you —"

"O don't be so silly, Christopher!" said Kate, scrambling to her feet. He would certainly be furious with her for disobeying him but as long as he was furious he would at least have something more than horrors to think of — and so would she. What she could not bear were the times when she felt as though she were hiding behind the rocks in the gorge again, watching helplessly as he walked further and further away from her towards the shadow at the mouth of the Holy Well. "We have to find out," she said over her shoulder. "I don't mind Gwenhyfara. You leave her to me."

But the next day Gwenhyfara was in a very unpromising

mood — cold, silent, and so pale that Kate, looking at her, wondered if she might not have been having an attack of the weight. There was no rest that morning and no chance to talk. Kate was made to lie down and go through a long stretch of exhausting and complicated exercises at a frantic speed which left her no time to think of anything else. She twisted and turned on the stone of the floor, panting, and the redheaded woman's cross on its chain around her neck twisted and turned with her. At first she was aware of it simply as a hard lump of discomfort, thrusting into her breast. Then suddenly she felt a prick and a little dart of pain at the base of her throat. The weakened bar of the cross had snapped at last, and the jagged end was cutting through the ribbon she had wound about it.

"Keep your head down," said Gwenhyfara. "Stop craning it up."

Kate put her head down, hoping against hope that what was left of the ribbon would hold together. It would never have been a good time for Gwenhyfara to find out that she was wearing a cross made of cold iron, but on *this* day, of all possible days —

"Turn over and lie flat on your face," said Gwenhyfara. "No — with your arms out. Flat, I tell you."

Kate felt another and a sharper prick at her throat as the cross shifted under the new strain. The worst of the prong must still be covered by the padding; but the padding was not going to hold together much longer.

"Wait," said Gwenhyfara. "Someone is at the door."

That they might be interrupted was a possibility that had not even occurred to Kate, accustomed as she was to the undeviating daily order of the Hill — and at any other time it would have struck her as exceedingly strange. But at that moment she was in no state to wonder. She merely felt like a hunted rabbit seeing an unexpected hole in the bank. Gwenhyfara had risen and slipped out of the room, the door closing behind her. There was a murmur of voices from the passage.

Kate sat up and tore the chain over her head.

The ruined ribbon was still clinging to the crossbar, but so shredded and feathered by the prong that it was clear no more could be done with it. The jagged point would have to be bent back somehow or rubbed smooth on the stone of the floor. But she ought to have thought of that long ago. She ought never to have worn the thing at all. Now —

Now it was too late: the murmur of voices from the passage had stopped; there were feet at the door. She had barely time to pour the chain into one cupped hand and close the other over it, on the last infinitesimal chance that she might still be able to hide it.

Then the door opened, and the Lady came into the room.

"Stay where you are," she said to Kate. "That place will do as well as any."

Kate froze where she sat. She could think of only one reason why the Lady should sweep down on her like this, only one. There had been no anger in the voice — it was not the sort of voice that would ever show anger — but surely somebody must have overheard Kate talking with Christopher in the night and told her of it.

"Gwenhyfara has told me," said the Lady, "that she wishes you to be taught to speak as we do."

Kate gave such an uncontrollable gasp of surprise and relief that the Lady nodded reassuringly.

"You may well be astonished," she said. "But what she asked, I had already determined to give you. That, and more."

"More?"

"You have pleased me," said the Lady, "though that is a thing

I never thought to say to any of your kind. You have pleased me. It was not so much that you chose to keep your mind at the beginning, but that you held to it afterwards, when you had seen my land and the burden that it laid on you — and I did not make the seeing easy, or the burden light, for I had to test and be sure of you."

Kate could only stare at her dazedly, and the Lady shook her head, almost as if she too was in some way perplexed by what had happened.

"Even now I do not know how you come to be what you are," she said. "The shape of your mind is new to me. But since you have shown that you can live as we do, then it is fitting that you should live as we do, and not like a beast or a slave any longer. From this time you will be taken from among the mortal women; you will be taught to speak, and allowed to carry light, and to learn herb lore, and to find your way among the signs and the passages."

It was the last promise that brought Kate out of her daze like the clang of a bell. The signs and the passages — the Lady had said that she would be taught to find her way among the signs and the passages. Not walking behind Gwenhyfara, with no chance even to look for those "signs"; not left alone in the dark, when she could not hope to discover them. Once she and Christopher were sure they would not be lost in the dark maze of the Hill, they could do anything — get back to the castle — make off with Cecily before they were missed and traced. For someone who did know the signs and was allowed to carry light —

The Lady's clear voice was speaking again.

"Nor is that all I may give you," she said, "if you prove yourself worthy of more. There are not many of our kind left, and the most part have been scattered to the woods and byways, with few to serve or remember us except as a country woman may tell a tale by the fire or set out a bowl of milk for a luck charm at the door. It is only here in the Elvenwood that we can keep the old shape and order of a circle of power; and even here, the wardens are all departed and we do not live unthreatened any longer. But we are that circle still, and to be the least among us is to be greater than any princess of your kind who is alive on the earth. And what more could you wish for?"

Kate could think of a great many things she wished for more: water meadows, and a manor house, and an orchard of green apples, and at least a month's clear time to get herself and Christopher safe out of the Hill. She could not hope to learn the signs and passages in a day.

"I will not speak more of this now," said the Lady, "for later you will understand me better. It is a hard thing to be a princess, and still harder to be a Queen, as I am; and bodily grace and fair speech and lore are not all that you must learn if you are to be one of us. It will be time enough to talk of more when you have seen the teind paid."

"And when will that be?" Kate ventured, holding her breath for the answer. If they had a month — if they had even a week —

The Lady came a step nearer, and stood looking down at her gravely.

"Between twelve and one of the clock tonight," she said. "For this is the day which in your world is called All Hallows' Eve; but in ours, the Feast of the Dead."

Absolute shock has sometimes a curious power of both numbing and clarifying the mind. Kate did not even move. She could tell that she had not moved because she could see her own hands, clear and still and flat like hands in a painting, resting against her knees. The hands were clasped lightly over the weight of the coiled chain, and the brown leather robe fell away under them in stiff motionless folds to the floor. She thought, very slowly and calmly: "Gwenhyfara must have known this morning, and she has had the care of him for a long time now. That was what made her so pale."

"Look at me," said the Lady.

Kate looked up, seeing with that strange concentrated clarity, every line of the beautiful face: the proud mouth, the fine delicate bones, the eyes under the lifted lashes, very dark and deep. It was the same face she had seen gazing at her from the shadowy bank in the forest, by the fire in the evidence room, under the blazing lights in the great cavern. Only the eyes had changed. There was no brilliance in them now, and no mockery. They seemed almost weary, intent and sad — or rather, filled with something that would have been sadness if it was possible to imagine any human sadness so wholy free from the least touch of human misery or human longing or human shame or human compassion or human regret.

"I told you it would be hard," she said. "Do you think it is easy for any of us to see the teind paid? But if the land or the people are weak and in need, how else are they to get power again?"

"Another way."

"There is no other way," said the Lady. "All power comes from life, and when that life is low in the land and the people, they must take it from one who has it, adding his strength to their own, or perish. That is the law which the gods have laid on us; and they themselves cannot alter it. Do not even those of your own faith believe that in the beginning your strength came to you out of a death?"

Kate hesitated. The only answer she could think of seemed wild to the point of blasphemy, but there was no help for it: she would have to put the thing into the only sort of language that the Lady might possibly understand.

"What need is there for another teind, then?" she asked, trying desperately to keep her voice steady. "The time for that has passed by. It was finished and done with when Our Lord paid it freely, to add His strength to our own; and His power is enough for us all."

"I have heard that tale," said the Lady, "and it is not as you say. I will not deny that your Lord paid the teind, nor that it would be good to have had some part in it, for He was a strong man, and born of a race of kings, and His teind must have been a very great one. But that was long ago, long ago in His own time and place. Its strength is spent now. The power has gone out of it."

"It has never gone out of it," Kate answered, her voice beginning to shake as she searched for the right words, because everything might hang on them. "All power comes from life, as you said yourself, but the life that was in Him came from the God who is above all the gods; and that is a life that knows nothing of places and times." She paused, and the Lady said almost sharply: "What more?" She was leaning a little forward, her head bent as if she were trying to hear some unfamiliar sound in the distance.

"I — I mean," Kate stumbled on, "that with us there is time past and time present, and time future, and with your gods perhaps there is time forever; but God in Himself has the whole of it, all times at once. It would be true to say that He came into our world and died here, in a time and a place; but it would also be true to say that in His eternity it is always That Place and That Time — here — and at this moment — and the power He had then, He can give to us now, as much as He did to those who saw and touched Him when He was alive on the earth."

"Do you mean," asked the Lady slowly, "that His power is in you?"

Kate stiffened, the color pouring over her face.

"Oh, no, no, no!" she cried in a sort of panic. "That was not what I meant. You must not judge it by me. Christopher is the one who has it."

"There is no thought of that in the Young Lord's mind," said the Lady, "or the Guardian of the Well would have learned it by this time, and so I would know it."

"He does not know it himself."

"That is fools' talk," said the Lady. "How could anyone have a power like that without knowing it?"

"I cannot tell," said Kate. "But he was named for a man who bore the whole weight of Our Lord once, on his own shoulders, and His power was with him, even though he —" her voice suddenly wavered and broke, "*he* did not know it, either, and thought he was caring for a child."

The Lady drew a long breath. Then she lifted her head at last, and her eyes were shining.

"This is a great thing you have shown me," she said. "For it means that when we take his life tonight, we can take the Other Life also, to add its strength to our own; and that is even more than I thought we could get from him."

It came over Kate in a rush of despair that she might as well be trying to climb the Hill of Glass in the fairy tale. The Lady's mind was completely set in its own conception of "power"; and against that every argument she could raise would simply glance off as if from some impenetrable crystal.

"Go on," commanded the Lady. "Is there nothing more you can tell me?"

"No," Kate answered dully, sick with defeat. "There is nothing at all. Only —"

"Yes?"

"Will you let me speak to him?"

"He is under silence," said the Lady. "Only the Guardian of the Well may speak to him now. And what would you say to him if you did?"

Kate shook her head blindly. She was at the end of her strength, and the unnatural clarity of thought and purpose that had sustained her was falling away into a kind of stupefied exhaustion. "Please," she said. "Let me speak to him."

The Lady slipped the gold bracelet from her wrist and stood turning it meditatively between her hands. "I did not know," she said, "that the Young Lord was so dear to you."

"So dear to me?" Kate stammered. "So — so dear to me?"

"I mean," said the Lady, in her unmoved crystal voice, "do you love him?"

"Yes," said Kate helplessly, watching a little point of fire run around the rim of the bracelet as it caught the flame of the candles from the bracket on the wall behind her. "But why should you care for that?"

"Because of the teind."

"What?"

"Have you no wits?" the Lady demanded. "Or do you think that I am such a fool as to take you there now? You would only be trying to claim him."

"But how could I claim him?" Kate was staring at her dazedly again. "How *could* I?"

"You know that well enough." For one instant a flash of something that might have been purely human annoyance appeared in the Lady's eyes. "There was a woman of your kind once whose lover taught her the way to do it, and afterwards the tale was made into a ballad called *Tam Lin* and sung up and down the common road for anyone to hear it."

"I never heard the whole ballad," said Kate. "I don't how she did it."

"Then I will not tell you," said the Lady, "and neither will I be such a fool as to let you see the teind paid now. You could not bear it. The pain and the grief would only break your mind, or turn it utterly against us. That I will not have. It will be long, and very long, before there is another teind, but you must wait until then. In this I can give you no choice. The present teind is not for you. You must put it out of your mind, as if it had never been."

"I cannot put it out of my mind," said Kate despairingly. Her eyes were still on the point of fire caught in the Lady's bracelet.

The Lady began to swing the bracelet very gently to and fro. The point of fire moved in a slow curve from the right to the left of the arc, and back again.

"Why should you not?" she asked, almost in a whisper. The icy crystal hardness had gone out of her voice, and it was like music, very low soothing music. "It will do you no good to remember him. Let him pass from you. All things change and pass in the end, and when they are past we must rest and forget. That too is a law of the gods. When the summer is over, the land must sleep, root and stone and water and earth: the seed in the furrow, the beast in the hole, the leaf on the tree giving itself to the air, lightly — lightly — no weight staying it — to fall to the ground and to rest. To rest and to rest, safe on the ground, deep under the snow, with nothing to trouble it, only to rest."

That was the last Kate heard clearly: the words were all blurring and weaving together, and she was aware of them only as murmuring rhythms swinging to and fro, to and fro, to and fro, like the point of fire in the Lady's hand, rising and falling and rising and falling, weaving together, over and over again, lovely floating sounds, inexpressibly consoling. She could feel the stupefied exhaustion of her mind melting deliciously into softness and warmth, as if down, down into the velvet and fur of a bed. Her lips parted in a long sigh of content and acquiescence. Her head fell forward, swaying on her shoulders. The hands clasped in her lap slumped against her knee, and the jagged prong of the broken crossbar caught the center of her left palm.

It was only a glancing prick, but the little momentary discomfort broke the rhythm of the circling sounds and roused her for an instant out of her lethargy. She thought: "This is a spell. She is trying to put a spell on me," her mind wavering and stumbling against the pull and drag of the music, unable to break loose from it. She felt her brain beginning to go again as the prick faded; the circling sounds shut in about her; and then, with a last effort of will, she closed her hand and brought it down on the jagged prong as hard as she could.

A white-hot flash of pain ripped up her whole arm. The point of fire spun around, dancing crazily; the music shivered into roaring fragments. Then her eyes cleared. She was back on the floor in Gwenhyfara's cell, with the candles burning on the wall behind her; and the point of fire was only the reflection of a flame caught in the rim of the Lady's gold bracelet. One of her hands was throbbing abominably, and a hot stickiness was oozing up through the coils of the redheaded woman's chain into the palm of the other. The Lady's voice was speaking somewhere over her head.

"Rest," she was saying, "rest, and forget. The seed to the furrow, the beast to the hole, the leaf to the ground, and all to rest and forget."

Kate had a sudden furious impulse to rise to her feet and announce that she was not a seed in the furrow or a leaf on the ground; it was as much as she could do to stay where she was, her head drooping, and continue to let her shoulders sway very slightly to the interminable, murmuring chant. "Oh, get on!" she thought, in an agony of impatience. "Get on with it, can't you?"

"Sleep," said the Lady. "I will leave you to sleep now. Lie down, lie down, close your eyes, lie down, lie down, and sleep and forget."

This was a little more promising. Kate closed her eyes obediently, and — the art of falling had been the first that Gwenhyfara had taught her — slid to the floor in an exhausted heap, taking care to end on her left side, with her back to the Lady and her face turned away from her against the stone.

"Sleep!" said the Lady in a wholly different voice: clear and penetrating and imperious. "And do not awake until I return and command it. By seed and beast and leaf, I command you to sleep and when you awake to remember nothing that you know of the Young Lord, Christopher Heron: neither that he paid the teind, nor that he was dear to you, nor that you ever saw him, nor that you and I spoke of him together. All that part of your mind I have taken into my own hand, and it is gone from you. Sleep and forget."

There was an instant's silence, and then the faint rustling stir of her feet coming nearer.

Kate lay still, sickeningly afraid that she was about to bend down and make sure that the spell was working as it should. But apparently it did not occur to the Lady even as a possibility that she might have missed her mark. The feet moved past Kate's inert body and on without pausing; there was a little clink as she lifted the branch of candles off its bracket to light her out of the room. The faint rustling stir retreated slowly and died away.

Kate let the cross drop from her hand with a gasp of relief,

and stood up. It was pitch dark, but she knew where she was and long practice had given her a certain ability to find her way blind over any ground that was familiar to her. She paused a moment, picturing the shape of the cell in her mind; then she moved very quickly and lightly across to the door and out into the passage beyond.

She had no time to think or plan. Her one idea was simply to get to Christopher as fast as she could. What she would do if she met the Lady returning, or encountered another troop of the Fairy Folk, she did not know. How he and she were going to make their way out of the Hill without losing themselves, or reach the castle, or find Cecily, she did not know either. All that would have to take its chance now. Any chance was better than none.

She turned into the passage that led to the great cavern, her feet gathering speed. She knew every inch of the way here, every irregularity and change of surface, every step, every fold in the stone. There was nothing to stop her. The Fairy Folk seemed to have withdrawn to some other part of the Hill. The passage was completely silent and felt curiously empty, as though she were running about through the stillness of a deserted house.

The first check came at the two doors halfway down the passage. They had always been closed and locked before whenever she had passed them, but now she could feel that they were open, wide open, drawn back against the wall. And somewhere ahead of her — it was not possible to tell how far away — there was the faintest flicker of light.

Then she realized that the door into the great cavern must be open too, and what she had seen was nothing but the glow of the candles that were always left burning in honor of the Lady on the wall behind the stone chair. The glow vanished as she plunged through the narrow entrance to the last passage and turned to her left.

"Christopher!" she called. "Christopher, we —"

She stopped short, feeling again the silence, the curiously empty quality of the air.

"Christopher?" she said questioningly.

There was no answer.

XII ॐ

All Hallows' Eve

Kate said again: "Christopher!" and took a step forward, groping for the mesh. Her outstretched hands touched something hard in the darkness, and it moved a little, with a faint sighing sound.

The hidden door in the mesh was open: not broken or torn, as if he had forced his way through it and escaped, only open, wide open, like the other doors, drawn back to the wall. It came away loose as she caught at it and hung swinging, clappering gently — almost idly — against the stakes and knots of withy that framed the dark open entrance to the room beyond.

Somewhere in her mind a long-forgotten memory stirred and came back to her — her own six-year-old voice protesting that she was cold, and her nurse's answer, kind but uncompromising: "No, leave the door open, Mistress Katherine. On All Hallows' Eve you should always leave every door in the house open, to let the dead pass through."

After another moment the door stopped moving, and the silence fell again, complete, unbroken, and final. The room beyond the door was empty. She did not even have to go into it to be certain of that.

Presently she turned and began, very slowly, to make her way back towards the outer passage. She was not going anywhere, or thinking of anything. She had nothing left to think of.

There was only one place they would have taken him — back up the gorge of the Holy Well, to the Standing Stone, where the teind had been paid in the old days. She could not get out to him, and she could not "claim" him, like the lady in the ballad; she did not even know how the lady had done it, and she was utterly without help. The old dream of Sir Geoffrey riding down the forest road followed by a long line of heavily armed men was only a dream. It was clear by now that Randal must have failed them, and there was no reckoning on Sir Geoffrey any longer. The castle people were all under Master John's thumb, and too afraid of him to be of any use. The village people might possibly turn against the castle in some last extremity, but at midnight the village people would be asleep in their beds, and there was no way that she could reach them or rouse them. The only part of the Hill where she could find her way blind was along the path that ran from the great cavern to Gwenhyfara's cell. Without light and the signs, even the Lady herself would be lost among the other turns and passages: Gwenhyfara had said so. Kate had never learned the signs, and she had no light. There was no light in the whole Hill except for the candles that the Fairy Folk kept in their own hands, and the —

The — the —

"Oh, you idiot!" she cried out, and began to run.

The door of the great cavern was still open, and through it, distant and shimmering, came the glow from the four clusters of candles that were always left burning, in honor of the Lady, on the dais wall at the far end, behind the stone chair. She was so accustomed to seeing them there that until that moment she had not given them a thought. She had never even looked at them closely.

She went down the hall and looked at them now, her heart

thudding violently but her eyes suddenly clear and as coldly intent as the Lady's own.

There were three candles to a cluster, set in branched holders like the one Gwenhyfara usually carried, and the holders placed on flat sconces that jutted out from the wall. The candles themselves were thick and fairly tall, eight or nine inches high, church candles, the finest wax. They would go on burning for a very long time.

The sconces were set high on the wall, and she had to clamber up on the stone chair – feeling a flash of wicked pleasure at the sacrilege – to lift the nearest branch down. She could not take more than one: the wound in her palm had almost stopped bleeding, but her whole left hand felt numb to the wrist, and she was unable to carry anything except in her right. All she could do was put out two of the three candles to keep them for a reserve supply before she turned to go. The single remaining flame dipped and fluttered dangerously when she started to run again, and she was forced to rein herself down to a walk, pacing like an acolyte in a church procession back up the hall and through the door to the outer passage.

She had no choice in the matter: it would have to be the path that led to the waterfall and out into the glade with the oak tree. There must be other ways out of the Hill – the way by the Holy Well, and the way back to Lord Richard's tower; but she could not tell in what direction to begin looking for either of them. At least she knew where the path to the glade with the oak tree started: at the two closed doors halfway down the outer passage. It was there that she had been cowering when the Fairy Folk overtook her on the dancing night. She remembered the sudden rush of feet, and the clear voices singing, and the torchbearer with his head flung back, thrusting his way past her. Then the rest had come crowding up, and they

had all run together through — through — which door had it
been? the first, or the second? She had not seen it clearly. Everything had happened too fast, and there had been too many
other bodies pressing about her to be sure. But that need not
matter. She wanted a passage. With luck, the wrong door
would lead only to a sleeping cell or a storeroom.

Her luck was out. The doors were still wide open, pulled
back like the others against the wall; but when she stopped at
last and raised her light to look, she found that both of them
led to passages, narrow tunnels that sloped upward for a few
feet and then vanished in darkness. There was nothing whatever to distinguish the first from the second, and Kate could
almost hear Christopher's voice saying dryly: "One of their
tricks?"

She beat off the thought of Christopher and what might be
happening to him before it drove her frantic, and turned from
the doorways to the doors themselves. She had to push them
free of the wall with the point of her foot — for her left hand
was past using, and her right taken up with the candle-branch
— but in the end she swung them back and made herself stand
still and look at them in turn.

One thing at least she was sure of. The Fairy Folk would not
have lied to her. They might trick or mock her kind for the
sport of the matter, but they would somehow do it by telling
the exact truth. If Gwenhyfara or the Lady had said that there
were "signs" to mark the passages, then signs there would be.

There were no signs. Both doors unmarked, and as far as she
could see, there was nothing to choose between them.

She set her teeth, and relighting the other two candles, looked
again.

The first door was made of plain oaken boards, with bronze
hinges and a leaf-shaped bronze thumb-latch.

The second door was exactly like it.

No, not exactly.

Somewhere, as the light of the candles swung from one door to the other, she caught something — a flicker, the very faintest possible flicker, of a difference. Not the height, or the breadth, or the timbers, or the hinges, or —

The latch. The pattern of the latch, where it broadened out to make a holding place for the thumb. On one door, it was shaped like an oak leaf. On the other door, it was ivy.

For a long moment, Kate stood still, her head up, hardly breathing, as though the oak leaf thumb-latch might somehow vanish if she moved. It was all coming back to her again, the rush of feet behind her on the dancing night, and the clear voices singing together, question and reply —

> *O where is the Queen, and where is she now?*
> *Go out by the oak leaf, with never a bough!*

and then suddenly her head dropped forward, and she was rocking between fury and exasperated laughter.

It was there before her, the bronze oak leaf that had never hung on a bough, the sign that marked the passage, the key of the Hill. And she had had it in her hand ever since the day that she had sat on her horse beside Sir Geoffrey and heard the same words blowing towards them through the misty rain. Randal must have learned the words on one of the nights when he was allowed to come back and harp for the dancers. It would be like them to teach him that song and then let him go singing the truth, the exact truth, over half the roads in England, since he himself would know nothing of what it meant, and everyone else would take it for a jingle of the lunatic he was. Her mouth hardened fiercely as she thrust back the oak leaf door with her shoulder and walked into the arched tunnel behind it. There were some things she thought that she might forgive the Fairy Folk, but what they had done to Randal was not one of them.

The new passage was neither rough nor treacherous under-foot, like the way from Lord Richard's tower; it had been made for running dancers, and it unwound before her as smoothly as a ball of old Dorothy's embroidery silk. Twice more she came to doors, and once to a cross-passage, but always the sign of the oak leaf was there to guide her, carved in the stone of the wall or worked into an ornament for a hinge or a latch. Presently the air grew fresher; she heard a murmuring splashing sound somewhere ahead, and wondered, with a lift of her heart, if it was the waterfall that masked the rock arch at the end of the passage. The path took a sharp curve to the left, and there suddenly opened out of the darkness the dimmed pearly moonlit glow she remembered. She stooped her shoulders to shield the precious candles from the spray, and was through it so quickly that only one of the flames went out.

The glade lay before her, silent now and empty of dancers, but still drenched in moonlight so brilliant that it broke through even the heavy shadow of the oak tree and showed a motionless dark figure curled up there among the roots. The light was running like silver rain down the strings of the harp that rested against his shoulder.

"Fairy woman," he whispered, "fairy woman, fairy woman, is it a dancing night?"

Kate hardly heard the question. Her mind was so wholly taken up with its one overwhelming concern that she did not even feel any surprise at finding him there.

"What time is it?" she whispered back. There was such a hard knot in her throat that she could barely speak. "Randal, for the love of heaven, tell me what time it is."

"A little past ten," replied Randal obediently.

"*Ten?*"

More than a hour until midnight, almost two: and even one seemed at that moment like time everlasting. Her worst fear, the fear she had not dared to think of, had been that she was already too late. "You did say ten, Randal? Are you sure?"

"The big clock in the courtyard arch was striking ten when I went down the hill from the castle to here, and it's no more than a mile away."

"The castle? You've been at the castle tonight?" Then with an effort Kate remembered that she must keep her voice quiet and easy, not to confuse him. "Is Sir Geoffrey there, Randal? Did you give my letter to Sir Geoffrey?"

"What letter, fairy woman?"

Quiet; *quiet.* "I'm not a fairy woman, Randal," she said quietly. "Don't you remember me? Kate Sutton? Mistress Katherine?"

"Why have you changed yourself into a fairy woman, then?"

"I've not changed, not in myself, Randal. I haven't changed at all. Do try to remember. I gave you a letter for Sir Geoffrey, to put into his own hand. What did you do with it?"

Randal drew back a little. "Sir Geoffrey was angry with me." For the first time since she had met him, he sounded petulant and even sullen. "I did as you told me," he whimpered. "I carried it with me all summer long and never forgot it. You wanted him to come back by All Hallows' Eve. I counted up the days it would take him to ride here, counted them up carefully, to be sure I was doing just as you told me. *By* All Hallows' Eve was what you said."

"Yes," said Kate, dismayed, remembering how she had blundered over the message. "Yes, I did."

"Then why was he angry with me? There was time enough,

and more. We rode like the wind, and it was not my fault that he fell over the rope."

"What rope?"

"Someone had stretched a rope across the road in the forest, and it was so dark that the horse couldn't see it." (*Master John,* thought Kate instantly. The mean little trick to bring down any chance pilgrim or traveler who might try to reach the castle that night did not taste of the Fairy Folk.) "Sir Geoffrey was first in the line, and he fell striking his head. So I left his men trying to recover him, and ran away in the dark. I don't like it," said Randal simply, "when people are angry with me."

"But what became of Sir Geoffrey? Was he hurt? Hurt badly?"

"That's more than I know. I went down to the castle from there, to see if I could get a bit of bread, but they were all asleep, and then the moon made me remember that it might be a dancing night. *Is* it a dancing night?"

"No, I'm sorry," Kate murmured, her mind trying frantically to grapple with the new problem. A blow on the head could mean anything. Sir Geoffrey might have been stunned for a moment — or an hour. He might not come to himself for days. He might even (face it) be dead. Most certainly she would be a fool to count on his reaching the place in time. With a sigh she thrust the old dream away again. "Randal —" she began.

But Randal's wandering gaze had flitted off to something else. "There's blood on your hand," he announced. "Why is there blood on your hand?"

"I ran a sharp piece of steel into it," said Kate. "Randal, how did the lady claim Tam Lin in the ballad?"

"I can tend the hurt for you," said Randal proudly. "The Fairy Folk showed me how to do it one night when I'd stepped on a rusted nail." He rummaged in the pouch at his belt and brought out a little silk bag containing a jar of ointment and a crescent-shaped knife. These he laid out on a ledge by the waterfall with all the gravity of a child playing doctor to a doll.

Kate bit back a cry of impatience. If she snapped at him or did not let him have his own way he might think she was angry and run from her as he had run from Sir Geoffrey. "It's no great matter," she said. "My hand can wait."

Randal took the hand and frowned over it professionally by the light of the candles. "No," he said, "for this is the kind that festers the soonest if you let it close up on you. Hold still now," and bending back her fingers, he cut the wound open with two quick slashes, one across the other, and then told her to hold it under the running water of the fall to let it bleed out. The water was icy cold and numbing to the pain; after a moment Kate took a deep breath and asked for the second time:

"Randal, how did the lady claim Tam Lin in the ballad?"

Randal shook his head. *"Tam Lin's* not a song to sing so near the Queen's hall," he said reproachfully. "I told you that long ago, on the rock by the little stone house."

"You don't have to sing it to me," Kate implored him. "Only tell me what she did. Whisper if you like. Then nobody can hear us. Please, Randal. What did she *do?*"

Randal opened the jar of ointment and bent to salve Kate's hand, his head very close to hers. "Tam Lin told the lady to pull him down from the white horse and then hold fast to him," he answered hurriedly, under his breath. "A terrible hard thing to do."

"Is it so hard to pull a man down from a horse?" asked Kate, taken aback.

"Not if he wants to come. But then the Fairy Folk laid a spell on him to make her let him go."

"What spell?"

Randal's voice dropped even lower. "They changed his shape in her arms," he whispered. "Some say to a cold snake, and some to a burning fire, and some to a great bird, and some to all of them in turn; but still she held him fast, so in the end he came back to his own true shape and knew her face, and then the Fairy Folk had to set them free."

Kate's first impule was to dismiss the tale of the shape-changing as an invention of the ballad maker's; however, she had seen enough of the Lady's magic by now to feel sure it was at least based on a distorted account of something that had actually occurred. But — she told herself firmly — the poor lady in the ballad had not known that the Fairy Folk's magic was nothing but medicine or illusion, and she had been all alone. There was still one place where Kate could hope to find help.

"Randal," she said, "how do I get to the village from here?"

Randal had produced a roll of linen strips from his bag and was busily bandaging her hand. "You follow the little stream from the waterfall out of the forest until it runs into the river, and the river into the open land," he told her. "And put your candles out, or you'll have the woods on fire. I myself will come with you, to show you the way."

The bank of the little stream was very dark under the shadow of the interlaced branches, but beyond the forest the open vale with its scattering of trees looked almost day-clear. The moon, now completely full and even more glorious than it had been on the dancing night, was riding up the heavens through a whole attendance of stars, so bright that Kate could only hope fervently that nobody on the Hill was watching for strays on the road. With its crest of battlemented walls and towers shouldering the sky, the great mass of the Hill looked much larger than it usually did, larger than she remembered it, larger and more formidable the closer they came.

A light was burning in the gateway above them.

"Randal."

"Yes, Mistress Katherine?"

"Could a heavy man — or call it a line of heavy men, one at a time — get into the castle by your secret way over the wall behind the stables?"

"That's no way for a heavy man, Mistress Katherine. Only the cat or I could climb the stable roof."

They plodded on. Kate tried to quicken her pace a little, but the effort did nothing but show her how dangerously weary she was, too weary to move fast, and the slow walk down the long bright road seemed to go on forever. Somewhere along the way Randal had put a supporting hand under her arm, but she could not remember when he had done it. The castle kept growing larger and larger.

"Mistress Katherine."

"Yes, Randal?"

"Why don't you go up there, and not to the village?" Randal pointed to the light in the gateway. "Up there is where you belong."

"I want to go the village first."

"No, you don't. The village people are afraid of the castle folk. A little village boy threw a stone at me once."

"They won't throw stones now. I've friends in the village," said Kate, "and they'll know me."

"That they will not." Randal was certain. "*I* knew you'd changed into a fairy woman because of the way you carried yourself, but when they see you in the light, they'll take you for a bogle out of the woodlands and shut their doors in your face."

"But —" Kate began, and then hesitated. It had not until that moment occurred to her to think how she would look: blood-stained, disheveled, grotesquely hung about with animal skins, and shrilling at the doorsill on the Feast of the Dead.

"I can tell them who I am," she argued. "They'll believe me then. I'm sure they'll believe me."

"Not they. The air's full of ghosts and evil things walking the earth on All Hallows' Eve. You can beat on their doors and tell them who you are till it's morning, and nobody will listen to you."

"They *must* listen. I want the men to go up to the castle with me."

"The men from the village?" Randal turned at the foot of the path up the Hill to stare at her as if she were demented. "Up to the castle? On All Hallows' Eve?"

"They must go with me, Randal. They *must*, I tell you. We'll have to break down the gate. There's no other way to get in."

"Why don't you just walk in at the gate?" suggested Randal diffidently.

Kate's hard-held patience broke at last. "Because the porter locks and bars it the minute the sun goes down," she snapped at him.

"Not on All Hallows' Eve," Randal protested. "On All Hallows' Eve they leave every door in the house open, to let the dead pass through."

"Oh, Randal!" gasped Kate. It was true, of course; she ought to have known it would be true, only she had forgotten again. "Randal, I — but what of the porter? The porter's there. He'll be keeping a watch on it."

"The porter's asleep. He won't wake when you pass him. Sir Geoffrey's whole troop of armed men could ride straight in, the horses galloping, and there'd still be no waking him. He's too fast asleep."

"What do you mean, there'll be no waking him? Is he drunk?"

"No. He's asleep, I tell you. They're all asleep up there. Every door in the house is open, and they're all asleep by the hearth, every single one of them, like the enchanted folk in a tale my grandmother told me. You come and I'll show you." He tugged at her sleeve.

Still Kate held back. Randal's account of the sleeping castle did sound very much like a tale his grandmother had told him. Perhaps the tale had come back to his crazy mind because he had seen the porter dozing, or a couple of kitchen maids nodding by the fire. Perhaps it might be wiser at least to try the village first.

Beside her Randal's voice said suddenly:

"What's that?"

A crimson glow like a return of the sunset had appeared in the western sky. It pulsed for a moment above the battlements, and then rose higher and brighter, throwing the walls and roofs and turrets forward into darkness. It came from the far side of Lord Richard's tower.

"Somebody's lighted a fire up there," said Randal, mildly surprised. "I thought they were all asleep."

But Kate was no longer listening. He might have mistaken the time from the first, or the slow walk from the forest might have taken even longer than she had thought: it did not matter. All that mattered was that the time had gone by; there could be no weighing of the chances any longer. In one last rush of strength she had not known that she possessed, she snatched her sleeve from Randal's hand and went flying up the path to the gate.

The gate was open and the porter was sprawled out on the bench by the door of his hutch, breathing heavily, his empty

supper bowl and tankard next to his hand and his great raw-
boned dog curled at his feet. The man's breathing changed to
a gurgling snore as Kate ran past him. The dog did not even
stir in its sleep.

Beyond the gate, the bailey court lay empty and so still that
she could hear the laborious ticking from the castle clock in its
place on the wall above the archway to the inner court. The
numerals and hands of the clock were elaborately gilded, and
shone bravely under the red glowing light in the sky.

The shorter hand pointed to eleven, the longer one to six.
At the next tick, there came first the whirring sound and then
the loud clanging two strokes that marked the half-hour.

Kate's breath caught in her throat, a little whimpering sob.
It was not twelve of the clock yet. What she had seen was only
the first lighting of the fire.

Randal had taken the porter by the shoulder and was shaking
him, but his head only fell forward and flopped from side to
side like a rag puppet's. "I told you there'd be no waking them,"
he observed with calm satisfaction. "You see now how it is
with him?"

"Yes," said Kate. "I see now." Fool, fool, not to have seen
it as soon as Randal spoke of the enchanted sleep. Master John
himself had said that only one or two of the castle people knew
about the teind-paying. Why should he risk being found out
by any of the others, when all he had to do was ask the Lady
for a sleeping drench, and then give the household a barrel of
good ale to be merry with, because it was All Hallows' Eve?
They would wake in the morning, when the night was over and
nobody the wiser. She thought of the empty tankard by the
porter's hand. That would be Master John's doing, the miserable
little sneak-cup. The man had been drugged to keep him
quiet, and so had all the rest of them, by the sound of it.

"The rest of them are in the great hall by the fire," said Randal, running ahead of her up the terrace steps.

There they lay, gathered around the hearth of the great hall, the pages in one heap like a basket of kittens; Humphrey with a chambermaid's head against his shoulder; the cook holding a pan of apples, two of them peeled and the knife on the floor beside him just as it had slipped from his hand. In the place of honor, Sir Geoffrey's own armchair, close to the glowing embers, old Dorothy sat sleeping, with a child on her knee.

"Look!" said Randal, pleased. "That's the little yellow-haired girl who gave me the slipper on the dancing night."

Kate, with one foot already on the first step of the stair leading to the upper floor and the battlement walk, paused and looked back. Somewhere at the back of her mind she could still feel fear, and great pain, and a dreadful dragging weariness, but in her extremity she was hardly aware of them. The same unnatural clarity of thought and purpose she had felt once before in Gwenhyfara's cell had come back to her.

"Randal," she said.

"Yes, Mistress Katherine."

"Would you like to know how you can please Sir Geoffrey again?"

"Sir Geoffrey's angry with me," said Randal.

"But he won't be angry any longer, not if you do just as I say. Take the little yellow-haired girl in your arms and carry her down to the trees by the road at the foot of the castle hill. Can you hide?"

"The Queen of the Fairies herself couldn't find me if I chose to hide from her," said Randal.

"Then hide the child and yourself near the road; and when Sir Geoffrey comes —" she caught herself on the edge of another disastrous mistake, and added hastily, "Sir Geoffrey *or any of his own armed men,* give her to them and tell them to come straight out to the Standing Stone where the fire is. They'll be pleased with you then, very pleased. I promise you," and with a reassuring nod, she turned and ran on up the stairs.

That last race through the silent house went past like a dream. Nothing of it remained in her mind afterward but a row of doors standing open, and a glimpse of moonlight pouring in at the oriel windows of the long gallery and lying in lattices on the polished floor. Then the night air was cool against her face again, and she was out on the battlement walk that went along the top of the outer wall, pelting along the narrow way, past Lord Richard's tower, making for the steps that led down to the little circular courtyard with the archway out to the Standing Stone. From the wall above the archway she could see anything in the hidden valley just below if she had light enough. And there was certainly light enough. The glow in the sky was all around her as she dropped to her knees to get under the shelter of the parapet, and crept forward to look.

On the wide flat stretch of ground that lay between the Standing Stone and the castle wall an enormous fire was burning. It had evidently been soaked with sweet oils and spices before it was kindled, for it was already flaming sky high, and the air blowing toward her was full of a fragrance like church incense, but somehow different, shriller in the nostrils, sharp and wild and strange. Two dark forms, stable grooms by the look of them, were moving about tending the fire, and a little apart, standing quietly, his hands linked behind his back, one small fat figure with the gleam of a steward's chain around his neck.

The fire was so brilliant that when Kate turned her eyes away and tried to glance past it to the valley, she could at first see nothing at all. Then little by little, the tops of the cliffs appeared,

shimmering faintly in the moonlight above the dense shadows
that hid the deep floor of the gorge. From the shadows, rising
and falling through the perfumed wind and the hiss of the
flames, she heard the sound of voices in the distance. They
were singing together, a slow, sad, heavy chant. First one
point of light and then another broke the darkness, a long line
of lights like a skein of birds flying. Master John and the castle
people had drawn back against the wall.

One by one, pacing slowly, the Fairy Folk came up over the
brow of the steep drop to the gorge. They were dressed now in
dull winter-colored garments, mist gray, earth brown, fungus
yellow; and instead of candles they carried heavy torches that
flared and crackled sullenly on the night air. They were still
singing, but there were no words to that song, or else they were
not in a language Kate knew.

The procession ended with the torchbearers erect in two lines
curving like horns from either side of the Standing Stone.
Only the dark mouth of the path and the wide circle of turf
before the fire were left clear. The chanting voices lifted to a
wailing cry and then fell away into a dead silence.

In that silence a figure on a black horse emerged from the
darkness at the mouth of the path. It was the Guardian of the
Well. Even by the double light of the torches and the fire, he
was still hardly more than a vague, uncertain shape, a shadowy
head, a long bare bony arm that looked as though it were dripping with water. Nothing but the horse stood out clearly, and
even the horse did not rear and neigh in panic at the sight of
the flames, like a natural animal. Instead it walked forward,
step by step, to the center of the circle and stopped there. The
gray creature slipped down from its back and moved slowly
across the turf to a place at the left of the fire. By chance or
cunning, it was the one place where some trick of the shifting

light made it almost impossible to see him. The horse remained standing like a rock, exactly as he had left it.

The Fairy Folk gave another cry, and to the sound of their voices a second rider appeared at the mouth of the path. This time the horse was brown, a little smaller than the first one, lighter and more finely made. The figure on its back could not be seen at all. It was covered with a brown veil that hung from head to foot, hiding it completely, and it was only when the fairy women sank down one by one into the Queen's bow as she passed them that Kate knew who she was.

The brown horse came forward and stood still beside the black one. The Lady dismounted and in her turn moved slowly across the turf to a place at the right of the fire, opposite the Guardian of the Well.

The castle people were moving too, walking into the center of the circle, the two grooms first and Master John behind them. The grooms took the horses' bridles and led them off through the archway into the courtyard, Master John following them demurely, very much as Kate had seen him follow the serving men out of the great hall a hundred times when his duties for the night were over. The sound of the horses' feet came up from the courtyard, moving away, faster and faster, as if both man and beast were trying to get under cover as quickly as they could. The Fairy Folk were already closing in to fill the break in the circle where the castle people had stood against the wall. The chant rose again, louder now, and somehow different: fierce, triumphant, and imperative, like a call or a summons.

And as if in answer, a third rider on a white horse came up over the brow of the hill into the dark gap at the entrance to the path.

He paused there for an instant, very clear against the shadows of the valley beyond, for everything about him caught and

held the light. His whole head was covered with a golden
mask like a helmet which hid it completely. But whoever had
made the thing had evidently seen Christopher, for the golden
hair and the rigidly set, beautiful face might have been his own
except for the dark empty holes where the eyes and the mouth
ought to have been. The light gleamed on the helmet, and
shone over his short golden tunic, and was thrown back glittering
from the golden armlet on his left wrist and the wide flat collar of
golden links studded with great crimson jewels that lay around
his shoulders. Even the hoofs of the white horse glinted faintly,
as though they had been shod with silver.

Then the rider touched the horse's side with the heel of his
golden sandal and came riding deliberately down into the ring.

Christopher had once warned Kate that the Fairy Folk believed that he had done with life already, and were training him
to will and accept his own death; but what she had thought this
meant was some enchantment of the sort she had seen at the
Holy Well, that would turn him into a mindless clockwork
horror again. Yet what she saw now was in its own way even
more terrifying. His face was hidden, but in the lift of his head,
in the touch of his hands on the reins, in every line of his body,
there was the same remoteness that she had heard in his voice on
the worst of his nights. The circle of the Fairy Folk with their
torches might have been so many of the distant stars for all the
heed he paid to them. Kate had a sudden strange feeling that
even if she herself stood up and screamed out to him, her voice
would come to him only as a faint meaningless sound, too far
away for him to hear it.

The white horse turned in the center of the circle and stood
still as the others had done, facing the fire. The cries of the
Fairy Folk had died down again into a low murmuring chant,
hardly louder than the sound of the flames. Then, cutting

through their formless whispering, a voice rose out of the shifting shadows to the left of the fire. It was soft, almost gentle, but curiously clear; and as it spoke Kate understood at last what Christopher had been asking God for the strength to endure on the night when she had come upon him praying in the darkness.

"Teind-payer," it said. "Teind-payer, teind-payer, will you be nothing?"

Kate saw the golden mask turn in the direction of the voice. The Lady had told her that "only the Guardian of the Well could speak to him now" — and in this, as in other matters, she seemed to have been telling the exact truth, for evidently the voice had reached him; he heard it; he was listening. Then, with the same clarity, as if he were pronouncing the words of some ritual, he answered:

"I will be nothing."

"Will you keep the life that is in you, or will you be nothing?"

"I will be nothing."

"Not yet," said the voice, "Think. Will you keep the strength of your body, the force of your will, the power of your mind, the courage of your heart, or will you give them up to us, and be nothing?"

"I will be nothing."

"Not yet," said the voice. "Think again. Are you free to be nothing? To whom are you bound? Have you a father?"

"No," said Christopher.

"Have you a mother?"

"No," said Christopher.

"Have you a child?"

"No," said Christopher.

"Is there a woman you love?"

"No," said Christopher.

"What holds you back, then?"

Christopher's hand, with the heavy gold armlet on the wrist, went up and touched the jeweled links of the collar around his neck. The torchlight and the firelight and the moonlight ran in a shining wave over the gold and crimson splendor as he moved.

"How can I be nothing," he asked, "with all this upon me?"

"Throw them away, then," said the voice. "Jingle and trumpery: why should they trouble you? Such gauds are valueless. Throw them away."

The last thing Kate saw before she turned and ran down the steps to the courtyard was Christopher slowly drawing the armlet from his wrist. She moved so fast that when she reached the archway it was still in his hand.

The gray creature's voice rose again out of the shadows before he could let it drop.

"Not yet," said the voice. "You have all heard the teind-payer speak for himself. Does anyone here speak for the teind-payer?"

The voice paused; and then, as if with one accord, the Fairy Folk turned their heads away from the golden rider and stood gazing at the ground.

"Once more," said the voice, "does anyone here speak for the teind-payer?"

There was no sound or movement. The whole circle was completely still. Kate, shivering like a puppy in the shadows of the archway, found herself listening frantically for some-thing — anything — to break the stillness: armed men galloping in at the gate, Sir Geoffrey, her father, Master Roger, the Lady Elizabeth —

"Once more, and for the last time," said the voice, "does any-one here speak for the teind-payer?"

Kate thrust her way between two of the torchbearers and ran across the ring to the white horse's side, facing the gray creature, the Lady, and the fire.

"Well, yes," she stammered uncertainly, and braced herself for what was coming.

But nothing came. Nobody cried out in rage or astonishment, nobody so much as turned to look at her. The gray creature remained half lost in the shadows, the Lady hidden behind her veil, the Fairy Folk gazing at the ground. Christopher did not appear to know that she was even there. He went on holding the armlet in his hand, with the golden mask looking away from her, at the fire; and as for pulling him down from the horse, one glance was enough to show her that she might as well try to pull down an equestrian statue.

"Christopher," she said in a desperate rush. "Christopher, listen. Cecily's safe. She's been taken away out of the house and hidden. You don't have to go on with this foolishness."

Only the gray creature answered, and then it was not to Kate that it spoke.

"Teind-payer, teind-payer, do not deceive yourself," the voice murmured. It was not speaking ceremonially now, like a priest, but kindly, persuasively, like an old wise man, a counselor. "Do not listen, do not look aside to the right or the left, fix your mind on what you have chosen, remember the warnings. The King of the land in the old days had many trials to pass through before his death-time was over; and one of them may have been a test of his will, to see if his courage and strength would fail him at the last. I cannot tell you more of this — it is not allowed — but I am permitted to ask you questions. What did you hear? A voice trying to turn you from your purpose? Whose voice was it? A friend's? Someone you know perhaps? Someone you trust? But can you be certain — *certain* — whose voice it was? Our kind are all shape-changers, and they can take on any voice or appearance they please. Can you —"

Questions, thought Kate savagely; why even now couldn't the thing tell a plain lie, like an honest man?

"Christopher, if you think I'm not —" she began indignantly, but the gray creature's voice closed over hers before she could finish the sentence. Whatever strange custom they were following, it evidently obliged the contestants to speak in turn, each waiting for the other; and her turn had gone by.

"Can you even be certain that it was a real voice you heard, and not your own fear of the fire speaking? There are many voices in the mind, and the loudest may be no more than an illusion born of a wish or a fear. You need not tell me what it said to you: I know. How many times have you longed with all your soul that you could hear the child was safe, out of the house, hidden away — and you free to break through the mesh that held you, clear yourself a path to the gate, and be gone? How often have you dreamed that it was true, and then awakened to find it was only a dream? But what you see before you now is not a dream. You are awake. You can ride that horse out of the circle this moment, if you choose, and not one of us will lift a finger to stop you from going. But will you go? Fail your brother again, and go? Leave the child behind to pay the teind in your place, and go? Live with that knowledge for the rest of your life? Or will you hold to your purpose, and come?"

The long bony arm shot out in a curious undulating gesture towards the fire. And as if at some signal, the Fairy Folk lifted their own arms and made the same gesture, the flames of their torches pouring and curving on the air between them. Softly at first and then harder, their feet began to beat the ground; the torches dipped and curved again; the whole circle was dancing. Not wildly and joyfully, as they had around the oak tree, but with a fierce deliberate intensity, the torches making patterns on the air that opened and drew together and opened again, faster and faster, in a curling net of fire that caught at the heart and pulled it irresistibly towards the calling voice. Even Kate found that she had, without knowing it, taken a step in the direction of the fire — and she had not spent a nine weeks' death-time listening to that voice and schooling herself to answer the call when it came.

"Come," said the voice.

But Kate, looking up at Christopher in an agony of fear, saw that for that one moment at least she had reached and held him. He was still silent, turned away from her, gazing at the fire; the golden mask was still as blank as ever; and with his left hand he was still trying to draw the armlet out of his right. But apart from that his whole body was motionless, as rigid as if it were locked in the grip of two equal and opposing forces, contending together, neither able to break free of the other. Nor was there now anything remote or passive in that quiet. The right hand was clenched so hard over the armlet that she could see the heavy metal twisting under the strain.

"Christopher, Christopher, be still," she implored him. "That's all you have to do — be still a little longer; keep yourself from moving. It's almost over. Sir Geoffrey's coming. He's on the road now. Don't you remember? Randal took him the word weeks ago, and he knows, and he's coming."

The gray creature lifted its shadowy head a fraction, and the dance stopped.

"Weeks ago?" murmured the voice. "Why is he not here, then? Ask yourself, teind-payer. Do you in your heart of hearts believe that he will come? Why should he? Has he ever truly cared for you? Why should he? Who killed his mother?

Who wrecked the life of his father? Who hated his wife? Who lost his daughter? When have you ever — until now — brought anything to anyone you love except heartbreak and shame? How do you know but that if you go on you may not do it again? One act now, and you are free forever. Why not? What have you to live for? What have you —"

As it spoke, the voices of the Fairy Folk began to rise again, this time not in a cry or a chant, but in one low, sustained, unbearable moan that ran, crawling cold as a snake, through every nerve of Kate's body. The sound mingled with the words of the gray creature, blurring and distorting them, so that for one moment Kate thought first that they were coming from somewhere deep in her own body, and then that it was some other voice speaking — her mother's voice: "Go away, child: I can't bear the sight of you"; her old nurse's voice: "There, there, Mistress Katherine, we can't all be as pretty and loving as your sister"; even Alicia's voice crying sweetly: "O Kate, Kate, I do wish you were like me! Truly I do!" The next moment all the sounds had faded and were lost in a voiceless aching misery that came down on her spirit like the insufferable sense of the earth and the stone pressing about her at an attack of the weight — and then in a rush of shame her thoughts came back to Christopher. If it could do this to her, what was it doing to him?

"And you can be free of the shame and the fear," the gray creature was repeating softly. "One act, and you are free of them, free of them forever. More: you will be honored in your death; it will be a proof of your worth that even your brother will be compelled to understand. What else have you to live for? Ask yourself, teind-payer. What else have you to live for?"

"The manor," said Kate.

"Manor?" For the first time, the voice hesitated, fumbling

over the word, and it came to Kate with a strange quick pride that whatever else Christopher might have told it, he had not told it about the manor.

"Yes, the manor," she hurried on. "And the village, and the house, and the ditching and the drainage, and the orchard and the dairy." She was throwing in everything she could think of, frantically, as she might have tried to fill up a broken dike with the first stones that came to her hand. "You never did decide where you wanted to build the new dairy."

But the gray creature had instantly recovered from its slip.

"Manor?" said the voice smoothly. "You? What sort of end is that for a man? To pass your life digging last autumn's rot into the dirt so that this autumn's rot may be dug into it again next spring? Breed animals to use and to kill? Breed like an animal yourself, and rear sons for stronger men to use and kill in their turn? Build a house that may be swept away into ruin by one storm of wind or one lighted candle in the hand of a fool? Tend and guard those who will give you no thanks for it? And all this while with no more to hope for than that at the last you may die of old age, a witless bag of bones drooling on a feather bed? No, Young Lord. That will do well enough for those who are born to be servants and scrubbers. But with some men it is otherwise. They are born great, and if their greatness cannot show itself in their lives because of some curse or affliction, it may yet be made plain in their death. Why else did your poets make the tale of the phoenix, who among all the birds is the only divine, if not because it alone will plunge gloriously into a holy fire and burn its own mortality away to nothing?"

The voice had changed again. It was lifting, quickening, breaking into a great triumphant cry that went soaring up and up, so high that for an instant it almost seemed to Kate that something had flashed past her, a golden splendor, forever beyond her reach.

"And why else, when the King of the land paid the teind in the old days, did the people lead him to this place in glory, adorned with gold and precious things like one of the gods, if not to honor and praise him because he alone had the greatness of spirit to spurn this earth out from under his feet, and be free of it like the god he looked?"

"*God?*" said Kate, revolted. "You don't look like any god to *me*, Christopher Heron! You look like a piece of gilded gingerbread, that's what you look like, one of those cakes they sell at a fair!"

Christopher stiffened. "That's a fine thing to say to the King of the land at his death-time," he retorted. "Nobody but *you* would think of such a — O Lord!" She heard him gasp as if she had struck him; then with a sudden movement he thrust the golden mask back from his face, and the white horse reared up, neighing indignantly, as it was wrenched around on a savage rein. His own yellow hair, matted and dark with sweat, lay plastered over his forehead, and he was breathing in great pants, like someone coming up out of deep water; but the eyes he turned on her were alive and furious. "O Lord!" he said again. "It *was* you! I might have known it! What in the name of all the fiends are you doing here? Run! — Kate, you fool! you pest! you abominable meddling little pumpkinhead! Run, I tell you! I'll hold them off until you get away."

Any reply that Kate might have made was lost in a burst of cries from the Fairy Folk, cries of rage and despair and something that sounded dreadfully like disappointed hunger. The circle broke into a wild confusion of sound and movement. The air was torn with shouts and wheeling lights and high sharp screams like the mewing of seagulls as the Fairy Folk flung down their torches and went flying down the dark gorge to the Holy Well. The wide flat stretch of grass before the fire was littered with torches, burning where they lay. And from somewhere in the distance over the wall there rose a new sound — the far clear note of a horn.

"That'll be Geoffrey." Christopher mopped his wet forehead with his arm and grinned at her shakily. "Shall we go tell him he's come too late for the show? Quick, Kate! Don't stand there gaping like an idiot! I have to get you out of here." He let the battered armlet fall to the grass and reached down an imperative hand to her. "Up, lady! I'm going to carry you off on my saddlebow."

But Kate, to her own astonishment, found that her knees were buckling under her and all the fiery torches on the ground were rushing together and roaring up into darkness. Christopher, flinging himself down from the white horse's back, was only just in time to catch her as she fell.

XIII ❧
The Changeling

Kate was awakened by a light shining in her face. She murmured sleepily, "Yes, Gwenhyfara," and opened her eyes.

She was lying on the coverlet of a great carved bed, its four towering posts hung about with embroidered curtains which had been drawn to darken the room. But somewhere beyond them the sun was out, and a long ray was slanting in through a narrow gap where they did not quite meet on one side of the bed. She thought, "I'm dreaming," then, reaching dazedly for the pull-ring of the curtains, "No, the other was a dream; it was all only a dream," and fell back with a little cry as a sudden jag of pain ran through her left hand.

The hand was only a paw of bandages, with the pain a jangling throb in the heart of it. The other hand was chapped and reddened from weeks of scrubbing, the knuckles swollen and callouses on the palm. It was covered with spots of blood and candle wax, streaks of grime, soot, and scratches where the twigs along the path had caught at her. The leather sleeve falling away from the wrist was stained and worn, the edge of the fur lining almost rubbed away. But through the gap in the curtains she could see the familiar windows of her own room, a fire dancing on the hearth, and an old woman bent over the fire, stirring something in a bright copper pan.

"Ah, Mistress Katherine!" She turned around to smile at

Kate cozily. "I thought you were never going to waken. Sir Geoffrey says you'd best keep to your room and not trouble your mind with questions today. So you drink what I've made you like a good girl, it's chicken broth with an egg beaten up in it, and then I'll put you properly to bed." She poured the contents of the pan into a silver porringer, and advanced on Kate with a tray.

"Dorothy!" Kate sat up. "Dorothy, what's happened? Is Cecily safe? Where's Christopher? Did they catch the Fairy Folk? And the Lady? Whatever became of the Lady?"

Dorothy sniffed. "I'm sure I don't know what you mean, Mistress Katherine," she retorted. "What Lady? You're the only Lady we have now."

"You know well enough," said Kate indignantly. "The Lady who rules over the Fairy Folk. Those in the Well. The People of the Hill. Where do you think I've been all this while?"

"Master John said you'd run away with someone."

"The Young Lord?"

"Someone," said Dorothy, avoiding Kate's eye. "I believed what Master John told me. Sir Geoffrey left the house in his charge. Didn't I have to believe what Master John told me?"

"And where's Master John now?"

"You'll have to ask Sir Geoffrey that. He must have gone away in the night. I was asleep myself; I don't know. I was never one to pry and meddle with the business of the great folk; and besides —" her voice dropped and she looked directly at Kate for the first time. "I was so afraid, Mistress Katherine," she whispered. "We were all of us so dreadfully afraid of them."

Kate thought of Master John's fat white fingers sinking into the flesh of Dorothy's arm, and his story of the prying servant who had gone to walk in the Elvenwood and never come out again.

"Then let's not speak any further of it." She finished the last of the broth and swung her legs over the side of the bed. "Are my clothes still in the garderobe, Dorothy? I want to get up."

Dorothy was so relieved that she went off to fetch the clothes without a murmur and stayed to help Kate put them on. Kate was glad of the help: she could not arrange her hair one-handed, and dressing was no longer a matter of slipping her arms into the sleeves of a loose robe and clasping the belt. She had almost forgotten how heavy and elaborate the dress of the world was: linen shift, under petticoat, upper petticoat, kirtle, gown — merciful heavens, what a welter of skirts! — the bodice fenced with whalebone, the starched discomfort of the collar. Nor did anything really fit her any longer. The coif and hood seemed to have become too small for her hair, the starched collar too large for her neck; the bodice was too tight under her arms and fell away from the new slenderness of her waist, dragging the skirts down with it into ungainly swathes, as if the whole dress had been meant for an entirely different person. Even the face in the mirror did not look like the one she remembered.

"You've changed, Mistress Katherine, that's what it is," Dorothy pointed out, doing what she could with pins. "No, don't try to hitch that up through the girdle; you're only making it worse. All your dresses will have to be taken apart and made over, and that's the brief and the long of it."

"All of them?" said Kate in dismay, and glanced involuntarily at her old scrubbing robe, lying like a heap of discarded skins on the floor.

"Every single one of them," said Dorothy firmly. "And don't you go looking at that nasty heathen rubbish, Mistress Katherine, it's not fit to be worn. Just you stand still there like a good girl while I fetch you my sewing basket."

"Later," said Kate. She could see that if she did not put her foot down at once she would soon be celebrating her return to the world by "standing still there" all the long afternoon while Dorothy clucked around her with the sewing basket. "Later," she repeated. "I have to go and speak with Sir Geoffrey now. Where is he?"

"Sir Geoffrey said you were to keep to your room and not trouble your mind today."

"There's something I want to ask him. It's great folks' business," Kate added wickedly, "the kind you say that you never want to pry or meddle in. Where is he?"

"I don't know, Mistress Katherine. The last time I saw him he was out looking at the water."

"What water?"

"He said you weren't to be troubled about it until you'd rested."

"Was Christopher with him?"

"The Young Lord? Oh no, Mistress Katherine, how could he be, seeing that he's — but you're not to trouble your mind about him either, Sir Geoffrey says, and it won't take me but a minute to fetch the basket. No, don't, Mistress Katherine, do be quiet, you mustn't —"

She followed Kate to the door and out into the hall, still expostulating, just as Sir Geoffrey emerged from the long gallery and came striding towards them. He was frowning as if something perplexed or troubled him, and the narrow white bandage around his head made him look even grimmer than he usually did.

"Be off with you, Dorothy," he said briefly. "Mistress Katherine, I thought you were keeping to your room today. Don't you ever do as you're told?"

Dorothy vanished around the corner in a flicker of skirts, and Kate ran to him.

"Sir Geoffrey, where's Christopher?" she demanded.

"Gone," said Sir Geoffrey.

"Gone where?"

"Away. He left very early this morning, as soon as it was light."

"But he couldn't have — he can't be —" Kate protested. "Why? Why should he go away now?"

"Because I sent him."

"But you can't have! Not now! Surely not now, after all he's — you haven't forgiven him? Even now?"

Sir Geoffrey stood regarding her.

"No, I haven't forgiven him," he replied gravely. "But I asked him to forgive me." The old smile flashed up into his eyes; he put both his hands on Kate's shoulders and very gently shook her. "So you can take that look off your face, and don't let me see it again! I said there was no need for you to trouble your mind about him any longer, didn't I? He's only gone to London to take Cecily to live with her aunt Jennifer, as she ought to have done a year ago, God pardon me for a fool! But yes, I did send him away and I sent Cecily away, and believe me, my girl, if it weren't for the Queen's own strict command, there's nothing I'd sooner do than send you off straight down the road after them."

"But why? I mean, what's wrong? Surely, now that you and your men are here, there's no reason —"

"Oh, but there is," Sir Geoffrey interrupted her, "and a good reason too. Come along with me, and I'll show you." He tucked Kate's hand into his arm and drew her with him back into the long gallery and out onto the battlement walk. "I didn't want to tell you, at least not until you were rested, but —" He checked his long stride as they passed out of the shadow of Lord Richard's tower and stood for a moment looking down at her face in the sunlight. "Saints above, how you've changed, lass!" he said abruptly. "What in the world did they do to you?"

"It's nothing; none of my clothes fit, that's all," Kate answered, flushing. "Sir Geoffrey, will you *please* tell me —"

"I want you to see something first." He stopped on the walk above the archway, almost where she herself had stood the night before, and pointed over the parapet.

"There," he said.

The fallen torches had been carried away, and all traces of the great fire had vanished. The grass turfs had been neatly laid in again over the burnt earth and the ashes, so that the wide flat stretch of rough lawn between the Standing Stone and the castle wall looked very much as it always had. Beyond the Standing Stone she could see the sharp drop to the floor of the little valley, the great boulders and the rocks below, the thread of a path winding among the litter of stone as far as the last dip down to the cave and the Holy Well — but beyond that last dip the path disappeared. She could make out nothing but a bright line along the ground between the cliffs, shining in the afternoon sun, and glimmering a little as if it were very faintly moving.

"Water coming up out of the Holy Well," said Sir Geoffrey's voice beside her. "They must have broken some sort of dam or known how to block the river so as to flood the caves and the valley if anyone tried to break in, and they had almost an hour to do it. First I was delayed at the foot of the road to the gate when Randal walked out of the trees with Cecily — wanting to know if I was pleased with him now, the poor loon! — and meanwhile Christopher was in the house carrying you up to your bed and finding himself some armor and weapons. Then when we came together at last we began by looking for the secret passage from Lord Richard's tower and searching the whole place for

Master John — no, we didn't find him; he must have left by
some bolt hole of his own as soon as he heard my horn and
knew the game was over. We *did* find the stairs in the keep,
but they were flooded already; and by the time we came to the
valley the water was pouring out of the Well cave in torrents
and no one could go that way. Christopher thinks they must
have escaped from the Hill through some other tunnel and got
away into the Elvenwood. But for all I know they're still lurking
about there — and that's why I made him take Cecily off to
London with a good strong escort so early this morning, and
why I came within an inch of sending you with them, Queen or
no." He stood looking over the parapet with the troubled frown
in his eyes again. "Who's to say what the creatures will do next?
They may even feel they've some sort of right to kill the child
or my brother."

Kate shook her head. "No, not now," she said. "I know them.
They won't touch Cecily now because Christopher paid the teind
for her, and they won't touch Christopher because someone was
able to lay claim to him. They won't touch anybody. The Lady
did say that she'd kill the mortal prisoners if the Hill were
attacked, but once they're beaten and driven out of a holy place
all they can do is wander away and never come back to it.
Gwenhyfara told me so herself. They're probably miles from
here by now, looking like gypsies or tinkers, and if they ever meet
again, it will only be for a dancing night."

"You're sure of that?" Sir Geoffrey was still frowning. "God
knows there's nothing I'd sooner do than let them go. The last
thing I want is to raise a stinking scandal about my wife's family
and send the whole countryside off in a state of frenzy hunting
for witches and heretics. Nine-tenths of the folk they'd rake in
and ruin would be real tinkers, or real gypsies, or the miserable
castle people. But what am I to do? We have to catch the

creatures. Otherwise, they'll be stealing some other child the next time they need a human sacrifice, and —"

"They won't, they won't," Kate insisted. "They can't form a circle of power or pay the teind in any holy hill that's been desecrated or broken, and the Lady said this was the only place left in all England where it could still be done. There won't be any more teinds now, ever again. They're finished."

"You're *sure* of that?"

"I'm sure of it," Kate replied steadily.

"Very well then," said Sir Geoffrey, and drew a breath so long that he might have been holding it for her answer. "Let them go."

"But can you?" asked Kate, frowning a little in her turn. "I mean, *can* you keep it a secret? How about your men? They must know what happened here last night. Can you trust them not to tell about it?"

"No," said Sir Geoffrey. "But there's not much they can tell. Remember that we came too late for the teind-paying, and they didn't see you or Christopher in those outlandish gauds you were wearing. All they saw was the castle people sleeping it off after a Hallow'een bonfire and a drinking party."

"Then why did you ride back so fast when you got my letter? Who's had Cecily all this time? Why aren't you still angry with Christopher? And they must have seen you were hunting for someone when you searched the house and the valley."

Sir Geoffrey laughed suddenly as she had sometimes heard his brother do when the strain broke. "My men and I were hunting for Master John," he said calmly. "And if they end by thinking it was all a plot of his to keep control of the whole estate by making trouble between the new masters, where's the harm? That was a good story he told you about someone stealing the child and then running away rather than face me when someone else found out the truth and sent me word to ride back. It's such a good story that it seems a pity to waste it — especially as it happens to be perfectly true. We'll only have to change a few of the names."

"And do you think the castle people will believe you?"

"The castle people have had a deal of practice in conniving at whatever belief would do them the most good," said Sir Geoffrey dryly. "All they'll want now is to forget they ever heard of Those in the Well. Though to speak justly, I think they really were terrified of the creatures, and won't shed any tears because they've lost your Lady and her Fairy Folk. If you ask me, nobody's going to miss them."

Kate nodded, remembering what Dorothy had said to her. Sir Geoffrey was right, she reflected: nobody was going to miss the Lady or the Fairy Folk, unless — it was a curious notion — unless she herself did. She put the thought away from her, and came back to the point.

"But there's bound to be *some* talk," she observed doubtfully.

"There's been talk about the Perilous Gard for hundreds of years," said Sir Geoffrey. "A little more won't hurt us. In a month or two, Randal will be making it all into a ballad, and after a while nobody will believe that it was ever anything more than a tale by the fire."

The long bright line across the end of the valley was widening now as the water continued to rise and advance. Kate thought that it must be well beyond the leper's hut already, and the flat rock where she had eaten dry bread with Christopher would soon be gone too.

"Nothing was carried up out of the caverns on the water?" she asked Sir Geoffrey. "Some of them may have been killed or drowned trying to escape."

"No, nothing at all," said Sir Geoffrey. "That's to say, it

wasn't a *body*, exactly. We did find a mass of old bones floating outside the Well cave, wrapped in some kind of thin gray raggedy stuff that was holding them together; but whatever it was had been dead a long time. The men didn't want to touch it, and I can't blame them; it wasn't a pretty sight. In the end we buried it in the ashes down there at the foot of the Standing Stone before we laid the turfs back, to get it out of the — Kate! Hold up, lass! What's the matter? You're as white as a ghost."

"It's nothing." Kate pulled her wits together. "Only, I — that thing you found — you're sure it *was* dead? It had been dead for a long time?"

"Lord, yes!" said Sir Geoffrey. "Didn't you hear me? There was nothing left of it but —"

He stopped short as a thin wailing cry rose from the archway at the foot of the wall beneath them. It was a cry of such pain and despair that even Sir Geoffrey stiffened, and Kate turned whiter still.

"What is it?" she gasped. "What's that noise?"

"I don't know," said Sir Geoffrey, in his grimmest voice. "But I'm afraid it's another one."

"Another *what?*"

"I was wrong when I told you that nobody was going to miss them."

The old white-haired pilgrim that Kate had once seen returning from the Holy Well had come back again. As they leaned over to look, they saw him pull himself away from his serving man's arm and plunge down the path to the valley at a hobbling run, rushing to and fro distractedly as he ran, and making sudden darts at the water, like a lost dog in front of an empty house.

"That's the second since this morning," said Sir Geoffrey. "The first one — but never mind that now: I'd better go down and do what I can to keep him from breaking his neck. Get back to your room, Kate. You're shaken enough as it is. You don't want to see any more of this; it's as if they'd run mad."

But Kate only went as far as the door of the long gallery and stopped there, feeling that she could not bear to be shut up again just then, even in her own room. Instead she found a corner of the wall overlooking the courtyard where a stone seat had been built in the old days for a guard or a watchman. The seat was in the sun, sheltered from the wind, and the stone was warm where it reflected the light. The light was so strong that she was aware of it even when she closed her eyes and leaned her head back against the warmth of the stone, listening to the murmur of the wind and the slow tick of the castle clock from the courtyard as it measured the time of the world.

In the days that followed, she spent many hours sitting there in the sun or walking back and forth in the high clear air on the battlements. Sometimes she stood looking down at the inner courtyard and the workmen moving in and out of Lord Richard's tower; Sir Geoffrey was giving the grain to the village to replace the crop that had been destroyed in the storm, and there was to be a peal of bells for the church at last. Sometimes she went as far as the stretch of walk above the archway and looked down the valley towards the Holy Well. The flood had stopped rising when it reached the foot of the Standing Stone, and not even an occasional pilgrim was still coming to wander about on the shore. There was nothing to be seen in the whole valley but a lake of deep water, green where it lay under the shadow of the cliffs and blue where it reflected the color of the sky. It might have lain there in unbroken peace since the beginning of time.

Presently, little by little, the sharp images of the old pilgrim, the choked passages, and the floating mass of bones began to recede from her mind.

She was left very much to herself, for Christopher had not returned and Sir Geoffrey was taken up with the work of the estate, but in those days she did not feel a lack of company. She did not even want it. All she wanted was to rest, to be let alone, to walk in the air and the light, or to sit for hours watching the birds wheeling in the great space over her head. The wound in her hand had not festered, but the palm took a long time to heal, and it was even longer before she stopped dreaming at night of flooded caverns where the blind fish nosed in the darkness about the steps leading up to a stone chair, or where Joan and Betty and Marian still lay in their beds, drowned in their enchanted sleep. It was useless to hope that the Lady might have taken the mortal prisoners with her when she escaped. The Lady would not break her given word, and — what was it that the redheaded woman had said to her once? — "The Fairy Folk cannot be moved by pity because they have no hearts in their bodies."

The redheaded woman — her name proved to be Susan — was up at the Hall now with her little boy. There had been no way that Kate could tell her how much she owed to her gift of the cross, but she could at least find out what she wished for the most and try to give her that in return. What Susan wished for the most was very simple: the dream of her life was to learn fine sewing and move from the village to a great gentleman's household. She and Dorothy soon became mighty gossips, with many whispered secrets and interminable confidences as they sat by the fire making over Kate's clothes with their heads together, nodding wisely to one another. Kate did not ask what they were talking about.

The days passed and became weeks: two weeks — three weeks — four. The weather continued to be fair and remarkably mild for the month, one of those rare quiet seasons, the "Saint Luke's summer" that came like a blessing from time to time at the very end of autumn. It was not until almost the first of December that Kate awoke to find that the wind had veered north in the night and the sky was the color of iron.

"There's snow coming," said Sir Geoffrey at dinner that noon. "I knew this weather was too good to last. Christopher had better start back soon if he doesn't want to find the roads blocked."

"He's been gone a long while," said Kate. "I thought he was just taking Cecily to her Aunt Jennifer's."

"He may have business of his own in London. Who knows? Perhaps he's found a girl he fancies at last." Sir Geoffrey pushed back his plate and rose to his feet, smiling down at her. "Would you care to ride over to the Elvenwood with me, Kate? I want to mark some of the trees for felling."

"In the Elvenwood?" said Kate, almost sharply.

"Why not? We're likely to have a great need of ship timber in England if the Queen dies and the Lady Elizabeth isn't fool enough to marry King Philip. That oak in your glade by the waterfall would go near to making a ship by itself."

"Not the dancing oak?"

"It can dance on the waves," said Sir Geoffrey. "Come along, lass. We won't be more than an hour."

Kate shook her head. She was not superstitious, but she did not want to see the dancing oak marked for felling, and she did not think she would care to put to sea in any ship that was fashioned out of its timber. "I'll keep to the battlements," she said.

But on the battlements it had grown bitterly cold; the stone seat was icy to the touch, and the heavy gray clouds hung so low that they seemed no further off than a roof of moving rock. In the end, for the first time, she was glad to get back to the warmth and shelter of her room, even though Dorothy opened the door as she approached and said in her most old-nursely voice: "Come in, Mistress Katherine, and see what Susan and I have for you to try on."

"I tried on that dress this morning," said Kate. "And it doesn't need anything more done to it."

"Ah, but this isn't the same dress," said Dorothy coyly. "You come and see."

The dress lay spread in splendor on the coverlet of the bed. It was silk brocade, the most beautiful Kate had ever seen, all deep glowing bronze with a sheen of gold where the light caught it, woven in a pattern of birds and acanthus leaves. The bodice was cut square across the breast and closely fitted, but the skirt was wide, falling in folds from the narrow waist and opening like a flower over a petticoat of yellow satin. The brocade sleeves of the bodice were closely fitted too, but dropped away at the elbow into great bell shapes that were lined with golden brown marten fur, turned back and fastened with sapphire clasps to show the fur and big wrist-length undersleeves of the same yellow satin as the petticoat. There were sapphire pins to hold the little square black velvet hood to the hair, and a sapphire pendant on a thin fine gold chain for the throat.

Susan and Dorothy stood beaming delightedly at the look on Kate's face.

"It's from all of us, Mistress Katherine," said Susan. "Dorothy thought of it, and Sir Geoffrey gave us the sapphires for it, and —"

"Aren't you going to try it on, Mistress Katherine?" broke in Dorothy, almost weeping with excitement and self-importance. "No, don't you stir a finger; Susan and I will see to you . . . The brocade and the satin and the fur were laid by in a chest, and I said to Sir Geoffrey . . . Give me that comb . . . 'Sir Geoffrey,' I said to him, 'it's not for me to speak, but I can't bear the thought of all that lying there going to waste, and Mistress Katherine with nothing but done-over clothes to her name.' No, don't look in the mirror till we've finished. I made just such a dress for my own lady Anne years ago when she was a girl your age, and the sapphires are what she wore at her wedding . . . There, Susan! wasn't I right? The bronze color *was* the one for her hair, and the blue to bring out her eyes. Turn round now, Mistress Katherine, and see how it becomes you before you go show yourself to Sir Geoffrey."

Kate looked at the glowing figure reflected in the glass, and for the first time in her life, flushed with pleasure at what she saw.

"Where is he?" she asked a little shyly. "I thought he'd gone to the Elvenwood."

"No, he's back. Go down, Mistress Katherine: you've no cause to be shy of him or anyone else in the world now. Humphrey said he was working on the books in the evidence room."

But Sir Geoffrey had come out of the evidence room and was talking to somebody in the great hall. Kate could hear his deep voice below as she opened the upper door to the dais stair, and paused there, hesitating: it might be better to wait until he was alone. He was standing by the fire, and beside him was another man, a cloak flung back from his shoulders and a riding whip under one arm. He was a tall, stooping man, with a lean ironic face and brown hair that was thickly flecked with gray.

Kate gave one cry, and then — forgetting her dignity, Sir Geoffrey, the new dress, and everything else on earth — ran headlong down the stairs into his arms.

"Aren't you going to kneel properly to your father and ask him for his blessing?" demanded Sir Thomas Sutton, hugging her as if he could not let her go. "I've come to fetch you away, Kate. The Queen sent me for you."

"Not Queen Mary?"

"No," said Sir Thomas. "Queen Mary's been dead these two weeks and more, poor soul. It was the Lady Elizabeth. Where have your wits gone begging, child? Didn't she tell you that she'd send me for you as soon as she had the power?"

"I — I never thought she'd remember," Kate stammered. "A little word like that."

"It's my opinion that that young woman doesn't forget anything more than she chooses," retorted Sir Thomas dryly. "Yes, she remembered — and a pleasant journey it's been, too, with all the bells along the road ringing for our new Lady, and some of your old acquaintance for company." He nodded towards the oriel window that looked out on the terrace. "There they are now," he said.

Through the glass — the Wardens had never been ones to grudge the expense, and the glass was as clear as crystal — Kate saw Christopher at the foot of the terrace steps, very splendid in blue velvet, with his own riding whip under his arm. He was smiling, but not at her, and he was holding his hand out, but not to her. The girl beside him caught at the hand and came running recklessly up the steps, stumbling over the flagstones in her haste, laughing and waving and calling out as she ran.

"Kate!" she cried, bursting into the hall on a wave of cold air. "Oh Kate, Kate, Kate, isn't it wonderful? Aren't you surprised to see us? I made Christopher keep back on purpose to surprise you. Christopher likes planning surprises, don't you, Christopher? Did you miss me? Were you very unhappy without me? I was dreadfully unhappy without you. Darling, where did you get that *antiquated* dress? No one at the new court is wearing those sleeves any longer. Just let me take off this cloak and I'll show you. Oh, Sir Geoffrey — it is Sir Geoffrey, isn't it? I should have spoken to you first of all, shouldn't I? You must think I've no manners. It's only —" said Alicia, looking around her radiantly with tears in her golden eyes, "it's only that I'm so *happy*."

"And no wonder," said Sir Geoffrey, smiling down at her. "But won't you come to the fire now, Mistress Alicia — it is Mistress Alicia, isn't it? You must have frozen on the road."

"I *love* fires," said Alicia. "And," she added hopefully, "hot wine."

Within a matter of minutes — it was her great gift — she had them all gathered into the warmth and light of the hearth, Sir Geoffrey talking as easily as if he had known her all his life, Randal gazing at her wonderingly from his corner with songs in his eyes, Sir Thomas watching her with an amused quirk of his eyebrow, Christopher leaning over the back of her chair laughing and teasing her outrageously. She too had on a new dress: of cream-colored wool, embroidered all over with a wandering design of bright flowers and butterflies in fine crewel work. It had long tight sleeves that ended in puffs at the shoulders, and a small close ruff of lawn set high about the neck. On her head she wore a round hat of rose velvet, with a plume of feathers in the band.

"Everything's new at the court now," she told them, straightening the hat. "No more dark, heavy colors, no more of those mournful little hoods. No, Kate, don't go away to Father; come here and sit by me. I want to feel you close to me so I can feel sure it really *is* you, and I've got you back." She slipped her hand through Kate's arm and laughed a little uncertainly. "You — you've changed somehow. Christopher, what have you been doing to change her so?"

"Don't lay it on me," said Christopher. "I hardly know her myself."

"It's not the dress," persisted Alicia. "I can't tell what it is, exactly. But you know how bony and how stiff in the back you always used to be?"

"Yes," said Kate. She could feel herself stiffening again at Alicia's touch like a troll-woman turning to stone as the sun rose.

"And now, suddenly, you're — Kate! Oh Kate, darling!" Alicia broke off with a little cry. "Your hand! Your poor hand! What did you do to it?"

Kate tried to pull the hand away — she had fallen into the habit of carrying it half-closed at her side — but Alicia took it back and spread it open on her knee. The palm was slashed over in a ragged double cross-shaped scar, still red and angry, and puckered around the edges. "Will you have that all your life?" breathed Alicia, her eyes wide with pity and concern. "However did it happen, my precious?"

"I hurt it, and Randal had to cut it open for me."

Randal had been glancing from Kate to her sister and back again as if something puzzled or troubled him; but at these words the drift of his thoughts seemed to change. "I did it on All Hallows' Eve," he began proudly. "The night that the Fairy Folk —"

"Mistress Alicia." Sir Geoffrey took hold of the conversation and steered it away from the danger point with a firm hand. "Supper won't be ready until five o'clock and you've a long day's ride behind you. Let Kate take you up to her room to rest on her bed for an hour or two while I see to your father."

Alicia followed Kate obediently up the stairs. "I do like Sir Geoffrey," she remarked, walking into the room, which in some mysterious fashion immediately became her own. "But I like Christopher better. I like Christopher *very* much . . . Oh Kate, what a bed! It's like lying on a cloud."

"Do you want to sleep for a little? You must be tired. Was it bitterly cold on the road?"

"I don't know about that." Alicia ruffled her bright hair and giggled. "Christopher said I made it seem like summer."

"I can't imagine Christopher ever saying such a thing," said Kate, remembering some of the things he had said to her.

"He's always saying things like that. You know, pretty things. He said to me once that being with me was like being out in the sun and air again when you'd been shut up in a dark place or like feeling well again after you'd had a long illness. Was he ill, Kate? I thought he might have been."

"No. It was only a manner of speaking."

"That's what he said when I asked him, but I wanted to be sure. He was looking dreadfully thin and worn down at first when he came to stay with us in London."

"Did he stay with you in London? I thought he was going to his sister's house."

"He was at his sister's when the Queen died, but after I came home and he met me, Father asked him to stay with us, so that we could all become better acquainted. He'd gone to see Father in the first place to bring him news of you, but after he met me, it was just as if he were one of the family. He and I went for rides, and we sang together in the evenings, and he told me about the manor."

"He told you about the manor?"

"The manor he was buying," said Alicia. "You know."

"*Buying?*"

"Hadn't you heard? There was some old manor near Sir Geoffrey's house in Norfolk that he wanted, and he was buying it, so — oh, how silly of me! I forgot. We were keeping it a secret. He said I wasn't to tell you."

Kate was beginning to feel as though she were caught in a nightmare version of the old question-and-answer story: What happened while I was away, Tom? The dog died, master. How did the dog die, Tom? When your home burned down, master. How did my home catch on fire, Tom? One of the candles at your wife's funeral, master —

"But he can't have bought the manor," she protested. "Sir Geoffrey said that it would take a fortune to set it to rights, and Christopher hasn't any money to speak of."

"Oh, he does now," said Alicia blithely. "I thought surely you knew about that. Everyone at the court now is looking for precious stones to make New Year's gifts for the Lady Elizabeth at her coronation; and there was some gold collar or other set with rubies that — I don't know just how it came about, but Sir Geoffrey said it was only fair that Christopher should have it to buy the manor if he wanted to. Oh Kate, those rubies! They're *huge!* Christopher showed me one he was saving out for a betrothal ring to give — but that really *is* a secret, and I promised him faithfully not to say a single word until everything's settled." She leaned back against her pillows and yawned suddenly, like a sleepy kitten. "I'd like to tell you about the ring, truly I would, but I can't break a promise, can I? You'll be sure to waken me in time for supper?"

"Yes," said Kate.

Alicia smiled up at her. "Dear Kate," she murmured contentedly. "It is so good to have you back. Now that I've been with you for a little, you don't seem so changed as I thought you were."

Kate closed the door behind her and walked away without thinking or caring where she was going. What else was there for her to do? She could not scream. She could not throw herself into the Holy Well lake, as two of the pilgrims had tried to do when they first realized their loss. She could not drag her own sister out of the house and lock the door against her. Presently, she would have to go back to her room and waken Alicia in time for supper. She would have to watch Alicia and Christopher sitting together all the long evening and telling each other secrets. She would have to dance at Alicia's wedding and marvel at the ruby in her ring. She would have to visit Alicia at the manor and hear about the place that she and Christopher had chosen for the new dairy.

Somewhere near her she heard a voice singing, and became aware that she was once again on the dais stairs, looking down into the great hall. Her father and Sir Geoffrey and Christopher had gone, and there was no one left in the hall but Randal, who was still in the corner by the fire with his back to her, crooning to himself.

> *As they were walking upon the sea-brim,*
> *(Binoorie, O Binoorie!)*
> *The elder pushed the younger in,*
> *By the bonny mill dams of Binoorie.*
> *O sister, dear sister, reach me your hand,*
> *(Binoorie, O Binoorie!)*
> *And you shall have my house and land,*
> *By the bonny mill dams of Binoorie . . .*

Kate did not pause to ask Randal what had brought that particular ballad into his mind. She slipped past him softly, before he realized she was there, making for the door to the terrace and the open air beyond it.

Outside on the terrace the winter dusk had begun to close in.

There was still enough light to see by, but on that bitter day the castle people were all sheltering from the cold, and the courtyard was as empty and silent as a desert. The silence was so deep that she could even hear, very faintly, the sound of Randal's voice from the hall:

> O sister, dear sister, reach me your glove,
> (Binoorie, O Binoorie!)
> And you shall have my own true love,
> By the bonny mill dams of Binoorie

Then, cutting through the distant music, another voice behind her said imperatively:

"Girl!"

Kate turned as if at the flick of a knife and saw what might have been a shadow standing against the wall on the dark side of the oriel window.

"Who's there?" she cried. "Who is it?"

The shadow detached itself from the wall and took the shape of a slight dark woman dressed like a gypsy, with an old red cloak wrapped about her shoulders and a tattered scarf tied over her head. There were rings in her ears, and she was carrying a flat rush basket over one arm.

"Pretty lady," she said. The voice had dropped and changed into a curious singsong, half whining, half coaxing. "Pretty lady, pretty lady, will you buy some hazel nuts for your Christmas feast? Rare herbs to season your Christmas ale? Cross my palm with silver, and I'll tell you what fortune is laid up in the stars for you, pretty lady."

"Don't!" Kate interrupted her, fiercely. "Don't talk like that! Not to me! I can't bear it! What are you doing here? Get away quickly, before someone sees you!"

"And why should they not?" asked the voice. "A poor gypsy

woman selling herbs to the lady of the castle, the great lady, in her fine silken gown? Choice and rare herbs, my lady. Only a penny a bunch."

"But that cannot be what you came for," Kate insisted. "What *are* you doing here? I thought it was against the law of your kind to return to a holy place once you had left it, and how ever did you get in? The passages are all blocked by the floods."

"Have no fear," said the Lady in her own voice, with a fine edge of contempt to it. "The passages are still blocked. Did you think that I or any of my people would creep back to this house to rob or to murder you for what you have done in the past? If ever I avenge myself on you or the Young Lord, it will be after another fashion. I came by the secret way over the wall behind the stable that Randal found, and I will never take that way again. I cannot return to the holy place for more than this one hour, and even for this one hour the gods will ask a heavy price of me."

"Then why did you come at all?"

"I came because I had to speak with you," said the Lady. "And briefly, for my time grows short. Geoffrey Heron has been in the Elvenwood marking trees. I wish you to tell him that whatever else he cuts down, he is not to touch the dancing oak."

"I can ask him," said Kate, a little doubtfully. "But how can I keep him from doing as he chooses?"

"I think there is not much that Geoffrey Heron would deny you if you asked it of him," replied the Lady. "And since I cannot keep him from doing as he chooses, I must in my turn ask it of you." The words were very quiet, almost colorless, but Kate knew what it must be costing her to say them, and spoke quickly before she had to humble herself any further. It never occurred to her to refuse. She had taken too much away from the

Lady already. "I will ask it of him then," she said. "And gladly too."

"And what will you ask of me?"

"Ask?"

"In return," said the Lady. "I have never in my life taken something for nothing, after the way of your kind. I would not beg a favor or a boon even from the gods themselves, and least of all would I beg one from you. I asked you to speak for the life of the dancing oak because nothing else would save it, but do not deceive yourself. I am your enemy. I feel no kindness for you, and you are a fool if you feel any for me. I only want to pay you back — to the uttermost farthing, as the priests of your faith would say. You have given me the wish of my heart. Very well: suppose I give you yours?"

"You cannot know what mine is," said Kate, "and even if you did, you would not be able to give it to me."

"Our kind do not speak of what we do not know," said the Lady, unmoved. "When I came here searching for you, I stood by that window and watched you sitting by the hearth: you and the Young Lord and the girl in the embroidered dress. I could not hear what you said, but I saw her face when she looked at him, and your face when you looked at her, and his when he looked at you both. Will you let her take him from you? She is one of those who takes as she pleases, like the spring wind."

"She is my sister," said Kate, "and she has always taken as she pleases. But what am I to do? I cannot make her other than she is."

The Lady took a step forward, and put one hand into the basket on her arm.

"I would take her walking upon the sea-brim if I stood in your shoes," she observed softly. "But that would not give you the wish of your heart." She drew her hand from the basket again, and holding it out to Kate, very slowly opened the closed fingers. There was something dark lying on the whiteness of the palm — a little round dark thing like a dry and wizened berry.

"See to it that the Young Lord has wine again when you are all merry around the fire tonight," she said. "And then, at a time when he is looking up into your face, drop this secretly into his cup. I give you my word that it is not a noxious drug or a poison or any other unclean thing. But it is a very powerful charm, and the one he sees at that moment he will care for as he cares for no other woman. I cannot tell you how long the spell will hold — most love spells do not last forever — but it will surely last long enough to win him from your sister, and while it lasts he will be entirely your own. Put out your hand and take your payment from me."

She moved forward as she spoke, and Kate found herself retreating before her, backwards, one step, two steps, three, until she was brought up against the balustrade of the terrace. The Lady's hand was still stretched out to her, glimmering white like a moth in the dusk.

"Take it," said the Lady. "I tell you again: it will do him no harm. Do you doubt that I am speaking the truth?"

"No," said Kate.

"Do you think you can win him without it?"

"No," said Kate.

"Do you want your sister to have him?"

"No," said Kate.

"Will you take it, then? I cannot give it to you. You must take it from me."

"No," said Kate.

"What do you mean?" said the Lady, with the edge of contempt on her voice again. "And speak quickly, for my time is very short now. What are you afraid of? That the Young Lord may look down and catch you at it? Have no fear. The charm is only a small thing, easy to hide in those fine silken sleeves, and it will be lost in the wine soon enough. He will never know what you have done. No one will ever know."

"I am not afraid that he will catch me," said Kate.

"What else then? Who is to know?"

"Well," said Kate, almost apologetically, "I would."

"Then why," the Lady retorted, "have you been listening to me?"

Kate sighed. It was almost dark now, and she was very cold. The stiff rustling brocade of her gown felt as if it were made of ice.

"Because I am a fool," she said, "and my sister has had the better of me all her life. But do you think I learned nothing from the time I spent in your land, when you let me live as you do?"

"I thought you had gone back to the ways of your own kind."

"And so I have," said Kate; "but I am not Joan or Betty or Marian, and there are some things in which I would still choose to live as you do. I will take a payment from you gladly, if a payment will please you. But pay me another way."

The Lady closed her hand and let the basket slip away from her arm. She was now little more than a shadow, outlined against the faint light coming through the oriel window. In the dusk, it was impossible to see much except the mere shape of the dress, the cloak, the hair, and for that moment at least she looked like herself. She did not speak again. Very slowly, and with grave deliberation, she bent her head and sank down before Kate in the great bow that the women of her kind made to a Queen. Then she was gone.

Kate did not see her go because she was crying, as she had not cried since she was a small child. She did not know why she was crying, and she did not sob or shake or make a sound: only stood there with the heavy, unaccustomed tears thick and hot on her cheeks. Her mind seemed empty of everything but a confused sense of sorrow and pain, like the grief of a wound she would have to bear all her life.

It was not until the door of the hall opened behind her and the light streaming from the doorway filled the air with dancing points of fire that she even realized it had begun to snow. The flagstones were white already, and darting through the hot tears on her face and mingling with them were quick feathery touches of cold.

"Kate!" said Christopher. "Good Lord! What are you doing here?"

"Nothing," said Kate, turning her head away from the light. "Let me alone."

Christopher went on standing in the doorway.

"I told you the first time I met you that I didn't want you to die of a cold or an ague," he remarked. "Have you gone out of your mind? Come into the house before you freeze to a statue! I've been looking for you everywhere. I want to talk with you."

"No," said Kate. Christopher was the last person in the world she wanted to talk with at that moment; and after what she had just been through with Alicia and the Lady, only good breeding kept her from adding that she had had her bellyful of talking.

"You can go and talk with Alicia," she said. "It must be nearly time I went up to wake her."

"I've been talking with Alicia for the past two weeks, and your father and your mother and the whole skein of your other kin," said Christopher. "Now I want to talk to you, without your sister and my brother and Randal and your father all breathing down my neck. There's a good fire in the evidence room, and bolts on both the doors."

"I know that," retorted Kate waspishly. "Master John locked me up there."

"Master John is a man after my own heart," said Christopher. "What was it that he said to you on that occasion? That you could come or be carried? Well? Which is it going to be?"

Kate stalked into the evidence room ahead of him and knelt down to warm her hands by the armchair on the hearth. The snowflakes and the tears were already beginning to melt into ugly wet splotches all over the beautiful new dress; and she could hardly keep herself from saying to Christopher — most irrationally — "Now see what you've made me do!"

The evidence room was only dimly lighted by the fire and no longer quite so tidy as it had been in Master John's time, but it still looked very much the same: the big table covered with papers, the shelves, the account books, the new candles in the seven-branched holder on the mantelpiece. Christopher calmly bolted the other door and followed her over to the fire, stooping down to pick up a twig from the wood-basket.

"What do you want that for?" asked Kate hurriedly.

"Only to light the candles; it's very dark in here."

"I'd liefer have it dark, thank you."

Christopher threw away the twig and sat down on the floor at the other side of the hearth. "Very well then," he said amiably. "Now I come to think of it, I like the dark myself; it takes me back to the bad old days when we sat together like this under the Hill. And now suppose you tell me what the trouble is."

"Nothing."

"Don't speak that word," said Christopher. "For some reason I've taken a dislike to it. And don't try to cozen or deceive me! There's something you have on your mind. I can hear it in your voice. Do you think I could sit beside you and listen to your voice for as long as I did without coming to know it?"

Kate was startled almost out of her wits. It had never occurred to her that Christopher might have come to know every tone and shade of her voice as well as she had come to know every tone and shade of his.

"At least I never pestered you to tell me what you had on *your* mind," was the only retort she could think of.

"True," said Christopher, conceding the point. "Let that pass, then. I want to talk to you about the manor."

"You don't have to. Alicia's told me already."

"O Lord, I might have known it!" said Christopher. "Hasn't that girl any more brains than a buttercup?"

"*You* seem to have found her easy enough to talk to. She likes you very much, all the pretty things you say to her."

"Who doesn't say pretty things to a kitten? I like her, too. I like your whole damned family." Christopher's temper, never very long-suffering, was visibly beginning to fray, and he sounded like nothing so much as a small boy unjustly defrauded of some promised treat he had been looking forward to for a long time. "So she told you about the manor, did she? What else did she tell you about? The ring, and all the plans for the wedding, and every last penny in your dowry?"

"*My dowry?*"

"It is customary in this time and country for a father to give his daughter a dowry when she marries. It is also customary for the aspiring suitor to go visit his home and ask him for his consent. What did you expect him to do? Turn you over to me sight unseen? In your petticoat?"

"Turn me over to you?"

"Can't you understand English? You. Me."

"You're marrying *me?*"

"Who else would I marry?"

"W-w-well," Kate stammered, "Alicia."

"O God!" said Christopher, with finality.

"But she *likes* you."

"Kate! Unkind! How can you? Marry Alicia? Think of it!"

But Kate was past thinking coherently of anything. A whole part of her mind seemed be loosening, dissolving, vanishing away, as strangely as if the Standing Stone itself had suddenly crashed down and turned into a handful of dust, and there was nothing but green grass in the place where it had stood for so long. Over the grass a white kitten with golden eyes was chasing butterflies in the spring wind.

"Alicia," she said witlessly.

"*Will* you stop maundering about Alicia?" demanded Christopher. "I'm not marrying Alicia. I'm marrying you."

Kate shook her head as though to clear it. She was still very uncertain of herself and the world and everything in it. "I'm not marrying you," she protested. "I can't be marrying you."

"Yes, you are," Christopher informed her. "And give me leave to remark, my girl, that when you've been spending all your nights with a man for weeks on end, it's high time you married him, or so your mother should tell you."

"I might have known you'd only say something silly," retorted Kate, stung by this injustice.

"That sounds more like you," said Christopher approvingly. "But what's so silly about my wanting to marry you?"

"You don't want to marry me. If you'd wanted to marry me, you'd have said so, long before this."

"It's hard for a man to ask a woman to marry him with an eight-foot wall of stakes and withy between them, especially if he happens to be dead at the time."

"But why should you want to marry me? Why do you?"

"Well, you might say it's because I need you." For the first time, Christopher's voice sounded a little uncertain, as if he himself were not very sure of his ground. "You know how it is with me, Kate. I've been going to waste all my life, like the manor. It's not bad land, but it's too heavy and if the dead water backs up in it —"

"And what am I supposed to do — keep you drained?" Kate interrupted him indignantly. "Next you'll be telling me that you want me to ditch you and manure you!"

"Perhaps that wasn't the most fortunate way of saying it. But I can't think of the right words."

"There aren't any right words. You don't even love me. You know you don't. They asked you on All Hallows' Eve if there was a woman you loved, and you said there wasn't."

"I've never thought of it like that," said Christopher. "How could I? If you were any other woman, I could tell you I loved you, easily enough, but not you — because you've always seemed to me like a part of myself, and it would be like saying I loved my own eyes or my own mind. But have you ever thought of what it would be to have to live without your mind or your eyes, Kate? To be mad? Or blind?" His voice shook. "I can't talk about it. That's the way I feel."

"I — I didn't know," Kate's voice had begun to shake too, uncontrollably. "I didn't think — you never said — you've never even looked at me as if —"

"Look at you! Geoffrey says that all I did this afternoon was stand there and gawk at you like a mooncalf from the minute I walked into the hall! It was *you* who weren't looking at me. Everyone else could see it plainly enough."

Everyone else: Sir Geoffrey, and her father, and Alicia, and the Lady standing at the oriel window, seeing — what had she said? — "her face when she looked at him, and your face when you looked at her, and his when he looked at you both." The Lady had known. Her eyes missed very little, and she was subtle beyond belief. She had been speaking the truth when she said that she would not avenge herself on Kate or the Young Lord by anything so cheap as robbery or murder. Kate was in no state to trace out all the intricacies of the many truths she had told her, but she did find herself wondering what it was — exactly — that she had had in her hand. A dry berry? A hedge-fall? A withered leaf, like the fairy gold she had given poor Randal? It did not matter, as long as Kate went on thinking all her life that Christopher had spoken those words to her only because he was under a spell.

"Well?" said Christopher. "What more do you want?"

"Nothing," said Kate.

When they finally came out of the evidence room, Randal was still crouched by the fire, crooning to himself. But now he appeared to be engaged on a new song, rather than an old one. His head was bent over his harp, and trial scraps of dialogue and snippets of refrain were floating about the air of the hall like the tag ends of silk and thread when Dorothy was cutting out a dress. Only one stanza had as yet taken shape as they stood listening in the doorway:

> *Nine and twenty ladies served in the Queen's hall,*
>   (Follow, my love, come in at the door!)
> *But bonnie Katherine Sutton was the flower among them all,*
>   (And we'll never go down to the Well any more.)

Sir Geoffrey had been right. Randal was making it all into a ballad, and after a while nobody would believe it was ever anything more than a tale.